THE LAST RESORT

Marian saw with shock exactly what Reginald Montague thought of her. The bribe he offered her—not to wed Lord Darley—was shamelessly blunt, and her refusal infuriated him.

"Are you so greedy that you would make my friend's life miserable in return for what he could do for you?" he demanded.

"I have no intention of making his life miserable!" Marian's voice rose an octave as she glared at him.

"You will make his life hell," Reginald declared. "I will do everything within my power to prevent that from happening!"

"Is that why you are forever tempting my temper? Do you think to expose me as a shrew?" Marian said.

There was only one way for Reginald to halt her tongue. He put his arms around her, clamped his mouth to hers, and set about teaching her there were more pleasant things to do with her tongue than wield it in anger—and much to her dismay, Marian found that there were. . . .

The Genuine Article

The Genuine Article

Patricia Rice

A SIGNET BOOK

SIGNET
Published by the Penguin Group
Penguin Books USA Inc., 375 Hudson Street,
New York, New York 10014, U.S.A.
Penguin Books Ltd, 27 Wrights Lane,
London W8 5TZ, England
Penguin Books Australia Ltd, Ringwood,
Victoria, Australia
Penguin Books Canada Ltd, 10 Alcorn Avenue,
Toronto, Ontario, Canada M4V 3B2
Penguin Books (N.Z.) Ltd, 182–190 Wairau Road,
Auckland 10, New Zealand

Penguin Books Ltd, Registered Offices:
Harmondsworth, Middlesex, England

First published by Signet, an imprint of Dutton Signet,
a division of Penguin Books USA Inc.

First Printing, October, 1994
10 9 8 7 6 5 4 3 2 1

To Katherine Bernardi,
whose devious mind will put her name
into print any day now.

One

"**H**ave you ever thought of marrying, Reginald?" The speaker sat sprawled across a bench in the Cock and Crow on the London road.

"Whyever should I?" His companion seemed completely taken aback by the question, as if it were one that he'd thought would never come under consideration, somewhat akin to asking whether a Turkish emperor wore corsets. He set down his mug and gazed across the table at his friend with serious concern. "Your mother after you again?"

The young man ignored the question. "A man ought to get married sometime, you know."

Reginald snorted. Some men snort and look piggish. Reginald was not one of those men. Expensively if not elegantly turned out in doeskin pantaloons, linen cravat, and double-breasted green riding coat, he managed only to look haughty when emitting this inelegant noise. His dark hair was rakishly disheveled, not by design but by the force of the increasing wind they had stopped to avoid.

He crossed one Hessian-booted leg over the other as he scanned the occupants of the tavern. His attitude was such as to show that he did not expect a sensible reply to his challenge: "Give me one good reason why I should marry."

The young man squirmed unhappily and pulled at his high, starched collar. The starch, which fashion's arbiter Brummell insisted made a gentleman, left red weals on Darley's neck, and he gazed enviously at Reginald's unstarched but pristinely white linen. Reginald had told Brummell he'd rather wear hemp than starch, and rather

than being ostracized for his boldness, he was considered a
top gallant. Darley was quite certain that if he had said such
a thing, he would be scorned by all.

"Why, a man should marry to have children, I suppose."

Reginald quirked an eyebrow in Darley's direction.
"Whatever for? I suppose if I were inclined to a nursery,
Madelyn would agree for a small sum. It's not as if I need
an heir, after all. That's Charley's duty."

Darley glumly sipped his ale. "A wife would see to your
house and that sort of thing, keep things neat and orderly
and keep the cooks from quitting, I suppose."

Reginald was growing amused. "I have servants to keep
things neat and orderly, and Jasper is most functional when
it comes to keeping the servants in line."

The younger man ripped at his cravat until it loosened,
then moved his neck gingerly inside his collar. "Well,
there's entertaining, then. A man needs a wife at his side
when he entertains. A good hostess can be very helpful."

Reginald waved at a waitress to bring more ale. She had
been keeping an interested eye on both of them since they
walked in, so the service was excellent. He waited until she
had departed with a saucy wink before answering Darley's
last nonsensity. "Whyever would I entertain at home?
There's nothing of any interest there, and no one to talk to.
A man only needs a good club for entertaining. He's more
likely to be entertained with good wine and good sense at
his club in the company of other men than with listening to
the simpering ineptitudes that typify polite conversation in
the company of women."

Darley gave it up. "And of course, you always have
Madelyn if you need a woman in your bed. I only wish I
were in your position."

Reginald gave him a look of sympathy. "Being your father's only son is a sad thing, but you're not earl yet. Tell
your mama you are looking for the perfect countess and
will settle for no less."

Darley didn't look appeased. "That's easy for you to say.
Your mama has been gone these many years. You don't
know what it's like to be harped at by the woman night and
day. I have come to think that if I can find a gentle, quiet

maid, I would be much better off under her care than at home."

"Maybe so, but it has been my experience that the tenderest of maids can turn into dragons once harnessed by marriage. I would be wary, if I were you, Darley, or you could find yourself in worse suds than with your mama." Reginald drained his glass and reached for his hat. "It looks as if the sun's back out. I'll be on my way then. Promised Charley I'd put in an appearance for the heir's birthday. I'm so grateful for his existence that I'll go to any lengths to please him. Don't go getting yourself leg-shackled before I return."

Darley merely looked more miserable as his gaze went longingly to the door. Upstairs, his mother and sister were adorning a private parlor. It had been mere chance that he'd found sympathetic company in the tap room. He lifted a mug in farewell and watched Reginald march out, a hale and hearty fellow with no cares in the world.

Maybe he would be as bold as Reginald if he had the other man's height. At five-eight, Darley was merely average. Had he not been an earl's son, he would go unnoticed by the larger portion of the females of his acquaintance. He was not so well set-up as Reginald—the padding in his coat was necessary. His dark coloring did not meet the popular taste, and he was quite certain his long thin nose had been compared to a quill point by more than one clever miss.

Of course, Reginald could not be called handsome in the traditional sense, either, but women seemed to flock to him anyway. It had to be his height and the breadth of his shoulders. Women liked to feel helpless and protected, and men of Reginald's size always made them feel that way, Darley supposed. He gazed gloomily down at his knee-high boots. Perhaps he could have the heels extended.

"I could wish that we had our new clothes now, Marian. Did you see how elegant that lady in the carriage looked? Such beautiful fur she had on her collar! And the feather! It drooped at just the right angle. Do you think I will ever reach such heights of sophistication?"

Since Jessica had stopped growing at age fourteen, she

wasn't likely to reach any heights at all, but Marian conscientiously refrained from mentioning that fact. She was already learning her new role well, she decided in a moment of self-congratulation. The old Marian would have said what she felt without thinking.

"There is no use in spoiling a good gown until we are somewhere to be seen. You know there is no money for more. And you know you are always spilling something on your bodice or dragging your hem in the mud. Poor Lily cannot get all those stains out, especially with the silks."

Jessica looked resignedly out the window at the rapidly falling twilight. They had stopped early for fear of the thunderclouds lining the horizon. That meant they would not arrive in London for another day. "I know you have said we will arrive early to give us more chance to choose, but do you really think we will take, Marian? Whatever shall we do if we do not?"

Marian didn't have to look in the mirror to know she would not take. Her dark hair, eyes, and complexion were not at all the thing. Worse than that, she had the tongue of an adder and a mind quicker than that of most men. If men despised anything more than a woman smarter than they, she didn't know what it was. But Jessica had no such problems.

"You will take, Jessie, there is no doubt of it. You will look just like the fashion plates, all golden slenderness and dimpling smiles, and your nature is as sweet as any gentleman can desire. You will have swarms of beaux. You need only choose a rich one."

Jessica clapped her hands anxiously as she turned back toward the room. "But I am not clever like you, and not only do I not have any dowry, I do not have any family connections."

Admittedly, that was the fly in the ointment, but Marian did not say so. "Nonsense," she disagreed heartily. "Our mother has the very best connections, else how would she have married my father? If she can capture a marquess, you surely deserve an earl."

"Yes, but her father was the younger son of an earl. My

father was merely a country squire. It is not at all the same thing, you know."

And a poor country squire at that. Poor and not very bright when it came to business, Marian added to herself a trifle waspishly. That wasn't in keeping with her new style of behavior, but surely she was entitled to think what she might for a little while longer. Her stepfather had been a kind and generous man. There, she had thought something pleasant to balance out her unkindness. Poor James Oglethorp had just been so mightily impressed at landing the beautiful widow of a marquess that he had lavished everything he owned on her. The fact that the widow had been left with only a small trust fund for herself and her daughter had meant little until the crops had turned bad two years in a row. Marian quite sincerely believed that her stepfather had died of a broken heart when he no longer had a cent left to lavish.

So here they were, the next best thing to penniless, and their mother was no longer young enough nor wealthy enough to attract the best of suitors. It was left to Marian and Jessica to save them all from penury. Marian was quite determined to do it by herself. Jessica was too tender-hearted to take any wealthy man who came along, but Marian was no such thing. She had already gleaned enough information from her gossips in London to know which gentlemen to set her hat for. She had only to focus her attention on those few gentlemen until one of them came up to the mark. She was clever. She could determine what he liked in a woman and be that, just long enough for him to fall for the act. He would be wedded faster than he could get the words out.

She had already decided that was about the only way to do it. Her wayward tongue would otherwise give the game away sooner or later. She would be sweet and demure and empty-headed until the band was on her finger and her husband's pockets were at her disposal. Then she would set about educating him.

Still, there was Jessica to reassure. Patting her sleeve gently, Marian disposed of her sister's arguments. "There have been Oglethorps in government since there was a government to be had. You will make a fine politician's wife, I am certain. You need only look around and find the one you wish and smile at him for him to come tumbling to your feet. We shall both be married by June, just you wait and see. Now let me go find Lily and see what detains our dinner."

Since the chambers were so small, Lady Grace and Lily had taken a separate room from Jessica and Marian. Not wishing to disturb her mother if Lily were already downstairs, Marian made her way down the narrow hall. Her mother had not been well since the death of her second husband. Marian was quite certain it was the pressing worry of their non-existent finances that had her in the dismals. Once they restored the family's security, Lady Grace would be fine. Until then, she was best left undisturbed.

The front room of the inn was fairly deserted at this hour. Most of the patrons had settled in for the evening meal, either in the tap room or in private parlors. Apparently the last coach had already gone through, so there were no new arrivals expected. Marian glanced down at the worn wool of her brown traveling gown and decided no one would look twice at her if she went toward the kitchens. She wasn't dressed much differently from Lily.

Before she could act on that decision, the front door swept open with a rush of wind and rain.

"Miss! Don't leave yet. Be so good as to tell me if there is room left in the inn. I don't fancy traveling farther in this."

Wide-eyed at being addressed in such a manner, Marian turned to gape at the jackass who brayed so loudly. He wore the caped driving coat of a coachman and seemed to have lost his hat. His linen was loose and unstarched, and his boots were coated in mud. He was of an unseemly height, and the haughty arrogance of his handsome features was reflected in his manners. No doubt he thought himself God's gift to women. She'd seen louts like that before. They smiled at poor naive country girls, charmed them out of their virtue, and then when they were in the family way, either left them or lived off them until the next one came along. Marian had little use for men, and less for scoundrels.

"'Tis a pity then. Mayhap you'll enjoy the stable instead." She turned and started for the kitchen once more, but a large gloved hand caught her shoulder and swung her around. She glared at him in astonishment.

"Whatever have I done to you to deserve such treatment?" He released her shoulder and began to peel off his soaked gloves.

"You exist. That should be sufficient reason." Without excusing herself, Marian turned on her heels and once more sought refuge in the rear of the inn.

"I trust you don't need this employment," he called after her, "for I mean to tell your employer of your behavior."

Fury colored Marian's cheeks that he could think her no more than a common servant. Her gown might not be of the best quality, but surely he could see she was no ordinary maid. Without stopping to think, she swung around to face him again. "I thought you a braying jackass when first you walked in here. I must congratulate myself on my perceptiveness. Please do talk to the landlord. I will be happy to speak to him personally and tell him I heartily recommend the stable for you. That's where we always keep the animals at home."

Reginald's eyebrows shot up toward his hairline as the young woman stalked out of sight in the direction of the kitchen. He had undoubtedly made a foolishly hasty judgment, but the young lovely had retaliated with an unexpected and totally unladylike vehemence. Still, he couldn't help grinning just a little at her retort. Perhaps if she had been less lovely he would have found it less humorous. But delivered from rosy lips surrounded by a creamy complexion and enhanced by a wealth of very dark hair, the setdown achieved a certain savoriness he could appreciate.

Perhaps she was some lady's maid. If so, she was probably as unattainable as the lady herself.

Shrugging off the incident, Reginald rang the bell for the innkeeper. He seldom had the opportunity to exchange insults and witticisms with the fairer sex. He didn't see any particularly good reason to begin now, or he would chase her down into the kitchen and see if she took as well as she gave.

Two

Marian caught Jessica's wistful look in the mirror as she fastened the heavy braided gold chain around her neck and tested the effect of the exquisitely mounted ruby against her tawny skin. She turned and straightened her sister's seed pearls gently.

"You know I would give it to you if it would serve any purpose, but not only would it not suit your coloring, you are only seventeen. A young unmarried lady must not wear jewels. I cannot possibly pass myself off as less than my twenty-two years, so I must take advantage of what few assets I have." She turned around and frowned at the ornate jewel. "I only wish I could sell it so we might live a little more easily."

Jessica shook her head and sent a cascade of golden curls flying. "No, it is all you have of your father's inheritance. It must be very old and valuable. We could not sell it. Mother would be distraught."

Marian sighed in resignation. She was much too practical to be sentimental about family heirlooms, but she was also wise enough to know her sister was right. Mother would be more than distraught were the piece to be sold, although to Marian's mind, one piece of gaudy jewelry was the same as another. She was certain a lesser piece would be just as effective as ornamentation, and the difference could go a long way toward buying the silks and muslins needed for their foray into society.

"Well, we are not in dire straits as yet. Lily's handiwork will keep us outfitted a little while longer. If only our heights and coloring were a little closer, we could exchange clothes and then have twice the wardrobe." Marian sighed at the waste as she pulled on her elbow-length gloves.

Jessica glanced down at her gown of pale tulle over a delicate ice-blue silk, then over at Marian's more daring gown of rich gold accented with wine-colored trimmings. She smiled slightly. "I don't think so, Marian. Even were you blonde, you would not wear this."

That was probably so. Jessica often hit closer to the truth of things than Marian wished to acknowledge. She frowned at her reflection and played her fan as her mother had taught her. Her frown deepened. "I will never be sweet enough or silly enough to capture Lord Darley's interest. Perhaps I should set my cap for Mr. Henry. He is said to be quite wealthy and an older man may be less inclined to wish for a younger woman for wife."

Jessica started for the door. "Don't be silly. Mr. Henry must be at least forty, and he's practically wall-eyed. Lord Darley is a very handsome young man, and he seems quite pleased with your attentions. I only wish I were bold enough to attract a man as you can. I do not dare even look them in the eye."

Marian could tell her she would do well when she was older and more sure of herself, but Jessica wouldn't want to hear that. She wanted to believe she would be able to help the family fortune by marrying soon and well. Marian was just as determined that her sister should wait until she was in a better position to choose a husband suited to her gentle nature. To that end, she must capture a suitor quickly. Then Jessica would be free to relax and enjoy her season as a young girl should.

Lord Darley was the ideal candidate. A wealthy viscount rumored to be in search of a wife, he had fallen readily for Marian's bold smile, then believed the shyness in her hastily lowered lashes. She had listened intently to every word from his mouth, adroitly given him her fullest attention without offending the company around them, and never uttered one cross or ill-chosen word in his presence. She had easily determined he was slightly shy around women, but he seemed good-natured enough to make a suitable husband. She might wish for a man who was taller than she and a little more forceful in character, but that was not to the point. He was a man who would gladly lend a hand to his bride's family and not complain when Marian began to show signs of intelligence after the vows were said. She could not find one flaw to her plan.

"Is Mama ready? We shall be fashionably late but in plenty of time to find partners for the supper dance. Then if she is not feeling well and we must leave early, we will not have wasted the better part of the evening." Marian efficiently tugged on her gloves as she started for the door.

"Lily was fixing her hair when I left. I think Mama is feeling better now that she has found some old friends with whom she might chat while we dance. I think she was worried no one would recognize her after so many years away."

Again, Jessica's observation was exceedingly astute, Marian realized as she hurried down the stairs. Her steps were quick for a purpose. They had only the one male servant to serve as footman and butler and guardian of the house in general, and they were all half afraid of him. Hired London servants were so much haughtier than the simple country folk back home. It would not do to keep him waiting by the door longer than was deemed necessary.

They had hired a carriage along with the house for the season. The house was not in a fashionable neighborhood and the carriage was quite plain and ordinary, but there had been no sense in going too far in debt to pretend they were what they were not. Their lack of dowries had been the main reason for Marian's decision to use subterfuge in her own presentation. They must be judged on their looks and characters and breeding alone. Knowing full well she was deficient in all categories but one, she felt justified in blurring the image a little.

Allowing Lady Grace to nap late had delayed their arrival until after the usual stream of carriages at the door. The three women entered the elegantly appointed salon after the reception line had dispersed, and the footman's announcement of their arrival went virtually unnoticed. Marian had no complaint about that. They would have gone unnoticed had they arrived at the height of introductions. A Lady Grace and a Miss Jessica Oglethorp were of little consequence in a glittering assemblage such as this. It was only their mother's connections through her family and first marriage that allowed them entry at all. Even Marian's courtesy title held little meaning since her father's title had passed on to a distant cousin. She would never be a countess or a marchioness, only a Lady Marian—until she married. She glanced around unhurriedly for Lord Darley. His wife would be a viscountess and some day, a countess.

He came hurrying forward as if he had been waiting for them. Marian felt sincere gratitude for his eagerness. She might even learn to love a man with such a generous character. She just felt sorry she had to deceive him to distract him from her own true nature. She was quite certain he and his mama would not approve of a woman who read Coleridge and Hannah More and thought the majority of the aristocracy little better than useless wind chimes.

"Lady Marian!" he cried happily, taking her hand. As an afterthought, he added a polite bow to her family, "Lady Grace, Miss Jessica, it is good to see you." When they nodded shyly and moved discreetly away, he turned his attention back to the object of his interest. "You look in fine fettle this evening, my lady." He colored slightly as he realized the slang was not particularly applicable to a lady.

Marian hastened to reassure him with a shy swirl of her fan as she hid behind it. "You put me to the blush, sir. The ball is quite lovely this evening, is it not?" Simpering idiocy did not come easily, but she was satisfied she had done it properly when he looked more at ease.

"Indeed it is. Will you honor me with a dance or two? I hope I have caught you in time to inquire."

She offered her card. "As you can see, I have just arrived. You may have your choice, although I believe Mr. Henry requested that I save him a cotillion."

He dashed his name across the supper dance and looked up at her daringly. "Might I have the final waltz also, or is that saved for someone special?"

Marian wished she could blush at will, but she could not. She merely hid behind her fan again to pretend she was blushing. "I would be honored, but you must not hold me to account if my mother grows tired and we must leave early."

Growing more sure of himself with every passing simper, he said, "Then you must hold an earlier waltz open and send word to me if she begins to tire. And if she does not, we will sit out the dance together."

"You are too kind, Lord Darley. You cannot know how much I appreciate your thoughtfulness." Marian laid her hand on his arm as he offered to lead her over to her mother.

"You may show your gratitude by agreeing to go for a drive with me in the park tomorrow. I have just bought a prime set of grays and am eager to see them sprung. I would be honored to have you by my side when I introduce them."

Marian batted her lashes in eager surprise. "Why, that would be lovely, sir! Tell me about your horses. Did you buy them at Tattersall's?"

Since horses were the one topic he could converse upon with great animation and intelligence, Darley launched into a colorful description of his new acquisitions. Such animation from the usually quiet viscount drew attention around the room, but the young couple appeared oblivious to the whispering.

Mr. Henry arrived to claim his cotillion, and several other young gentlemen took the opportunity to claim her remaining dances. Marian glanced anxiously at Jessica, who was doing her best to disappear into the woodwork, and with a pleading look from beneath her lashes, she sent Lord Darley in that direction. With a pleased smile and a polite bow, he went to do his duty by her sister.

Relieved to know that Jessica wouldn't be left holding up the potted palms, feeling gratitude for the young viscount's generous understanding, Marian allowed herself to be escorted onto the dance floor. With a man like Lord Darley for husband, she might even lose some of the sharp edges to her tongue, for who could complain in the presence of a man who sought to please at just the bat of an eyelash?

Her sense of well-being and satisfaction lasted well

through the next few sets, until she happened to glance up and catch the entrance of a tall, dark-haired man dressed in casual elegance. She started nervously and looked away, for though she could not place him immediately, she was certain that she had seen the man before, and equally certain that it had not been under pleasant circumstances.

She had been more than charming to all the young men she had met these last weeks, even the ones with no wealth and no brains. Marian attributed her feeling of unease to nerves. Things had been going too smoothly. She was leaping at shadows. There was no reason she could think of that this particular man might have a poor opinion of her.

She watched him surreptitiously when she could. In a room full of stiffly correct swallow-tailed coats, starched linen, and elaborate cravats, he seemed at ease with his coat unbuttoned and his cravat in a single fold and his collar all-too-obviously unstarched. His height and grace of manner made him appear as elegant as any man around him; that in itself was intimidating. Marian had to work hard to achieve any semblance of elegance herself, and she did so by copying the standards of those she most admired. This man obviously set his own standards.

She would not be cowed by a man who was patently out of her class. He must be a duke or a marquess or some such, far too elegant for even this crowd. She did not know why he had come, but he would most certainly leave soon and she would not ever see him again. She smiled winningly as Darley came to claim his supper dance.

Marian did not see the immediate frown upon the elegant man's face as he watched Darley lead her into the set.

Reginald turned to the tall woman beside him. "That is the young woman about whom you spoke? There is something familiar about her, but I do not think we've been introduced."

Lady Agatha Darley smiled with satisfaction. "She only arrived after you had left to visit your family. She is the daughter of the late Marquess of Effingham. I believe her mother's lines are through the Earl of Avon. Eminently suitable, don't you think? Perhaps a little older than I could have wished for Geoffrey, but I understand her stepfather kept the family in straitened circumstances. Now that he is gone, the mother has come to town to marry her daughters off. Not for everyone, I think, but Geoffrey has no need to marry for money. That is in his favor. She seems quite a charming, pleasant young woman."

Reginald frowned and narrowed his eyes as he watched the young couple circle through the dance. The pair were nearly of a height, and he could see the foolish grin on Darley's face as he looked into his partner's eyes. As the woman's face came more into view, he took a sharp breath. There couldn't be two of them alike in this world. Flashing dark eyes and heavy chestnut hair were not that common in these parts, nor was the dark complexion. Even the richness of her gown could not disguise the sharp-tongued servant he had encountered at the inn.

Charming and pleasant were certainly things that she was not. In how many other ways could she have deceived the good-natured Darleys?

Three

D arley courteously summoned one of his friends to escort Jessica into supper with them so that she wasn't forced to sit with her mother and her cronies. Jessica managed a shy look of delight before turning her attention to the young man in painfully high collar who was to be her escort. The young man blushed red when she turned beguiling blue eyes to him, before assuming an air of cool aplomb as he seated her and asked what delicacies she preferred from the table. Marian noted their antics with amusement from the corner of her eye while ostensibly keeping her entire attention on Darley's rhapsodies over some other man's stable. She was quite inclined to despise this Reginald Montague on sight simply from the extensiveness of said stable.

Perhaps she could educate Darley somewhat in the arts. He obviously had a superb memory if he could recite bloodlines clear back to whatever that confounded racehorse's name was. Perhaps he could learn the classical artists and she could interest him in collecting. That might give them some common ground to converse on. It would be even better if she could persuade him to read, but she had learned at an early age that gentlemen weren't inclined toward the literary arts.

Planning Darley's improvements, Marian wasn't aware of the approach of the elegant gentleman she had noted earlier in the evening. Caught up in her conquest, she had managed to forget all about him. His arrival at their table after Darley's entreating wave dashed all possibility that she would ever be so gifted as to forget him entirely. The gray-green eyes glaring down at her from his towering height slowly turned to just an icy gray as Darley made the introductions.

Reginald Montague.

The braying ass from the inn.

Darley's closest, dearest friend.

Disaster. Marian tried not to close her eyes and resort to prayer as she smiled innocently into those furious eyes. She was mentally counting her markers, racking losses against gains to see how she stood and if she had a chance of winning this hand. The odds looked about even, depending on how much of a gentleman Montague might be. If he told Darley of their encounter, all was lost. If he held his tongue and just disapproved of her, she might counter this disapproval of a male friend with the feminine wiles of a potential countess. She knew Darley's mother approved of her. That would load the odds in her favor.

She had to make him hold his tongue. She had spent three weeks setting her cap on Darley. She didn't have a great deal of time left to lose. There were second and third runners in the contest because she was a practical woman, but none of the others were as appealing as Darley. She wouldn't let this disagreeable Corinthian stand in her way.

"Lady Marian." Montague acknowledged the introduction with the barest of nods and none of the effusive greetings to which Marian had become accustomed. She wasn't a great beauty, but she was a new face, and the gentlemen seemed to react with pleasure to anything or anyone different from the usual. It wore off quickly, she knew, but generally most of them managed to be pleasant through the introductions. This man hadn't even the common decency to smile through that.

"Mr. Montague." She managed a syrupy voice and a light smile. "Lord Darley has been telling me about your stable. You are indeed a fortunate man as well as possessing a skilled eye for horses if all he tells me is true." A compliment like that on top of a subject about which most men were usually mad, generally put them at ease. She sat back and waited to see how he would react.

He merely gave a curt nod and turned to Darley. "Will I see you at the club later?"

The man was impossibly rude. Marian wasn't much accustomed to rudeness. She wondered if she kicked his shin under the table would he even notice. With a rump as stiff as his, he probably had no feelings below the waist.

She almost giggled at the thought. Some of her laughter must have escaped, because he quickly turned a wary eye in her direction. Marian pretended not to notice as she turned her attention to Jessica's young gallant, complimenting him on his elegant attire. He turned red but set out upon a learned discourse on the topic of available tailors.

Once Montague had departed, she gratefully returned her attention to the viscount. At least Lord Darley conversed intelligently without stuttering and stammering. Poor Jessica. Marian really was going to have to look into a proper suitor for her sister just as soon as she had Darley firmly attached, which wouldn't be ever if Montague had any say in the matter.

Marian listened with dread as Darley sang the man's praises. What hope was there for a mere woman against a man who knew the best tailors, stocked the finest wines, owned the fastest horses, and in general was the male epitome of perfection? It was quite apparent whose word would be believed first should it come to a confrontation.

Drat her dreadful tongue. She had held it carefully for three entire weeks. Would that she had held it one day earlier. She could see disaster looming with every pearl of praise falling from Darley's lips. She had to bite down hard to keep from asking why—if Montague were so superior—Darley did not just marry him. Obviously, they were well suited.

Finally, Marian could not take any more of it without offering something in her own defense. Biting her bottom lip and lowering her eyes to the table, she affected a small sigh. Into the brief lull of talk that ensued, she murmured, "I could never aspire to the heights of such a paragon of perfection. You must find me very poor company indeed in comparison. I do not think I could learn half so much as a man like that must already know."

Darley looked horrified. He reached for her hand and patted it. "Don't be such a goose. Of course you cannot. You are a woman. But if Reginald is a paragon of perfection, then it is only of his gender, for you are the epitome of all that I hold dear in the fairer sex."

Had she been herself Marian would have ripped his tongue out while informing him that a female—any female—was five times more preferable to a puffed-up ass who knew nothing but horses and tailors. But she gave him a gratified smile, took his hand, and allowed him to escort her from the supper room. She was quite certain her tongue would bear scars before the season ended.

To Marian's relief, there was no further evidence of the disagreeable Mr. Montague's presence after supper. And her mother was rested enough to stay for the final waltz, so she spent a whole interval talking with Darley as well as claiming the last dance. Gossip was already swirling. She smiled into his eyes, melted into his arms, and willed him to see her as his viscountess. She was quite certain she would be very good at the position.

Reginald Montague sat sipping brandy, glaring at the noisy gaming tables around him while he waited for Darley to tear himself away from the ball and his latest folly. The viscount was too good a man to ever see the scheming qualities of another soul, and he was too diffident around women to see beyond their pretty paint and manners. The last two mercenary witches who had tried to dig their claws into him had been routed easily by Lady Agatha. This time, the little fraud had managed to fool even that daunting lady. How many others had she deceived? Was he the only one aware of the lady's true nature?

If lady she were at all. Remembering her manner of dress and the fact that she had been all alone in an inn of a less-than-respectable nature, he had to doubt even that quality in the woman. The pretty young thing she had called sister seemed innocent enough, but then, looks were not the best cover to judge by. Even this spurious Lady Marian passed easily as a lady of quality in her fashionable gown, but her bold looks and saucy mouth betrayed her. The show she was putting on for Darley's benefit was very well done, so well done that Reginald thought she might be an actress. Perhaps he could investigate her true background. That would be the wisest course to take: confront Darley with cold facts instead of subjective opinions.

Having decided that, Reginald waited with less impatience for his friend's appearance. He hadn't been looking forward to informing Darley of his inamorata's despicable behavior. Now he could keep his personal opinion out of it. He would set Bow Street on the matter tomorrow. It shouldn't be difficult to determine lies from truth if she wasn't Effingham's daughter. He might even present the facts to Lady Agatha first and let her lead the way. Darley more or less always bowed to that lady's opinions.

By the time Darley arrived, Reginald was complacent with brandy and good intentions. When his friend took the seat across from him and demanded, "What did you think?" he managed a good-natured smile.

"I thought about the beefsteak I had for dinner, which horse I prefer in the spring meet, whether to attend Lady Jersey's fete or the boxing match, and any number of fascinating topics."

Darley scowled and sipped the port the waiter brought to him. "I mean Lady Marian. What did you think of Lady Marian? I know you did not stay long, but surely you could see she was an absolute diamond."

More like coal, Reginald ruminated, but to say so would only get his friend's back up. He answered honestly, "She is quite attractive." For a brunette, he amended to himself. Fashion didn't favor brunettes. He, himself, was inclined to be less concerned with coloring than character, but he was more peculiar, as well as particular, than society in general.

"Isn't she? I'm glad you agree. I was afraid after you turned your back on her this evening that you had taken her into dislike already. But she was much too good-natured to comment on your rudeness."

Remembering what he almost certainly thought was a snicker from the young lady in question, Reginald also had the courtesy not to comment. He rather suspected the lady might be a mischief-maker in addition to all her other faults. While Bow Street worked on her background, he might do some investigating of his own. It was possible the lady could be diverted from her course with the proper inducements.

"I had not realized she was anyone of importance," Reginald replied carelessly. "I shall take better note next time."

"If I must marry, she is all that I could wish," Darley said eagerly. "I could talk to her for hours. You know how my tongue gets all tied up around women, but she is not like that at all. She even shares my interest in horses and has made some very interesting suggestions. We get along famously. And she does not have an encroaching family who would be forever dangling on my coattails. All she has is a mother and sister who are very shy and circumspect. No daunting fathers or rakehell brothers to be fished out of the River Tick."

Reginald groaned inwardly as he rose from the table. This was much worse than he had suspected. He should never have stayed so long in Somerset. If Darley weren't his closest friend, he would wash his hands of him now. But Darley was the only one of his companions who had gone through school with him and understood his position and accepted it. Darley's friendship was very valuable to him. He wouldn't see it destroyed by a scheming, conniving female.

"What about the current marquess? Will he not have some say in the matter of a cousin's marriage, if that is what you are contemplating?"

Darley drained his glass and accompanied his friend as he left the club. "As I understand it, Effingham is an old curmudgeon who never comes out of the woodwork. Lady Marian and her family never say anything against him, but it is apparent he has never taken any interest in their welfare. They appear to be living on very limited means. If they will let me, I intend to correct that situation."

They strolled down the gaslit street in the direction of the park near which Reginald had only recently purchased a small lodging. Even at this hour the streets were active. Gentlemen strolled to and from their clubs. Carriages rattled by filled with elegantly dressed fashionables going from one entertainment to another. Street urchins lurked on every corner, eager to hold a horse's head for a penny or sweep the street of droppings so their betters might cross without endangering their polished boots. A watchman snoozed in his box, unaware of the young bloods drunkenly eyeing his weight and wagering on who could tip him first.

Reginald and Darley ignored the night life around them. Wandering from the gaslit street into the darker environs of the park, they continued their desultory conversation.

"You have all the time in the world, Geoff. Do not waltz hastily into something so permanent as marriage. You remember that mare you had to have because her bloodlines were so aristocratic and her price was so low? She turned out to be a nasty, mean-tempered sort and never bred true. Had you made a few inquiries, you would have saved yourself some trouble."

Filled with the generosity of spirit that comes with happiness, Darley laughed at the comparison. "I shall interview the lady's servants to see if she is biddable, but I don't believe I can inquire into her abilities to breed."

Reginald allowed himself a smile of amusement at the thought. At least Darley was not too far gone as to have lost his sense of humor. "I had not thought that before, but there's the advantage to marrying a widow. If breeding is what you seek, you would do better to marry a woman who has proven her ability by producing a son or two already."

Darley snorted with laughter, then without changing his pace or his tone of voice, he said softly, "Don't look now, but we are being followed."

Reginald carelessly swung his walking stick. "I know. Not very good at the game, is he?"

"Young, I'd say. Perhaps he's not been about long. P'raps we ought to break him of bad habits before they start."

"My thoughts exactly. Let me offer you a sip from my flask when we stop under this next tree."

With apparent drunken carelessness, they halted their progress in the thick darkness of shrubbery and trees at the far edge of the park. The quiet residential street corner not far from this spot offered little in the way of observers. Reginald slipped a flash from his pocket and handed it to Darley.

The slight figure following them was better at his business than they had anticipated. He wheeled out of the darkness, bumped lightly against Darley, mumbled a drunken apology, and had begun to stagger off again when Reginald reached out and grabbed him by the coat collar.

Jerking the thief up to his toes, Reginald said patiently, "The purse, sir. I believe you have misappropriated the gentleman's purse."

Dangling by his coat collar, the young man kicked his feet in an anxious attempt to reach the pavement. He managed a drunken whimper. "In my cups, sirs. 'Pologize."

It was too dark to discern much about him other than that he was slightly made, wore the remnants of a gentleman's clothing, and smelled badly. Since there were any number of people in the fashionable world who disdained bathing, the odor was nothing new. The fact that he spoke without the uneducated dialect of the slums did indicate an oddity, however.

Reginald deprived himself of the pleasure of shaking the young rascal until he dropped the purse. Instead, he ordered, "Darley, search him."

The young man struggled again. There was the vague sound of something brushing against the bushes, then he held his hands up in protest. His educated speech slipped slightly to the vernacular. "I didn't do anything, guv'nor. I'm just a poor man down on his luck. Search me, if you like. I been drinking, and I know that's wrong, but I've not done anything else."

Sighing, Reginald lowered the culprit to his feet but kept a firm hold on his collar. "Search the bushes, Darley. We should have just called the watch and allowed them to handle the rogue."

Darley cursed as the bushes tore at his elegant cuffs, but he finally located the small purse that had shortly before been in his coat pocket. He lofted it in his hand to show Reginald he'd found it, then returned it to his pocket. "Shall we wake the Charlie back there?"

The thief quivered. "I didn't do anything! I been lookin' for employment, I have. I haven't got anything to pay the nippers at Newgate. They'll throw me to the hounds. If they steal my clothes, I'll not be able to find employment anyways."

If he didn't have coins to pay the jailers at Newgate, he would undoubtedly lose his fine jacket and more. Reginald hesitated. He had no desire to allow a pickpocket back on the streets, but he didn't wish to see a young lad destroyed over a few coins Darley could easily afford. He hesitated long enough for the thief to look hopeful.

"I'm a good valet, I am. My father worked for the late Marquess of Effingham, and he taught me all he knew. The new one ain't got no use for valets or much else. I thought I'd make my way in London, but I can't get references from a dead man, and nobody'll look at me elsewise."

Reginald exchanged glances with Darley. They didn't have to speak. They both knew Darley had an old and trusted valet, a family retainer, but Reginald had never hired a man before. They had even discussed the possibility of his hiring someone besides the ubiquitous Jasper, who was more secretary and butler than valet. It seemed the time had come.

"If I let loose of your collar and you run, I'm calling the watch. If you don't run, I'll consider your petition for employment in the morning. I don't hire pickpockets in the general run of things, but I am feeling generous tonight. We'll see if I feel the same in the morning."

He loosed the culprit's collar.

The man looked around nervously, rocked on the balls of his feet, then evidently deciding he had nothing to lose if he stayed instead of running, he remained where he was. "Name's Michael O'Toole, guv'nor. I'll have your clothes looking a treat 'afore morning if you take me in."

Reginald scowled. "I'm more likely to lock you in a broom closet than I am to allow you access to my wardrobe. Come on, let's go. I've had enough of this evening."

The three of them traveled down the street in the direction of the silent houses ahead. The young thief's head nearly turned in circles as he took in the massive limestone buildings, ornate entrances, and spotless steps of his new surroundings. Breathing a sigh of deep pleasure, he awaited his fate.

Four

"We have invitations to Devonshire House." Lady Grace Oglethorp held them in her hand as if they were the Holy Grail, using the same note of wonder one would use at such an occurrence. "The young Duke cannot know me. How is this possible?"

It did seem distinctly odd, but Marian said nothing untoward as she took the invitations from her mother's hands. There were three of them, all very distinctly engraved in each name. There could be no mistake. "Perhaps he has a secretary who has acquired the guest lists of all recent entertainments, and he is sending invitations to everyone on those lists. Dukes are peculiar people. Perhaps they don't care if they know their guests."

Grace's eyes were alight with hope. "He is not yet married. Perhaps he has decided to choose a wife and is inviting all eligible parties."

Marian rather doubted that. She frowned, but she could think of no other likely reason for this unexpected good fortune. She did not generally believe in Cinderella stories.

Jessica stared in awe at the heavy vellum. "What does one wear to a ducal ball?" she inquired hesitantly.

A terrible silence fell at this question. One did not wear gowns made over from ten years before. One did not wear gowns made by one's lady's maid, however cleverly stitched. One went to a modiste and ordered the most exquisitely made gowns suitable to one's fortune and figure for a ducal ball. Their fortunes, however, could afford them a lace stocking apiece.

"I will find some way," Marian announced decisively. She was the family keeper of finances. She knew the value of tallow and wax and dealt out the candles accordingly. She had bargained Squire Oglethorp's remaining horses into this trip to London. She would have to be the one to find the funds for ball gowns.

"Not the ruby," Jessica whispered as her sister started toward the study.

Not the ruby. It was becoming a symbol of last resort. She needed to bring Lord Darley up to snuff before the ruby must be hocked.

She had no dreams of acquiring a duke for husband. Every ambitious mama in London had their caps set for the dashing Duke of Devonshire. The competition was far too stiff and out of Marian's means. But to be invited to a ducal ball gave a certain cachet that would see them in good stead in the future. She might only aspire to a viscount, but Jessica was lovely enough to look where she might, even if she was only an Oglethorp. Her appearance at Devonshire House would make that apparent to all the *ton*.

Retreating to the study, Marian opened the trunk that had been transported there at her request from their house in Wiltshire. Since Marian had always possessed a literary bent, no one had questioned her need for a trunkful of books despite the extra trouble it caused in transportation. Neither her mother or Jessica understood that this trunk held the remains of their fortune. Squire Oglethorp had inherited an extremely valuable library from a more literary ancestor.

She hated parting with any of them. Her fingers caressed the leather volumes of an earlier century. She had read all but the Greek and Latin ones. Her education had never been broad enough to include languages, living or dead. She would more readily part with those she could not read, but she suspected they were not nearly so valuable as some of the others. Her fingers found the ancient volumes at the bottom of the trunk.

She knew there was a good market in Medieval illuminated manuscripts. She had already sold several. It broke her heart to give up these last, because they were the most magnificent of all. The jewel tones of the illustrations cried out for admiration. The lettering lovingly penned in perfect script spoke of years of hallowed work. To part with such love and respect in exchange for the coins for ball dresses seemed sacrilege, but she must consider the living before the dead. Her mother and Jessica needed to go to the ball. They had no care at all for these old tomes packed away in a trunk. Marian would be the only one to suffer when the books were gone.

She had already made inquiries against the day this would be necessary. She had the names and directions of several respectable dealers in books and antiquities. All she must do was force herself to decide which of her lambs to sacrifice, and she could be on her way.

She chose several rare volumes from the fifteenth and sixteenth centuries for which she had already been given quotes. She knew they would not be enough for three gowns from a modiste. Sadly, she chose the smaller manuscript, the one in old English, with the carefully drawn flowers and herbs in the borders. Not only were the drawings exquisite, but the descriptions and uses of the various plants were of immense interest once she learned to read the highly ornate writing and odd language. She could imagine some monk making careful observations over a lifetime and having it faithfully recorded by some younger assistant eager to learn all he had to tell. The book cried out of history and love and patience. But it was worth far more than all the other modern volumes in her care.

She could not be so selfish as to keep this treasure when it might provide a future for her family. Wrapping it carefully in cloth, she included it in the satchel she would take to the booksellers'. She would obtain various appraisals until she knew which seller was the most knowledgeable and honest. It would be nice if she could find one who would appreciate the books as much as she did, but she had little hope of that. Men tended to be rather mercenary when it came to antiquities.

Calling for the carriage and her maid, Marian donned a bonnet and spencer and prepared herself for the expedition. Lord Darley had other appointments today, so she could not expect him to call or come by and ask her to go driving with him again. She would not be missed when her mother and Jessica went to make their calls. She could have the whole day to herself if she desired. She just wished the day could be spent on more uplifting activities.

By the time she had traversed the streets of London and haggled with three booksellers, she wished she could be anywhere else in the world but here. These men were avaricious monsters. They had no respect, no sensitivity, no concept of the preciousness of the volumes she had to sell. They gave her unfashionable gown a sniff, glanced through the leather volumes to check their condition, riffled the manuscript pages with raised eyebrows, and quoted figures as low as the ones she had obtained in Wiltshire. She had thought surely they would bring more in the enlightened population of the city.

The quotes were so universally similar that she had the horrible notion that there was some small imp running from stall to stall warning all the sellers that she was coming. The fact that these same vendors had been recommended by the vendors in Wiltshire added to her suspicions. It did not seem quite possible that they could all know each other and price all books the same, but it appeared that way.

Struck with the notion, Marian set her jaw and stopped the driver at the next sign of a dealer in books and antiquities. This one was not on her list, but it was in a very respectable section. She had seen a lady in fashionable muslin just leaving carrying a neatly wrapped package, and there were several elegant people admiring a display of jewelry in the window. She was quite certain this seller had the respect of the *ton*. She would see what he had to say about her books.

Lily exclaimed in weariness at having to stop at still another musty store, and Marian took pity on her. Lily was more family than servant. She worked for terrible wages and with a quiet steadfastness that endeared her to one and all. She stayed up late to help her ladies undress and rose early to mend and sew and press their gowns. She deserved a little rest now.

"I will be just a minute, Lily. Why don't you wait here

and admire the ladies' hats while I run in and see if the store owner is in?"

"I couldn't, miss. You oughtn't to be about without me. 'Tis not proper."

Marian climbed down from the carriage with the help of their driver. She turned to prevent Lily from following her. "I just saw a friend of mine enter. Surely that will be company enough?" It was a lie, but she wasn't above telling lies to make people happy. She had worked through the old debate about whether the means or the end were more important and came to the conclusion that it depended on the means and the end. In this case, the means were negligible and the end was by far more beneficial than a lie was hurtful.

Lily sat back and smiled happily, and Marian hurriedly carried the heavy satchel through the respectable portals of Aristotle's Antiquities Emporium.

She ought to have a footman, she realized, as she stepped onto a floor covered in thick Turkish carpet. Crystal glittering in glass cases made her think of the expensive reception areas of the grand houses she had been in these last weeks. Magnificent oil paintings adorning the walls reminded her of the museums she had visited at every chance. One did not attend these places without maids or footmen, clothed in one's oldest gowns, carrying battered satchels. This place was obviously not the vendors' stalls she had been frequenting.

She was terrified of being stared at and criticized, and started to turn and make her escape before anyone could possibly recognize her. Perhaps she could come back wearing one of her better gowns, and she could borrow a footman somewhere to help her carry the satchel. That would gain her a good deal more respect before she made her inquiries. Perhaps a place like this did not even deal with people like her. Perhaps they only dealt with kings and queens. Stomach tightening in anxiety, she started out, when a familiar voice taunted her from the interior.

"Lady Marian, I believe?"

She contemplated pretending she did not hear. Perhaps he would think he was mistaken. But men like that never made mistakes, she thought, grimacing; Only women like her did. He was Darley's best friend. She would have to try not to repeat her earlier mistake of rudeness. Besides, she sensed him coming up behind her. Pasting on her most pleasant smile, she turned to greet him.

"Good morning, Mr. Montague," she said softly, without any elaboration such as "Are you slumming today?" or "Have you had your morning drink of blood yet?" She kept her equilibrium by thinking these things only to herself while the elegant man in expensively tailored bottle-green coat and tight-fitting fawn breeches looked her up and down.

"Come slumming, have we?" he asked, noting her satchel.

Marian nearly choked as her own words came back to her without their ever having been uttered. The man had the tongue of an adder. She smiled sweetly, and was rewarded by his instant look of suspicion. "If I were, I was undoubtedly misled. You must excuse me, sir; I've left my carriage waiting." She liked the sound of that immensely. It made her sound like a royal princess.

A portly man with silver buttons on his vest and a monocle dangling from a silver chain came up to stand beside Montague. He quickly inspected the company and, without a word of warning, bent to open the satchel Marian had set on the carpet.

Marian made a startled cry, but the man's soft whistle of respect stayed her hand from slapping him away. Montague's fingers on her arm further held her.

"Jacobs knows the business inside and out. If you are a collector or purveyor of antiquities, he is the man to see."

The man called Jacobs reverently removed the Medieval manuscript from the satchel. Setting it carefully down on a glass counter, he donned a pair of soft white gloves before picking the manuscript up again. His expression was one of great awe and fascination as he delicately turned the pages.

"Surely you do not mean to sell this, miss," he murmured, his gaze never swerving from the pages.

Marian was aware of the sharp look from the gentleman at her side. She was not easily embarrassed, but the situation had her struggling for some semblance of dignity. All the *ton* undoubtedly knew the Oglethorps were not in funds. She would not be revealing family secrets by assuring him she must sell the manuscript. Her embarrassment came from the fact that it was this book that she was selling. She would rather it were the family jewels any day. Any lover of books would despise her for what she was doing.

"I must," she whispered, wishing Montague to the devil. It was much easier to be angrier at him for her humiliation than at the genial man who so respected her precious manuscripts.

Jacobs let the monocle fall from his eye as he glanced up at her. His sharp gaze took in her dowdy attire, the battered satchel, and the expression on her face. Without a word to her, he gestured to someone in the back. "Bring the lady some tea and a chair. Tell her driver to come around in half an hour."

Montague asked her sarcastically, "You do have a carriage, don't you, Lady Marian? I wouldn't want the poor boy to waste his time looking for it."

She bit her lip and prayed hard. Her nerves were on edge; her emotions were all-too-clearly on the brink of exploding. She really and truly needed to tell this braying jackass what she thought of him. She merely gave him a thoughtful look and accepted the gilded chair the boy brought for her.

Montague took out another chair and sat down without invitation, leaning over to rifle through the rest of the contents of her bag.

"Just precisely what do you think you are doing, Mr. Montague?" she asked tartly. It was impossible to be completely quiet with this arrogant monster.

"Seeing how much your soul is worth, Lady Marian," he replied idly, examining the dramatic hand-colored illustrations of her copy of *Odyssey*.

"It is not any of your business, Mr. Montague." She resisted the urge to jerk the book from his hands. She would behave as a proper lady; she would, even if it killed her.

Jacobs was still engrossed in the manuscript, much to the

detriment of other customers. The boy who brought the tea hurried to wait on a young gentleman looking for something in carved ivory. Neither looked to the trio poring over old books in the corner.

"I make it my business, Lady Marian. I am a collector of old books. These are extraordinarily rare and valuable. Have you some proof of ownership?"

Marian knew what it was to see red. Through a haze of fury she glared at the gentleman who so insulted her. It was quite possible that he was a handsome man. He had a strong chin with a cleft, and thick, dark, remarkably mobile eyebrows. She wasn't aware of ever having seen him smile, but his mouth had a handsome tilt to it. She wanted to bash him in the middle of his aristocratically patrician nose. She wouldn't be satisfied until the red she saw was his blood.

Clenching her gloved fingers, she turned to Mr. Jacobs. "I am sorry, sir, I have evidently come to the wrong place. If you will please return my manuscript, I will be leaving now."

Jacobs's small mouth fell open and he sent a beseeching gaze to the arrogant gentleman. He looked near to tears. Marian wished she had only to deal with him. Perhaps she could come back and find him alone later. She held out her hand demandingly.

Montague set her teacup in it. "You will be doing no such thing. You will break Jacobs's heart. Besides, I will wager every other vendor you've seen has offered you only half the sum these are worth."

Marian sent him a scathing glance. "Not one of them accused me of thievery, either. I would thank you to return the volumes to the bag, sir."

Montague retained his hold on the *Odyssey*. "I only wished some documentation to go with them. Volumes as rare as these will sell at a better price when their history is documented."

She clenched her hands around the teacup and tried not to look at him. She had always wished she could read the book he was holding now. The illustrations had held her captivated. She tried to remember the duke and the ball and her anxious family. "They belonged to my stepfather, sir. It would be a trifle difficult for him to come back from the grave to cite their history. Not that he would know it, anyway," she added a trifle bitterly. She might not be able to express all her anger and humiliation and sadness, but a dead man wouldn't care about sarcasm.

Montague's expressive eyebrows raised a trifle. "He was not a collector?"

"He didn't even know what he possessed, or he might have sold them with the paintings." There wasn't much use pretending anything else. She needed this honesty to balance the pressure of being polite to a man she despised and feared.

"But you knew?" He scarcely bothered to keep the incredulity from his voice.

If only she could smack him. Or throw the teacup at him. Or simply tell the ass what she thought of him. She would feel so much better. Marian tightened her lips and clenched her teeth. She couldn't speak through clenched teeth. She gave him what she hoped was a speaking glare.

Amusement flared briefly in his gray-green eyes, as if he understood her predicament. Then an expression of cool disdain dropped in place, and he was back to normal. "Of course, if you were a collector, you would know the value of the good squire's library. And if you were aware that antiquities have become very valuable of late, you need only make inquiries to ascertain their worth. If you were a true lover of books, you would not even think of parting with them."

There was the proverbial straw. With a great effort of restraint, Marian set the cup down, jerked the book from his hand, and stood up. "My opinion of you has not changed one iota, Mr. Montague. You are still a braying ass."

She returned the book to the satchel and reached for the manuscript.

Jacobs scrambled up and clutched it longingly to his chest, refusing to let it go.

Five

The situation was quite impossible. Marian was much too practical to be a watering pot, but she felt dangerously near to tears now. She could not leave without the manuscript. She could not stay in the company of the infuriating Mr. Montague. Tears might actually be the only solution, but she refused to allow the monster to drive her to them.

"Please, Mr. Jacobs, I must leave." She rose from her chair, holding out her gloved hand with what she hoped was a gesture of authority. She rather thought it looked more like a plea.

"Don't be ridiculous." Montague did not retrieve the *Odyssey* from the satchel, but stood up when the lady did. "I will give you forty pounds for it. I am certain that is more than anyone has offered you for all the books combined. The manuscript belongs in a museum, somewhere that it can receive the proper care and appreciation and can be shared by all."

Jacobs looked equally horrified by this suggestion. A man of obviously few words but eloquent expressions, he continued clutching the book and began to back away. Had the situation not been so rife with other emotions, Marian might have laughed.

Forty pounds. It was more than twice what she had been offered. Forty pounds could provide three gowns and all the accouterments and still leave funds for emergencies. She could not possibly turn down such an offer. Yet she could not possibly accept it from Montague.

When it seemed she still hesitated, Jacobs finally managed to squeak, "Fifty pounds, miss. I will give you fifty pounds."

Slightly startled, Marian glanced to her nemesis. She had thought the two were somehow together on this transaction, that Jacobs was an appraiser and Mr. Montague a rich collector. Mr. Montague's frown put an end to that theory.

When he made no further offer, Marian gave a hesitant nod. "Thank you, Mr. Jacobs, you are a true gentleman."

Positively glowing with relief, caressing the cherished manuscript, Jacobs hurried to the rear of the establishment to obtain the necessary funds.

Montague looked down his impressive nose at her. "He is not a gentleman, you know. He is just a wealthy Cit."

My, how she despised the man! Marian gave him a frosty look and disdained to answer.

He seemed determined to draw some comment from her. "You would have done better to hock your jewelry, you know. There are more people inclined to buy jewels than books."

He seemed intent on rubbing her nose in it. She saw no reason why she should not rub his as well. Back stiff as a poker, staring at the doorway where Mr. Jacobs had disappeared, she replied coldly, "Jewels? You mistake me for someone else, I am sure. Had I jewels to sell, I would surely have done so by now." Let him know that she had reached her last straw before she lowered herself to selling books.

"I see you are a liar as well as a mercenary, sharp-tongued little actress," Montague responded pleasantly. "The ruby and diamonds you were wearing the other night would bring a small fortune in a modern setting."

Another female would have had the vapors by now. Marian could see where that would be an extremely convenient ploy for avoiding such unpleasant situations. There was obviously little purpose in arguing with the gentleman, if gentleman he truly was. She didn't see how he could be, given his behavior. So a fit of the vapors would quite satisfactorily put an end to his obnoxiousness. She just wasn't inclined to falling into a heap on the floor. She was more than certain that Montague wouldn't bother to catch her.

Just thinking about Montague catching her gave her the vapors. He was exceptionally tall, and she didn't think the breadth of his chest beneath that coat had the benefit of padding. She tried not to think of just what lay beneath the gentleman's clothing. Obviously, her wits had gone to let at his insults.

"It is none of your business, but that necklace is my mother's, the only gift she retains from my father. Had I found some way of selling it without breaking my mother's heart, I should have done so long since. It is much more convenient to have a horse and carriage than to wear a stone around one's neck."

Montague raised his eyebrows. He had taunted her in all manner of ways, but she had not responded at all as he had expected. He had not produced ladylike tears, dramatic faints, or vitriolic insults. All in all, he had proved nothing about this enigmatic little harpy except that she was in desperate need of funds—and that she had the character of a stone Medusa when she wanted.

He almost had to accede to some respect for her intelligence and strength of character. He had tried to pretend he didn't see her despair at parting with the manuscript, but in light of her reaction to his suggestion of selling her jewels, he could see where her priorities lay. He knew very well what it was like to have to part with something precious, and like her, he had a distaste for wasteful ornamentation. He, too, would prefer to keep the treasure of words than the glitter of gold. But he'd be damned if he'd let her know that. It was more than obvious that this woman was not the sweet helpmeet Darley wished for wife. A woman made of steel and stone would walk all over the young viscount.

When Jacobs returned with the pouch, Montague made a show of counting out the sum for Marian's benefit. She held herself aloof from the transaction, but he noticed her eyes followed every movement. Had he attempted to pocket a single shilling, she might have leapt upon him like a tigress defending her young. He was well aware that her kind of hunger came from going without for too long.

When he was finished counting, Montague slipped the pouch into his coat pocket, picked up her satchel, and held out his arm to the young lady. "I think it best that I escort you home, Lady Marian. It would not do at all for a lady like yourself to be carrying such sums through London streets. Your carriage should be waiting by now."

Reginald could see the fury leap to her eyes, followed by suspicion. He wondered idly if she would snarl and pull a knife from that frothy little reticule or if she would remember her place and act as she ought. She did neither.

Apparently deciding he wasn't worthy of the treatment she gave Darley, she merely turned her back on him and walked out, expecting him to follow like a hired flunky.

That irritated him more than he cared to admit. It was much too early in the game for the little witch to be getting under his skin. If he was not careful, she would be married to Darley and he would have to endure this treatment for the rest of his life or write off the only true friend he had.

As he climbed into the carriage after her, Reginald had to admit that the contest was becoming personal. It was no longer a matter of saving Darley from himself, but of self-preservation. He eyed the perfectly respectable lady's maid beside her and counted another round lost. He had thought to catch her out alone again.

Idly, as if continuing a conversation, he mentioned, "It has become common practice to copy expensive jewelry. Thieves in London are rampant, and it is much more practical to keep the real jewels in a vault."

Lady Marian merely settled her skirts around her and looked through him as if he were not there. Her maid gave him a look askance, but being a good servant, she did not question his presence aloud. Knowing the importance of staying on the good side of a lady's servants, Reginald gave her a smile and would have tipped his hat had he been wearing one. Mostly, hats annoyed him, and he had a tendency to forget them at all times. The maid still looked a little wary.

He knew better than to condescend to make explanations to servants, but he had also learned at an early age how to make his way around any obstacle. Keeping his expression

pleasant, he addressed the maid rather than Lady Marian.
"Your mistress is a bit peeved with me at the moment.
Would you tell her I am most heartily sorry if I have of-
fended?"

Flustered at being addressed by an elegant gentleman for
the first time in her life, Lily fluttered her hands, looked to
Marian's stony expression, and glanced fearfully back to
the gentleman. "I don't think she accepts the apology, my
lord," she whispered.

"Mister. Just plain Mr. Montague. I suppose that ex-
plains the lady's reticence. She does not accept apologies
from those of lesser rank."

He was rewarded by a furious glare from the lady in
question. He had never seen eyes that flashed quite so de-
lightfully. It was no wonder Darley was head over heels. If
Reginald had not already seen her flash her true colors, he
might consider giving his friend a run for the money. Not
that marriage would be his objective. Smiling still, he
sought another perspective from which to reach her.

"Would you explain to the lady that I am quite circumspect? I do not go about boasting of my collection and I
would not presume to do so in the case of another collector.
The lady's secrets are quite safe with me."

The lady's shoulders seemed to relax slightly from their
stiff stance as she turned to look out the carriage window.
Her maid clenched and unclenched her fingers nervously,
uncertain how to address this situation. Having been rele-
gated permanently to hired flunky, Montague resolved to
put the maid at ease if he could not do so for the mistress.

"Will the ladies be attending Devonshire's ball?" he
asked cordially, as if conversing with servants was an
everyday occurrence. Considering his new valet, it might
become so.

The maid's face brightened. "Aye, they will. They are to
have gowns made by a modiste for the occasion."

Reginald raised his eyebrows. "I did not know gowns
could be made by anyone else."

Marian made an inelegant snort but continued to stare
out the window. The maid looked nervous at having spoken
out of turn. When she remained silent a little too long, Mar-

ian glanced back into the carriage. Reginald noted her expression of resignation rather than irritation at her maid's unwise words. It threw him momentarily off-balance.

"Most of the world constructs their own gowns, Mr. Montague. A few might hire a seamstress. Only the very rich and very fortunate can afford a modiste." As if that were lesson enough for the day, she turned back to the window.

"I cannot believe you are trying to tell me you and your family are trying to take London in homemade gowns." His gaze dropped to the drab bit of brown cotton she was wearing now. He could believe that was homemade. And so was the one she had worn at the inn. But he had seen her in evening wear as fine as any he had ever seen anywhere. What hoax was she up to now?

Marian gave him a scathing look and when her maid did not dare offer explanation, she replied, "I do not much care what you believe. You and your ilk no doubt go about running up enormous debts at tailors and trust in luck or families to pay them. We prefer to live honestly. Lily is a very fine seamstress. With her talents and our helping hands, we do very well, thank you."

The carriage was pulling to a halt in a less-than-fashionable but respectable residential side street some distance from the mansions of Mayfair. Reginald scarcely took note of his surroundings as he sought some means of resolving this situation peaceably. He found it hard to believe any word out of the woman's mouth, but then, he found it hard to believe that any impostor could sound so brutally honest. If he were to get to the bottom of her trickery, he would have to be more in her company. He could not do that unless he smoothed the feathers he had ruffled. Unfortunately, it was much more fun to ruffle them than smooth them.

"Then let me congratulate you on your fortune in finding such a paragon. I trust you pay her accordingly. Talent should be rewarded." He climbed down from the carriage as the door opened, pulling the heavy satchel after him, leaving the lady to stare after him in open-mouthed dismay.

She was forced to take his hand to descend. When she stood before him, she glanced deliberately at the pocket containing her money. Reginald toyed with the idea of making her ask for it, but even he could not sink that low. He removed the purse and handed it to her.

"If you truly wish to keep the rest of your library, remember what I have said about the jewelry," he reminded her in low tones as her maid waited a respectable distance away.

"I fail to see your interest in my jewelry, sir. In actuality, I fail to understand anything about you. My driver will return you to your destination." Carefully clutching the purse, she turned away.

Reginald watched her go with a hint of admiration. She had the proud manner of a duchess when her temper was riled. She had just successfully dismissed him as if he were a footman rather than the son of an earl. Of course, she no doubt thought him closer to a footman than an earl. He had a suspicion Lady Marian and her family had not exactly acquired a coat of town bronze yet.

He gave the driver the address of his residence rather than returning to the shop. Wouldn't it have delighted the lady to discover that he was owner of the shop and not a patron? She would have spread it all about the *ton* and forced him into permanent retreat. But he had dealt with much more sophisticated members of society without any of them ever having guessed that he was more than an eccentric collector of antiquities. He didn't think Lady Marian had any inkling that he wished to acquire her manuscript for resale, not for his own collection. He was quite annoyed with Jacobs for acquiring it as if he were bidding against him. It would be difficult to make a profit on fifty pounds. As much as the piece belonged in a museum, museums did not have that kind of money.

Maybe he ought to inform Darley that his beloved had an intellectual bent that included collecting rare medieval manuscripts. Darley had the funds to buy back the blasted piece and give it to her as a betrothal gift. Of course, once Darley realized the lady had real brains, he would turn into a rabbit and run. The viscount had been under his mother's thumb too long to want to spend the rest of his life with a wife of the same ilk.

Reginald toyed with various possibilities as the carriage rolled sedately through the streets. He had already hired a man from Bow Street to investigate the lady's background, but he was beginning to believe she was the genuine article. Even a very good actress could not produce that air of hauteur with which he had been dismissed. It was bred into the bones, he believed. An actress would overdo it, making some gesture or grimace to emphasize her displeasure. Lady Marian had merely turned her back and said everything by saying nothing.

He ventured to say that she was really a lady, but a particularly bad-tempered one. She must be practicing restraint while on the hunt for a husband. He had managed to crack that restraint a time or two today, but she had only once given vent to her real feelings. It would be amusing to see how long she lasted if provoked in front of Darley.

As Reginald stepped down from the carriage and tipped the driver, he turned his thoughts with satisfaction in that direction. Perhaps he could accomplish his goals before Bow Street accomplished theirs. He need merely be in company with the lovely Lady Marian and Darley to the extent that he ultimately wore down her patience.

How better to do it than to court the shy Miss Jessica?

Six

"O'Toole, give back the watch!" Reginald looked in the mirror as he fiddled with his cravat and yelled at his wayward valet. His new hireling was not adept with cravats, but his hands were exceedingly deft in other ways.

The valet innocently polished the gold watch with a handkerchief before handing it back to his employer. "It was just in the need of a spot of polish, my lord. A fellow needs to keep his hand in, if you know what I mean."

"I don't have a title, you needn't 'lord' me, and you had better keep those blasted hands to yourself from now on if you don't want to end up in Newgate. Thieving is a reprehensible habit for a valet."

O'Toole gallantly brushed an invisible dust mote from his employer's expensively tailored shoulders. The black swallow-tailed coat possessed not a wrinkle as it stretched over broad shoulders and narrowed to a taut waist. He was rather in sympathy with his employer on the matter of starched collars, but it was impossible to acquire the correct degree of elegance in the cravat otherwise. Instead, Mr. Montague had to aspire to strikingly done rather than elegant. Spotless linen, a fashionably embroidered white waistcoat done in gold threads, and a hint of color in the gold watch fob added to the impression. Except for the cravat, his master was a credit to his valet.

"'Tis not thievin' if I give it back," he replied insouciantly.

Reginald snorted, and picking up his walking stick and

hat, started for the door. "You need not wait up. I am quite capable of undressing myself. Just leave the maids alone. I cannot keep Jasper from sacking you if you can't keep your bloody hands to yourself."

From behind a shock of thick auburn hair and a nose full of freckles, O'Toole grinned easily. "The lasses can't leave a fella alone. You want I should spend the evenin' readin'?"

Thoroughly exasperated with his insolent servant, Reginald slammed the door on him and started down the stairs. Why in the name of all that was sane he had taken on the petty thief, he could not fathom. If he had any wits left at all, he would throw O'Toole out on his ear in the morning.

But the man knew his trade. He had polished every boot and shoe in the closet, saw that all Reginald's linen was bleached to a pristine white, and made certain every coat he owned was pressed and in good repair. And he had done it all at a minimum of expense. A man like O'Toole could be worth his weight in gold just in tailor and laundry bills. Reginald was not making such profits that he could afford not to take expenses into account.

He was well aware of this as he climbed into the carriage that he could only recently afford. It cost a great deal of money to keep up one's reputation as a wealthy aristocrat, which he needed to do to keep his business profitable. He had to be accepted into the best of homes and rub shoulders with the best society so that he could direct them to his establishment at every opportunity. Because everyone considered him a collector of excellent taste, they took his recommendations when they wished to make a purchase or a sale. It allowed him to skim the cream from the top and keep the best antiquities emporium in London. So far, no one had ever made the connection between the younger son of the Earl of Mellon and Aristotle's Emporium, and that was the way he meant it to stay.

But the carriage and the town house and the showy string of horses at Newmarket had been hard won. His family had wished for him to marry an heiress, had even picked one out whom they considered eminently suitable, but Reginald had refused the honor. He had nothing in particular against women, except that most of them seemed to be empty-headed and frivolous. Mostly, he valued his independence. He did not wish to report to a wife every day, or to be accountable to her for every penny he spent. He thought better of himself than that. He thought far too highly of himself, in his father's opinion. The earl had cut off Reginald's allowance after the argument over the heiress.

That had forced him to recognize his predicament soon enough. If he wished to be independent, he had to be independent of his family, also. He could not accept his father's money without accepting the strings attached. So he had taken what remained of his quarterly allowance, the funds he had invested in the market, and his gambling winnings, and set out to make his own way in London.

After all these years, he was finally on the way to being comfortable. He had run up excessive debts those first few years in his attempt to continue living as he had, but those debts were now paid. He had learned the difference between frugality and miserliness. It was not being tight-fisted to keep only one horse and carriage in town, but sensible, particularly at the high cost of upkeep in London. With the money saved, he could afford to buy manuscripts like the one presented by Lady Marian. Larger profits could be made on larger purchases, and the amounts grew from there, turning a penny saved into a fortune earned. He rather enjoyed the game.

But he could not afford to let society know he was a shopkeeper. Only Darley knew, and that was because Reginald had had to borrow the funds from him to buy his first inventory. Darley had been repaid with interest since and kept the secret very well. For a friend like that, Reginald would move mountains. He would also do his utmost to save that friend from a disastrous marriage.

Arriving at the rout where he had been assured he would find Lady Marian and her family, Reginald gave up his hat and stick to a servant, greeted his gratified hostess, and began the hunt.

This was not a *haut ton* affair. The assemblage was small and less than glittering, but everyone present was extremely respectable. Reginald mentally stifled a yawn as he found his prey. He had long ago lost interest in the malicious gossip, the required flirting, and the lavish entertainments for which the bulk of society existed. But it was necessary to attend these occasions to keep his ear to the ground for valuable acquisitions and to drum up new customers. That was the challenge that kept him going. Unfortunately, an entertainment such as this did not have the kind of recklessly wealthy guest that made his expensive inventory so profitable.

Reginald was here merely for Darley's sake. He smiled gallantly as the shy Jessica noticed his approach first. He was a cynical two and thirty, and she was a naive seventeen, but ambitious mamas did not object to age differences. He had no real intention of fixing the chit's interest though. He didn't think she was capable of fixing any interest at all at this age. He merely needed to dance attendance on her occasionally so he had some excuse to be close enough to rile her sister's temper in Darley's presence. The task shouldn't take as long as it would to light a candle, much less become romantically attached.

He bowed politely over Lady Grace's hand, nodded briefly to a suspicious Lady Marian, and paused in front of the lovely Jessica. "Miss Oglethorp, might I say you look ravishing this evening? Have you been introduced to my cousin, Lady Mary? She is right over there." He turned to her anxious mama. "Might I borrow your daughter for just a bit? Mary has been quite eager to meet her. I believe they are of an age."

Lady Grace gave her permission without a qualm. Everyone knew Reginald Montague. Although he was merely an "honorable," he was considered quite a catch. He came from a wealthy family and dressed with the arrogance of wealth, so it was assumed he was well to grass. There wasn't a hint of anything untoward to his reputation. He had been introduced by Lord Darley, who was the epitome of everything respectable himself. How could she possibly refuse Jessica this opportunity?

Knowing full well what was going through her mother's mind, Marian fumed. She knew the cad a shade better than her mother. She suspected the devious devil had something up his sleeve, for a man like that had little interest in a green girl like Jessica. Marian looked up with relief as Darley returned to her side with a cup of punch.

"Your friend Mr. Montague has graciously offered to introduce Jessica to his cousin," she mentioned with a small smile and a look of concern. "I do so hope she remembers her manners. She is very young yet."

Darley looked in the direction of her gaze with some surprise. This was not the kind of affair Montague generally attended, and his friend seldom bothered even speaking to his relatives. To go out of his way to make an introduction was a curiosity indeed.

"Let us go keep an eye on her if that is what you wish," he suggested, offering his arm. Not being entirely a fool, Darley knew his friend's sterling character was thoroughly corroded by cynicism, and he felt a certain sense of responsibility for the shy Jessica, since he had made the introduction.

Marian accepted his arm and they were soon part of the circle to which Montague had introduced Jessica. Marian's shy sister was listening with eyes alight at the quick badinage exchanged by these young people who had known each other all their lives, but Jessica was scarce offering a word herself.

Reginald easily made room for them beside him, giving Lady Marian a slight nod of acknowledgment. "You have joined us just in time to extol the merits of the Season's leading beauties and to lay your wager on which one will win Devonshire. I am sure Lady Marian has an opinion on the subject."

"Since I do not know the gentleman, I cannot judge what he prefers in a female, sir. Besides, I am not objective. I believe my sister is all that is perfection in a lady."

Jessica turned red as all gazes turned to her. She had no witty words to say in reply, and Darley gallantly jumped in to assist her. "Miss Oglethorp is indeed a rare orchid in a hothouse full of beautiful flowers. Like many rare flowers, it would take a wise man to recognize her worth."

Someone else laughed. "That leaves out Devonshire,

then. Unless she is an expensive and gilded wall hanging, he will not notice that she exists."

"He cannot look at all eligible females as wall hangings," Montague protested. "He must choose among them some time. Perhaps we could present Lady Marian in a gilded halo and cloth of gold. What odds could we take then?"

Marian flashed him a look of irritation but responded sweetly, "The odds would be very good that I would trip and fall under the burden of a halo, I'm certain. I have no aspirations to be a duchess."

Darley sent her an appreciative glance, and Montague hid a grimace. Round one, score one to naught. He turned to his young cousin. "Mary, you have been introduced to the gentleman. Do you think he would prefer a bookish female to a beautiful one?"

The young lady gave a trill of laughter. "Wherever did you mean to find a bookish female, Reginald? Do not look in my direction. I cannot remember seeing the inside of a book since I left the schoolroom."

Jessica spoke hesitantly. "Marian reads. She is all the time in the library."

A young gentleman eager to impress her with his wit leapt into the debate, "But what does she actually do there? The dark corners of libraries offer more interesting delights than books."

This conversation was growing entirely too risque for an innocent like Jessica. Marian sent Darley a glance, but Montague was the one to respond first.

"Harrington, there ought to be enough light in your pate from the holes in it that you never need a candle. Miss Oglethorp, would you care to accompany me to the buffet?"

Marian and Darley followed, leaving the more sophisticated young people to laugh and gossip behind their backs. Marian sent her escort a veiled look. How had Lord Darley taken the news of her literary bent? He was frowning slightly, but she could not tell if it had to do with her or with the foolish remark of the young gentleman. She was terrified of saying anything that would make him think less of her. Drat Montague for introducing the subject of books. She desperately needed to bring Darley up to scratch soon.

As they reached the table, Montague turned and offered Marian a plate. "A bluestocking, Lady Marian? I never would have guessed it."

He was deliberately provoking her. She could see it in the laughing challenge of his eyes. He wanted her to slap him or do something equally outrageous. Marian knew her temper and her sharp tongue were her worst weaknesses, and this man was aiming directly at them. She wasn't certain why he was doing this, but she didn't intend to play into his hands.

"I daresay there are a great number of things that you will never guess, Mr. Montague. It takes an open mind to see all possibilities." She serenely took the plate offered and began to fill it with dainties from the table.

Darley chuckled and reached to help Jessica slice a piece of cake. "The lady is much too quick to bite at your bait, old boy. Leave off and let us enjoy the evening."

If he continued to pick at her, he would only make a fool of himself, Reginald realized. Darley was so smitten that he could not see what was right before his face. The lady had all but admitted to being a bluestocking. Her quick wit and quicker tongue should have made him wary. But his friend simply couldn't see beyond a pleasant voice and a bosom too round for fashion. Admittedly, he was having some trouble looking beyond that enticing display himself. The lady's maid/modiste had an eye for emphasizing the positive without disregarding propriety.

"I apologize for any offense you might have taken in my cousin's company, Miss Oglethorp," Reginald offered as a sop to his conscience, "Mary's friends tend to be a bit fast. I had forgotten that."

Jessica gave him a blank look before hastily returning her gaze to her plate. "I thought they seemed very nice, but I do not understand what they said about dark corners. It is very difficult to read in dark rooms. Marian always lights a lamp."

In another moment, Darley would be rolling on the floor with laughter, Reginald thought with disgust. Courting Jessica was going to make an ass out of him, proving Lady Marian's roundly stated opinion. He would do better to court the lady herself.

Even as he thought this, something inside him began to hum with anticipation. Reginald glanced toward the lady as she bit into a piece of marzipan and licked delicately at her lips. She wasn't beautiful, but she exuded the sensuality of an experienced courtesan. He could see why Darley was smitten.

It would give him a great deal more pleasure to seduce the Lady Marian than to smile pleasantly at the lovely Jessica.

Then Darley would be forced to recognize the fickleness of his lady-love.

Seven

"Mr. Montague seems to be quite a pleasant young man," Lady Grace said absently as she made a neat slice through the seal of the next letter on the stack beside her. "I don't know what you hold against him, Marian."

Marian sipped at her morning tea and frowned at the hideous hunting picture on the wall opposite. "He is not at all what he seems, Mama. I cannot fathom why he showed such particular attention to Jessica the other night. And the flowers are completely out of character."

"The flowers were addressed to all of us, dear. You mustn't put much store in it. And what can you possibly know of the gentleman's character? You have barely spoken with him." She set one invitation aside in the acceptance pile, discarded several pieces of mail, and started on the next.

Marian couldn't admit that she had more than spoken to the man. It would serve nothing to tell her mother that they had exchanged insults on several occasions, for that would not reflect any better on her than on him. And she preferred not to discuss her means of obtaining funds. Her mother was inclined to be hysterical, and she would worry fiercely if she knew the kinds of places Marian had been visiting in order to sell the books. So she couldn't mention meeting the man at an antiquities emporium.

She crumbled her toast instead. "I suppose I must be pleasant to him for Darley's sake, but I cannot find it easy to like the man." She also couldn't say she didn't like the way he made her feel when he looked at her. That didn't seem at all the thing to be discussing over the breakfast table. But she remembered very well how Montague's assessing gaze had rested on her, and how it had made her skin tingle and her stomach feel quivery. Despite his reputation, the man was no doubt a rake. No other gentleman looked at her like that.

Her mother's puzzled exclamation from the end of the table made Marian turn her thoughts back to the present. "What is it? Surely we have not been invited to another ducal ball? Those gowns we have ordered will cost the earth as it is."

"Do you think we can cancel the order?" Lady Grace asked in a low voice, staring at the letter.

Growing alarmed, Marian put down her toast. "What is it? Do we need to return home? Has something happened to the house?"

Her mother handed over the paper with a frown of puzzlement. "I'm not at all certain, dear. What can this mean? I'm quite certain the squire said his man was all that was honest. Surely he would not be asking for such sums without reason. Perhaps he means they are debts that come due when the harvest comes in?"

Marian scanned the letter once with dread, then began again to be certain she understood correctly. Squire Oglethorp had always handled the family business dealings. He had a steward to manage the farm. After he had died, the steward and the family solicitor had dealt with the bulk of the family finances, leaving Marian only to manage the day-to-day business of surviving on the meager allowance given them. She could see that had been a mistake. She should have made more inquiries about the family's state of affairs.

"It says the taxes have not been paid and there is interest coming due on the mortgage," she murmured, more to herself than as explanation to her mother.

"We cannot possibly pay such a sum until the harvest comes in, can we? Why do they send this to us? It is their business to handle the farm, is it not?"

"They say there are no funds for paying the debts. They

have spent all on seeds and labor. We must borrow the money to pay the rest. If there is a good harvest, we can pay the loan then."

Lady Grace looked at her blankly. "How does one go about borrowing money? Isn't that what we have the solicitor to do?"

Marian folded the letter slowly. "He has found no one willing to extend such a loan. He thinks we might have better luck among our friends here in London."

Lady Grace picked up her teacup and stared at it in bewilderment. "We are to ask our friends for loans? That does not seem at all proper."

Crushing the letter in her hand, Marian pushed away from the table. "Do not worry about it just yet. Perhaps we can cancel the gowns, as you suggested. I will look into it."

Her mother looked relieved. "And I am certain Lord Darley is at the asking point. He will help us understand what to do once you are betrothed. We must wait until then."

Marian hurried out of the room and toward the study, her favorite hiding place since the town house did not possess a library. Canceling the ball gowns would accomplish little. Their cost was negligible compared to the sum quoted in the letter. She still had a goodly amount of the fifty pounds left after judicious negotiating over materials with the modiste, but even that sum wouldn't come close to touching the amount of taxes and interest due. Why hadn't someone informed them of the debt before? Perhaps if they had not come to London they could have scraped together enough to satisfy their creditors.

But the amounts would only come due again next year, and if the harvest failed again, they would be out of a home. They had to come to London to find husbands who could support them. Somehow, she must stall for time until she was safely wed. She had to bring Darley up to scratch soon.

Had she been a man, she could have gone down to her club and found a drinking buddy who would gladly extend a loan for a few months. Women did not have that alternative. She could not very well ask Darley for a loan. Perhaps when they were betrothed she could act helpless and ask his advice, but not before then. It might be weeks or months before Darley summoned the nerve to ask for her hand. This letter seemed to indicate that they didn't have that long.

Marian sat down in the massive chair behind the desk and stared helplessly at her trunk of books. She was certain Mr. Jacobs would be delighted to buy every one of them. If he gave her twice what she had been quoted previously, she might manage most of the sum needed, but she rather thought Mr. Montague was responsible for the earlier extravagant sum. Mr. Jacobs would surely not be so foolish a second time, without the wealthy gentleman looking on.

Thinking of Mr. Montague stirred the germ of another thought, one she wished she could shove aside. He had said the necklace was very valuable, and that there were ways of making copies, that many people did it. Would it be so very awful if her mother possessed only a copy of her precious necklace? It would still look the same, and she would still have the memory of her husband giving it to her. At the same time, they would have the money to save their home.

She didn't know if she could make herself do it. She got up and paced the room, from the glass-encased bookcase of musty tomes to the heavily draped window overlooking the mews. If she should ever be wealthy enough to have a study of her own, she would have it built with windows everywhere and draperies on nary a one. That was a fine thought, she realized, when she was about to lose the one study she owned.

Her mother had no desire to marry again, yet she needed a home of her own. With the proper care, the farm could produce again. It had made Squire Oglethorp wealthy once. It just hadn't made him wealthy enough for extravagance. By living carefully, her mother could be comfortable in a short time—if she still had the farm to live on. It would provide her an income for the rest of her life. Selling it would leave her subject to the whims of any husbands her daughters might acquire. That did not seem at all a satisfactory solution given the nature of men and the vicissitudes of life.

Perhaps it would be possible to just pawn the necklace

for a little while. She had heard of such things. It would be like borrowing money with the necklace as collateral. If it brought enough to pay off the debt and have a copy made, no one would know what she had done. Then when the harvest came in, she could retrieve the original.

That thought brightened the situation considerably. Had the stone been entirely hers, she would have had no qualms about selling it outright in order to ensure her mother's future. She held no sympathy for a father who had left her a mere pittance and a single heirloom to survive on. She was not in the least sentimental about the wretched rock. But her mother was.

She would have to ask Mr. Montague how to go about pawning the necklace and getting a copy made. She hated the thought of speaking to him at all, but he was already aware of their desperate need of funds. He had apparently said nothing to Lord Darley, and for that she had to be grateful. She simply could not lower herself in the viscount's eyes by admitting their financial desperation. She must seem sweet and unconcerned about such things until she had Darley's ring on her finger. She would have to work at making that sooner rather than later. In the meantime, she needed to deal with the obnoxious Mr. Montague.

She wasn't at all certain how to go about it, however. She couldn't very well send a note around to his house explaining the problem, and she couldn't count on finding him at the emporium. She must somehow wait until they met again and find a way to get him alone.

The thought of being alone with Reginald Montague was enough to give her the shivers. He was a tall man of considerable strength, she wagered. She had read enough stories of what happened to foolish young women who trusted themselves alone with such men. She would have to rely on the fact that he despised her. Surely men did not molest women whom they despised?

Fortune smiled on her for a change the very next day. While her mother and Jessica were out making calls, Marian chose to stay at home and read. She knew Darley had been called out of town this morning on some estate business, so she grabbed this opportunity to be alone. She found

the social whirl of London quite fatiguing after a lifetime of
rural serenity. Her sanity survived on these moments of
solitude.

When their manservant announced a gentleman caller,
she almost had him say she was not at home. But glancing
at the card presented, she took back that hasty thought.
Montague.

He had never presented himself here before. She could
not imagine why he was doing so now other than out of
friendship to Darley. If she were to have him brought up,
she ought to have Lily with her. She shouldn't entertain
him alone.

But she needed to speak with him alone. She couldn't
very well ask him about pawning the ruby in front of Lily.
Fortune had been kind enough to grant her this opportunity.
She had to have the courage to grasp it.

"Very well, Simmons, have him brought up, then bring
us some tea. I am certain Mama will be home shortly and
will wish to see him." She hoped that placated the stiff and
proper London servant's disapproval.

Montague looked surprised when he entered to find only
Marian present. He hid his momentary consternation well
when he accepted the seat offered.

"This is a pleasure, Lady Marian. I did not expect to find
you alone. Darley told me he was being called out of town
and asked that I look in on all of you upon occasion. Are
you already mourning his absence?"

He was twitting her, she was certain. She held her tongue
as a maid carried in the tea tray. When the girl was gone,
she attempted a pleasant expression. "You are refining
upon nothing, sir. Lord Darley is free to come and go as he
pleases, as am I. It would be presumptuous of me to mourn
his absence under those circumstances."

He nodded approvingly as he sipped his tea. "You do not
count your eggs before they are hatched, I see. A wise
woman, indeed. Do you set your sights on the duke then?"

Marian's lips tightened and she set her cup carefully on
the table. "If you have come to be insulting, sir, I would
thank you to leave now."

Montague held his hand up in a gesture of peace. "I

thought only to speak with you honestly as we have done previously. If you wish the usual drivel, so be it. Is not the weather very fine for this time of year? Would you care to go driving this afternoon?"

Marian scowled and handed him a plate of scones. "I cannot fathom what Darley sees in you, sir, but as we are on the subject of honesty, I will admit that there is a reason I allowed you up here unattended."

His expressive eyebrows raised. "I had wondered," he murmured. "I had not thought it was because you wished to seduce me."

She flung a pillow at him. He cleverly managed to divert the pillow while keeping a precarious hold on his teacup, thereby preventing a disastrous spill on his stockinette breeches. "That could have been uncomfortable," he murmured, carefully setting the china back on the tray. "Do you often indulge in these fits of pique? Is Darley aware of it?"

"You deliberately bring out the worst in me, Mr. Montague. If you tell Lord Darley about this visit, I shall have to inform him of your insult. I thought we were to call a truce."

"Why is it that ladies must turn jests into insults? Is it because they possess no sense of humor?"

"It is because their sense of humor does not rely on the vulgar, sir. I find nothing humorous in being accused of seduction, even if I had any knowledge of such things, which I don't. Your assumption that I do is insulting."

"The fact that you speak of such things with anger instead of fainting dead away tells me you know a great deal more than most ladies about these subjects. Let us cut the pretense, Lady Marian. You are no young innocent to wear white and pale at the mention of a man's inexpressibles. You are well-read and have a brain behind that pretty face. We will get on vastly better if you admit to it instead of playing the part of sweetness and light as you do with Darley."

So that was it. Entwining her fingers in vexation, Marian sent him a venomous glare. "I try very hard to be what is expected of me, sir. You do me no favors by encouraging me otherwise. But for the moment, let us set aside our differences. I need your help."

Montague looked interested at that. He even dared to retrieve his teacup. "Please go on, my lady. I am at your service."

She had a good reply to make to that, but she held her tongue. She needed his help, not his anger. "My mother received a rather distressing letter from her solicitor today. It seems we are in need of borrowing a rather serious sum to keep our home. It can be paid back immediately upon the harvest, but apparently the man has been unable to find a lender." She spoke succinctly, if with considerable distaste at revealing such matters to a relative stranger. She hastened to continue speaking before he could interrupt. "I might conceivably obtain much of it by selling the remains of the library, but you once mentioned the worth of my necklace. Is it possible to in some way use it as collateral for a small loan?" She breathed easier once she had the words out.

Montague considered the question carefully, swirling the tea in his cup. "You would wish to make a copy of it so your mother does not find out?"

Biting her lip, Marian nodded.

"And you do not wish to sell it outright?"

She shook her head. "I feel enough of a thief to consider even this. I know the stone is to come to me, but it is all my mother has."

"It suits your coloring more than hers," he said thoughtfully. "Your father must have been dark."

"I believe so. I was very young when he died. His portrait stayed with the estate, so I have not seen it since we left." She continued to watch him anxiously.

He took another sip of tea and watched her over the edge of the cup. "The current marquess cannot be called upon for help? Perhaps he would be interested in acquiring the jewel if it is an heirloom."

He wasn't going to help. Trying to hide her despair, Marian glanced at the mantel clock. Perhaps her mother and sister would be home soon to put an end to this distressing conversation. "I do not know the gentleman. He was in the

Americas when my father died, and as I said, I was very young. The solicitors arranged for our removal, I believe. From something the squire once said, I don't believe the estate was much in funds at the time. Apparently much of the unentailed land had been sold off for generations. I do not know the details. I just know I could not ask a total stranger for help."

Montague understood pride. He had too much of it himself. He nodded absently, then returned the cup to the table. "You cannot expect to obtain as great a sum by pawning it as by selling it outright. May I ask how much you need?"

The sum she quoted wasn't unreasonable, but it would take every penny of cash he could scrape together.

Montague sighed and stood up. "Go get the necklace. I think it is time we went for a drive."

Eight

W
here are we going?" Marian murmured as Mr. Montague wheeled his fashionable curricle toward the park. She had already noted with a great amount of nervousness that he had no groom in the seat behind.

"We shall show ourselves in the park as is expected, then make a slight detour to a jeweler. I shall have you back in your parlor in good time."

Marian clasped her hands in her lap and tried to look pleased. The ruby necklace in her reticule made that more than difficult. "It will take time to make a copy, will it not? How will I explain the absence of the necklace while it is being done?"

"Tell your mother that I am a great expert on jewelry and that I recommended it be cleaned to keep its beauty." Montague steered the horses into the park and joined the steady procession already there.

Marian was grateful that she was wearing one of her new London gowns as they met the stares of the *ton* in the park. The light jonquil yellow of her gown almost matched the tiny rosebuds and ribbons of her bonnet. She did not look completely dowdy, but she was aware of being nowhere near as fashionable as the other young lovelies in plumes and vivid carriage dresses. She told herself she did not care, but she disliked being judged and found wanting.

"How much will this copy cost?" She tried to keep her mind on business and not the picture they were presenting to the crowds. Mr. Montague looked very fine in his curly-brimmed beaver, driving his matched bays. His height made him seem exceptionally distinguished, but mostly it made her nervous. She was much more comfortable with Lord Darley beside her.

"The price of a few gowns, I daresay. Are you certain you would not prefer selling outright? Perhaps if you consulted your mother—"

Marian stiffened her shoulders. "We will make do with what gowns we have. I count them a fair price for my mother's peace of mind."

He sent her a long look before returning his attention to the fashionable crowd around them. He raised his whip in greeting to several young bloods and made nods to a number of dowagers taking the air. "You make it difficult to tell when you are giving me Spanish coin, my lady," he murmured while keeping an affable smile fixed to his countenance.

"Since it is utterly of no consequence to you, sir, it should not matter." She responded with the same insincere smile as she waved at an acquaintance.

"I stand corrected. There is Lady Jersey, smile pretty. I had not realized it has become fashionable to expose so much flesh in the afternoons. Do women not feel the chill?"

Marian nearly swallowed her tongue at this outrageous remark, said with the same smile and gallant greeting he had been using since they entered the park. She had some difficulty managing a pleasant expression while in the process of swallowing her tongue, and she nearly choked before Lady Jersey's carriage moved on in the other direction.

"You are a dreadful man," she remonstrated once she'd recovered.

"There is a phrase I remember from my misspent youth: 'It takes one to know one,' I believe is how it went." He serenely guided the horses out of the park and into the busy street.

"No matter what you think of me, you cannot call me a man," she reminded him. "And I fail to see in what way I am dreadful. It was not I who made that remark about Lady Jersey."

"But you were thinking it," he pointed out unreasonably. "Besides, 'dreadful' covers quite a few sins, lying and deceiving being among them, I am certain."

"If consenting to help me gives you liberty to insult me at will, I shall withdraw my request, Mr. Montague. You may return me home now."

"We are almost there, and it is your own behavior that gives me reason to insult you. Darley is my best friend. I will not see him shackled to a harpy."

Marian was given no time to form a reply. He curbed the carriage and swung down in one fluid motion, flipping a coin to a street urchin to grab his horses' heads before reaching to assist her out of the carriage. Now that the battle lines were drawn, she wasn't at all certain what she ought to say. Somehow, she had created a formidable enemy. She did not know what to do to combat his opinion of her.

So she said nothing, and allowed him to escort her into the jeweler's. While she examined the glittering displays, he spoke to the jeweler about insurance and values and the need to preserve family heirlooms. The jeweler seemed most sympathetic, and when he quoted his appraisal of the gem's worth, she nearly sank through the floor. She had been carrying that much wealth around her neck?

Montague made the arrangements for the copy to be made, received a receipt for the necklace, and returned to Marian's side. He glanced at the case of brooches she had been admiring.

"The ivory is very fine," he said, taking her elbow, "but I suppose it is the diamond that has caught your eye."

Marian started stiffly toward the door. "Had you asked me, I would have told you that the ivory would look very well with my new willow-green morning gown. I do not think diamonds would suit it at all." She swept out the door and toward the carriage.

He kept a strong hold on her elbow and steered her down the street. "I think we have time for an ice, don't you? We ought to have some pleasure from this day."

Marian turned her head to stare up at him in surprise. "I cannot imagine why," she said honestly. "We both dislike each other heartily. Why should we draw out the punishment?"

His lips curled in amusement as he glanced down at her. "Does that sharp tongue of yours not give you pain occasionally? I should think you would have cut your mouth to pieces if naught else."

She bit her tongue and stared straight ahead, saying nothing.

"All right, this time I was wrong. You were being honest, but you injured my high opinion of myself. It had never occurred to me that my company might be a punishment." He held open the door to Gunter's and helped her in.

"It is only reasonable to assume that since you find my company so unpleasant, that the feeling would be returned." Marian took the seat offered, nodded to a few acquaintances, and proceeded to play with her gloves rather than face the unsmiling man taking the seat across from her.

He gave their order before answering. When he returned his attention to her, he halted her fidgeting by the simple expedient of covering her hand with his. "When did I ever say that I find your company unpleasant? Challenging, perhaps. Amusing, occasionally. Certainly enlightening at all times. But I cannot remember one occasion of unpleasantness."

Immediately suspicious of this polite behavior, Marian jerked her hand away and glared at him. "You did not find it unpleasant being called an ass? You constantly complain of my sharp tongue; do you find pleasure in the pain of it? If so, you are a most unusual man."

Montague smiled, transforming his normally staid expression to one of charm. "I am that, I admit. Even Darley will tell you so. Can we not cry '*pax*' and be friends?"

"I cannot see how." Marian returned to worrying at her gloves. "You have all but stated your desire to keep Lord Darley from my 'clutches,' as I assume you perceive them."

The waiter placed the ices on the table and discreetly departed. Marian picked idly at hers. She would have delighted in the luxury at any other time. Now, her mind was elsewhere.

"You do not love him," Montague pointed out, heartily enjoying his confection. "All you see in him is his wealth."

Marian favored him with a look of annoyance. "It is not. Admittedly, I cannot marry where there is not wealth, for my family's sake, but there are plenty of eligible bachelors with plump pockets. It may be my duty to marry well, but I will have to live with my choice for the rest of my life. Lord Darley suits me very well, and if I suit him, I cannot see your objection. Marriages are made on a great deal less than that all the time. I have not deceived him in any way as to the portion I can expect."

Montague cleaned his dish during this tirade. When she was done, he answered calmly, "No, you have deceived him as to your true nature. Darley needs a quiet, biddable wife, one who will not run roughshod over him as his mother does, one who will make his life pleasant and not a living hell. I am aware, where he is not, that you are not what he thinks."

Marian folded her napkin and stood up. "That is your opinion. We will never agree on this matter. I wish to go home."

Her cold tone forbade any other alternative. Montague escorted her from the confectioner's and down the street to his waiting carriage.

As he climbed in beside her, he said, thoughtfully, "I realize I am not titled, but am I considered wealthy enough to deserve a place on your list of eligible bachelors?"

She stared at him in horror. "You and Jessica would not suit, I assure you. If I marry well, she may wait and marry where her heart lies. Do not try to confuse her into thinking it is her duty to marry elsewhere."

He gave her a thoughtful look. "You are a most unusual woman. Most would have assumed I meant to pursue them."

She settled back against the squabs. "You have already discovered I am not stupid. I would have to be extremely silly to be that vain."

A secret smile curled his lips again. "I can see you are

going to lead me a merry chase, my lady. Let us get you back to the house before your mother calls the watch."

"O'Toole, you do have your uses. The lady will be able to see herself in those." Reginald glanced down at the polished gleam of the knee-high boots his valet was returning to the rack.

"The lady is in the habit of admiring herself in boots?" the insolent valet inquired as he came up behind his master to brush off the coat waiting to be donned.

"Actually, the lady I had in mind is more likely to bite off my nose than admire my toes, but her young sister has an affinity for admiring floors. Perhaps my boots will keep her amused while I woo the elder."

The valet looked mildly interested as he helped his employer into the tightly tailored coat. "If you are going to continue escorting ladies through the park, you ought to have a groom. Did I mention that I often served as the marquess's driver?"

Reginald raised a disbelieving eyebrow. "Why am I inclined to doubt that?" he asked the ceiling as he adjusted his cravat.

"Well, if he were not dead, he could confirm it," O'Toole assured him. "And any nodcock can act the part of groom. All I need do is stand at the back of the carriage and look handsome. For a few extra coins, I am willing to sacrifice myself in your service."

There was some truth in that. If Reginald could be certain that the wretch wouldn't decide his horses were worth more than honest employment, he could leave his valuable animals in the care of someone experienced instead of relying on street urchins. And he might have less difficulty persuading Lady Marian from the safety of her home if she felt they would be properly chaperoned. His two-seated carriage wouldn't hold her lady's maid or sister, unless they wished to sit in the groom's seat. He hummed thoughtfully as he fastened his coat buttons.

"I suppose I would have to wear one of those devilish box coats in forest green or something equally dismal," the valet continued gloomily. "That would be cheaper than turning me out in a monkey suit of red and gold or something equally outlandish. I might even have something suitable in my own wardrobe if you will trust my discretion. I could be ready when the carriage is brought around."

"Your presumptuousness is scarcely outweighed by your arrogance, you young idiot. Have I said I need a groom?"

"You did not say that you did not," he replied reasonably. "And if I go out with you of an evening, you will know that I am not flirting with the maid."

"Or stealing from the wine cellar. Jasper keeps an inventory, you know. I think you owe me a few evenings' service to pay for that bottle of burgundy that has disappeared."

O'Toole did not look overly concerned with the accusation as he put away the gentleman's shaving gear. "I can offer my services on trial, as it were, for a few nights, until you see how well it will work out."

A thief, a groom, and a valet, all in one, Reginald thought to himself as he picked up his hat and stick. He was certainly getting his money's worth. "Then go find your bottle-green coat or whatever, and let us be on our way." He was going to regret this, he had a feeling, but he would never know for certain until he tried.

Actually, the idea of using O'Toole as his groom was an excellent one, if the man could be relied on. Reginald did not keep a stable in London. He stored his horses and carriage in a rental stall. He had to hire someone to look after them whenever he attended an entertainment not within walking distance. It was a pestilent nuisance, but he hadn't the funds to maintain a town house like his father's with a mews in back. Having someone within the household to handle the chore of ordering the carriage brought around and keeping the horses in hand would be convenient. He should have thought of it sooner.

Of course, O'Toole probably wasn't the ideal person, but he was available and willing, and Reginald did have several stops to make tonight. If it didn't work out, the thief could go back to amusing the maid in the evening.

He didn't go so far as to allow the wretch to drive, however. Reginald took up the reins himself as his valet adopted a suitably correct position in the back. The lad could emulate a duke if he tried, with his posturing and posing. He smiled at that. Perhaps he could introduce O'Toole to Lady Marian as a wealthy substitute to Darley. He wasn't making much headway with the lady on his own.

He wheeled up in front of the Earl of Tunningham's town house and sent O'Toole up to announce his arrival. Darley would appreciate the jest when he saw the messenger.

When the viscount came down to join him, he scarcely seemed aware of O'Toole's presence. He had been gone several days at his father's request on some estate matter, but it looked like the weight of the world had found him while he was gone. Reginald gave his friend a concerned look as he picked up the reins.

"You look like the blue dismals have wrapped around you, old boy. Anything I can do?"

Darley slouched in the seat to prevent wrinkling his trousers. "You've already been more than helpful, I hear. I understand you've been escorting Lady Marian in my absence?"

Reginald raised his eyebrows but kept his attention on his horses. "At your request, you'll remember. She's something of a handful. Did you know yesterday she wished to see Elgin's marbles, but because we had exchanged words the day before, she refused to get in the carriage with me? I had to leave the carriage and follow her and her sister through the streets to make certain they didn't get into any trouble."

"That doesn't sound like Marian." Darley crossed his arms over his chest. "If you don't like her, why did you drive her to the park and take her to Gunter's and escort her to Hatchards?"

Reginald scowled. "Because a certain friend of mine asked that I look after her, and I knew of no other way to do it. She's seldom available for a discreet morning call. The woman is all about traipsing across town every minute of the day."

"You could have suggested she wait until I was there to escort her."

Reginald finally sent him an incredulous look. "Wait?
Does she know the meaning of the word? I found her at
Hatchards without her maid because the multitalented Lily
had a gown to repair. I missed an appointment at Jackson's
because she desired to see the Tower and intended to go
with her sister if I couldn't escort her. The woman is a per-
petual motion machine. You try suggesting she wait until
you have time for her."

Satisfied, Darley drew a deep sigh of relief. "I apologize.
I'm not much with the ladies and you are. It's demeaning to
know I can be jealous of my best friend. If I weren't so
hen-hearted, I'd go to her mama immediately and press my
suit so I wouldn't have to put myself through this. What if
she sets her cap for Devonshire?"

Reginald kept his voice nonchalant to hide his alarm.
"She's too sensible by far to set her cap so high. A few
weeks isn't enough time to be certain of your affections.
Let the lady enjoy her freedom a while longer, while you
enjoy yours. A lifetime is too long to pay if you decide
wrong."

"I haven't thought of Marian wishing to enjoy her freedom a while longer. I suppose you're right. She's been
cooped up in the country all these years. She has a right to
spread her wings a little before I clip them. Do you think
she'll have me, though? I'm not much to look at, and the
ladies put a lot of store in that."

"They put a lot of store in wealth and titles too. She'll
have you, no doubt, rest assured on that." Reginald's tone
was wry.

Darley sent him a swift look. "What if her affections fall
elsewhere? All the wealth and titles will serve nothing
then."

Affections had nothing to do with anything when you
were up the River Tick, but Reginald refrained from saying
that. He managed to merely reply, "You must set your sight
to capturing her affections, then, hadn't you?"

Behind them, the spurious groom listened with great interest.

Nine

Reginald watched grimly as Darley headed straight across the room in the direction of Lady Marian. While listening to his hostess prattle about the highly successful squeeze of the crowd and the need to open a few windows in such unusually wicked heat, he managed to see Marian give Darley a slow, sweet smile that made even his own toes tingle. Damn, but she was good at what she was doing.

Excusing himself from his hostess and making his way toward the refreshment table, he watched as Marian made graceful gestures with hands that occasionally lighted on Darley's arm. He saw Darley laugh at some witticism that had her hiding behind her fan. She was no doubt batting her eyelashes for all they were worth, Reginald concluded dismally as he helped himself to the punch. No wonder Darley was smitten.

That complicated matters severely. He had no desire to lose Darley's friendship in a competition over a woman, particularly not a lying, deceitful woman like Lady Marian. If his friend's affections were truly attached, he would have to surrender the game and hope for the best. But he was rather certain Darley's interest was more in the lady's seemingly biddable nature and easy accessibility. He would not give up quite yet, not until he had made some attempt to show Darley the lady's true colors.

How he was going to do that without making a total clunch of himself was up for debate. The Bow Street Runner had come back with sufficient evidence that the lady was who she said she was. The ambitious detective had even attempted to interview the current Marquess of Effingham, only to be told he was away from home. The few servants the Runner had managed to interview had all been new and of little help, but Lady Marian's whereabouts had seemed to be common knowledge, and it had coincided with the truth. There was no evidence that the lady flirting with Darley now was anyone other than the daughter of the late Marquess of Effingham.

So Reginald was going to have to rely on his own abilities to unmask the lady's character. It would be no easy task. She had shown no particular interest in his suit these last days, and for good reason, he supposed. He had no title and as a younger son, his wealth was suspect. The lady wasn't so impractical as to fall for a pretty face. And she had already warned him away from her little sister. He could not fathom how he was going to play out this charade.

Feeling as if he were made of stone, Reginald made his way across the crowded room in the direction of the happy pair.

With a graceful flourish of long, skillful fingers, a silver coin appeared behind the groom's grubby ear. Lamplight glittered off the coin as the fingers bounced it lightly up and down, flashing silver against a gloved palm, until suddenly, it disappeared in mid-air.

"How'd you do that?" Suspicious, the old man in wrinkled livery glared at the smooth cotton of the now-empty glove.

"As I said, magic." Propped against the carriage, O'Toole crossed his bottle-green–clad arms over his chest.

"'Tis a trick. Show me how to do it." The old man shifted his glare to the younger man's grinning composure.

"It's not a trick. It's magic. One has to be born with the magic touch."

The old man scowled. "If 'twere magic, you'd be living like a king instead o' grubbin' stables."

O'Toole shook his head. "Magic cannot be used for

one's own profit. Greed destroys the power. Magic can only be used for the benefit of others."

The old groom glared at him stubbornly. "Then make me rich."

O'Toole laughed. "Your greed isn't any better than mine. Besides, making you rich wouldn't necessarily be for your benefit." He glanced toward the tall mansion glittering inside and out with lamps and candles and the sparkle of jewels. "Look at them in there. They got more than we can dream of, but do you think they're all happy?"

"Ought to be," the old man grumped, easing his aching bones onto a mounting block. "But they ain't all plump in the pocket. Some's not worth a bean more than we are. They just put on a good show."

"There's that, I suppose." The silver coin flipped in the air over O'Toole's hand again as he uncrossed his arms. "There's some that would leave the likes of us unpaid for years rather than give up their pleasures."

"Not my ladies," the other man answered loyally. "They do their own mending and the like so as to make sure we get paid every quarter day."

"Out to find rich husbands, are they?" The coin twirled in mid-air, disappeared, and reappeared as a penny.

Trying not to be impressed by this flashy display, the old man adjusted his baggy breeches. "Way of the world, it is. The young miss is a bit of a shy 'un, but my lady has already found 'erself a viscount. Belowstairs is waitin' a 'appy announcement any day now. The young gentleman is said to be generous with his pockets. We'll all be well to grass soon enough."

"Well, I'm sure congratulations are in order. Does the young lady seem happy with her choice? Not stuck with an old codger, is she?"

The groom shrugged. "'Appy enough, I'd say. 'E's not a well set-up sort, but 'e's young. There's nothin' to complain of."

"That's good. The young lady my master's been seein' has a devil of a tongue. She ripped up at him royally the other day."

The groom chuckled. "My lady 'as a bit o' temper too.

She's taken a friend of the viscount's into dislike. 'Eard 'er out on the street once a'tellin' 'im what she thought of 'im. And Simmons said as 'ow she threw a pillow at 'im the other day, near to knocked the tea from his 'and and into 'is lap. Mighty uncomfortable that would 'ave been, I wager."

The penny became two silver coins, then three, spinning and swirling in the lamplight between O'Toole's gloved hands. He was grinning happily as he watched the coins. "I daresay it would. Reminds me of the marquess I used to work for. Devil of a temper that man had. Wife was a quiet, pretty woman, didn't quite know how to handle it when he went off on one of his rages. Never took them out on her, though. He'd ride his horse 'til it came back lathered, apologize to the lads he'd combed over good, then go back to work with a smile as if all was well with the world again."

The old man couldn't help staring with widened eyes at the coins flickering silver in and out of the shadows. "That's the way of my lady, all right. Do summit wrong, and she'll scold until she peels the hide off your back, but do it right, and she gives you coins she ain't got to spare." He cackled softly to himself. "Teaches the young 'uns right quick to jump when they ought, it do."

"Lady like that needs a strong man for husband, I would think. The young viscount come back at her when she wields her tongue?" The coins disappeared in the wink of an eye. O'Toole leaned over to remove one from the old man's coat pocket.

"She ain't 'ad cause to wield 'er tongue at 'im far as I 'eard. They get along like peaches and cream." The groom began to surreptitiously search his other pockets.

"Odd." A second coin appeared behind a horse's ear. "The marquess used to yell at his daughter when she did something wrong, but then he loved her until she laughed after. When she got a bit older, she yelled right back. Sassy little chit. But anyone could see they adored each other. Seems like a lady with a temper ought to be that passionate about the one she is to marry."

The groom shrugged and stood up as several footmen ran down the steps to search out requested carriages. "Ain't fittin' for a young lady to yell at a suitor, now, is it?"

As one of the footmen approached them, O'Toole disappeared his spinning coins. "Keep up the illusion until the vows are said, eh? Makes sense, that."

He ambled off to his master's carriage at a gesture from a footman. The old groom scratched his head and watched him go. The red-headed young man made an odd sort of groom with his fancy speech and all, but he was a good enough fellow.

Carefully, just in case, he searched his pockets one more time. The silver coin in his breeches pocket glittered just the way he remembered when he held it in the lamplight. Just for good measure, he bit it soundly. Real, not illusion.

"Mama, I do not know how to bring him up to scratch." Marian ignored her image in the mirror and turned to her mother, who was attempting to straighten the bow at her back.

"If only James were here, he would speak to him. This cannot go on much longer without an announcement being made. Perhaps I ought to say something to the gentleman." This last came out with such doubt as to make the likelihood next to none.

Marian bit her bottom lip and turned around to examine the seed-pearl necklace at her throat. Mr. Montague had said the fake necklace would be ready in plenty of time for the ball. She tried not to think of her mother's gentle admonition. She was devoting a great deal of time to Darley, at the expense of her few other suitors. If Darley never proposed, her reputation could be tarnished and she would never find another husband. It didn't bear thinking about.

"I know it is all Mr. Montague's fault," she said out loud, then wished she'd bit her tongue. Hurriedly, she added, "I know Lady Agatha approves of me. Perhaps you could speak quietly of your concerns with her this evening, and she will make Lord Darley see his duty."

"She is rather a formidable lady." The doubt was not as strong but still evident in Lady Grace's voice as she stepped back to admire her handiwork.

Marian thought the lady quite congenial, but then, she was not prone to her mother's diffidence. She had been told time and again that had she been a boy, she would be the spitting image of her father, and that evidently included her character, too. The late marquess had been a neck-or-nothing type of man. She wished she could have known him better. It seemed a tragic fate that so vital a man could have been carried off by such a trivial complaint as an abscessed tooth that went neglected too long.

But with no father to press Lord Darley for his intentions, she was left to dangle at the viscount's will. She would be angry with him, if she did not know Mr. Montague was undoubtedly behind her friend's dilatoriness. She had two options: She could make Lord Darley see that his diffidence was hurting her, or she could rake Montague over the coals. Neither alternative seemed practical, but the latter would be exceedingly satisfying.

She could hear Lily answering the door belowstairs, and she hurried to tie her bonnet ribbons. Darley had been unable to attend the lecture with her today, but he had offered Montague in his place. Perhaps this was the opportunity she needed. Somehow, she would have to persuade the man that she was not the monster of deceit that he claimed.

As she ran down the stairs, she saw Lily speaking to a red-haired man at the door. He was wearing what ought to be a groom's jacket, she supposed, but it appeared to be rather fashionably tailored for all that. He was young and not overly tall, and his gaze was a trifle too insolent as he glanced up at her arrival. She almost imagined laughter in his eyes as he appraised her.

He hastily made a subservient bow and extended his hand with a note in it. "Mr. Montague regrets that he is unable to keep his appointment, but he places his carriage at your disposal, my lady."

Marian gave the note a hasty glance. She had no reason to recognize Montague's writing, but the hasty scrawl possessed his character. Irritated, she glared at the note as if its writer could feel her anger through the paper.

"At my disposal?" Marian gazed consideringly from the note to the young groom, who shifted uneasily at her expression. "Then I shall take my maid."

Lily hurried to fetch her bonnet. The groom appeared increasingly nervous at being left standing in the foyer, but he held his hat and managed to twitch only once or twice while waiting. Marian still regarded him with suspicion, but she had no experience at driving a carriage. She needed his help.

When Lily was up in the groom's seat and the groom was wielding the ribbons, Marian settled back against the cushions with a sigh of satisfaction. "Now, take me to Mr. Montague."

The groom looked startled and allowed the reins to fall lax. The horses shook their heads in impatience. "He says I was to take you to the lecture, my lady."

"He says he places the carriage at my disposal. I have a word or two I wish to say to Mr. Montague. Now where is he? Gossiping at Boodle's? Admiring horses at Tattersall's? Perhaps he is swindling some poor unsuspecting collector out of his books?"

The young groom sent the horses into a slow walk. He gave the lady beside him a sideways glance. "Greek curiosities, my lady. He is to see a man about some Greek curiosities."

"How lowering to be cast aside for Greek curiosities. Very well, then I shall have to see these curiosities, too."

The groom ducked his head and muttered something that might have been, "Yes, my lady." He clucked the horses to a faster pace.

It took only a few minutes to recognize they were heading in the direction of the proposed lecture and not of the shops where such things as Greek curiosities might be found. Marian gave the red-headed groom a sharp look. "Where are we going?"

"Where Mr. Montague said to take you," the groom replied with a hint of stubbornness.

She should have known Montague's servants would be as disagreeable as he was. The horses had picked up their pace and were now trotting neatly down Grosvenor. "Stop the carriage," she ordered.

He sent her a surprised look. "At which residence, my lady?"

"It does not matter. Just stop. I wish to get out."

The stubborn tone returned to his voice. "I cannot do that, my lady. A lady cannot walk unescorted through these streets. My master would have my position if I allowed that."

"Your master will never know if you just do as I say. I have no intention of going any further with you. Either you stop the carriage or I scream."

Behind him, Lily leaned forward nervously and whispered, "She will do just that. Please, do not cross her any more."

The freckles on the groom's nose wrinkled into annoyance as he glanced at the irate lady. "Give me time to come about. I will take you home."

Marian clutched her parasol and glared ahead, conscious that the young man beside her was larger and stronger than she was. She had never before had a servant argue with her. She wished she could box his ears.

"I do not wish to go home, sir. I wish to speak to Mr. Montague."

The groom brought the carriage around and headed it back the way they had come. Jaw set, he replied, "And just as your father wished his bad tooth would go away, you will not get your wishes, my lady."

He set the carriage to a fast pace, leaving Marian to stare at him in stunned silence.

Ten

"The fellow was, above all, insolent. You did say the carriage was to be at my disposal, did you not?" Still enraged and a trifle fearful of the encounter, Marian swirled about the drawing room, her skirts fluttering around her as she paced. She had excused the groom's knowledge of the circumstance of her father's death as common gossip. She couldn't excuse his behavior.

Reginald tried to hide his amusement. "I did not say it was to be used to track me down so you might ring a peal over me. O'Toole is a bit of a character, though, I'll admit. It would not surprise me to discover that he is not at all what he is said to be. But I cannot complain of his work, and I applaud his actions of yesterday. He did exactly right. You could not be left to walk home by yourself."

Marian clenched her fists and swirled around to glare at her grinning nemesis. "Did you come just to gloat? Or had you some other reason to be here?"

"I have had word that your necklace will be ready on the morrow. I wish to be certain that you are still desirous of pawning it. I can handle the transaction in confidentiality and bring you the sum as soon as it is concluded, if that is your wish."

Marian stared at the elegant gentleman lounging in the gilded chair. She had sent Lily off to fetch tea. They had only a few minutes for this discussion. She wished she could think faster. He was all that a gentleman should be, from the cropped curls at his brow to the polished toes of his Hessians. The only exception to his character was the laughter in his eyes and the tone of cynicism in his voice. She really ought to smack him for both.

He knew her dilemma. She did not wish to lower herself to dealing with those types who would loan money on a lady's jewelry, yet she could not trust him to return with the entire sum. Her necklace might be lost forever if she did. She had heard the terrible worth of the necklace and knew she could never obtain such a sum as a loan, but she did not know precisely how much she could expect. It would be simpler to sell it outright and live on the proceeds.

Marian did not have time to voice her decision. The door swung wide and her mother entered, waving a heavily sealed letter. "It's from him!" Her voice was breaking with excitement and trepidation.

"From whom?" Marian tried folding her hands calmly together as her mother entered, entirely ignoring the gentleman rising from the chair behind her. Lady Grace was not generally excitable. Marian sent Mr. Montague an uneasy look, but there was no simple way he could disappear.

"From the marquess! He has asked us to attend him at the manor. The note is from his secretary. It seems the marquess is something of an invalid. I cannot believe it! After all these years, why would he write to us now?"

Marian noted their visitor's frown. Knowing Montague was a great deal more informed about the *ton* than they, she took the letter from her mother's hands and scanned it carefully. Without comment, she handed it to Mr. Montague.

He raised one expressive eyebrow at the contents, then returned it to her. "It's been my understanding that the marquess had not been in England until recently. It is possible that he merely wishes to make your acquaintance."

Lady Grace nervously twined her fingers. "It has been nearly twenty years. He could have sent some acknowledgement sooner than this. I don't believe I shall go. I do not wish to go back there."

Marian clenched the heavy vellum and tried not to scream a protest. She had only been three when her father died and her world turned inside-out. She had very little memory of the manor house to which she had been born. She would dearly like to see it again, to find out if it jogged any memories of her father. But if the visit would be painful for her mother, she could not object.

Reginald gave her white-faced expression a thoughtful look before turning to Lady Grace. "The gentleman does not ask only for your company. He merely says he will send a carriage for your convenience. Perhaps you could return his note suggesting that you would prefer to bring your own escort? I am certain Lord Darley would be happy to accompany you, as would I. It might make . . . " he hesitated, in search of a proper word. Finding none, he continued vaguely, " . . . things a trifle easier for all concerned. After all, the marquess is the nominal head of the family."

Stunned at this realization, Lady Grace looked at the letter as if it were a snake that might bite. She met Marian's eyes, and the knowledge gradually sank in. If Lord Darley were to make an offer, it would most properly have to be made to the marquess first.

Shaking her head, Lady Grace took the paper. "If you do not mind," she murmured absently, "I would thank you for your escort. If you would excuse me?" She departed without making any notice that she was leaving her daughter alone with the gentleman.

Marian took a deep breath and walked to the window. "You know more about the marquess?"

"Very little." In truth, Reginald had made it a point to find out all he could, but his success had been limited. The marquess hid himself very well. "Mostly gossip. They say he is a recluse. None claim to have met him, leastways. The rumors only started a few months ago, so I suppose there is some truth to the gossip that he has only recently come to England. Does your mother not know anything at all?"

"All I know is what I have heard or overheard over the years. The manor has no dower house. Most of the lands were not entailed and were sold off over generations. The house and the park were entailed, however, and the solicitors said we must leave as there weren't funds for upkeep. We had a small trust left by my father and lived off it a while. There were rumors that the new marquess was an American and they had to send there for him, but that is all I know. What remains of the estate is in Hertfordshire, and we moved to Wiltshire when Mama married the squire. We heard very little there."

Reginald made an impolite noise. "If the estate was in sad shape, there would have been no particular reason for the man to return, particularly if he was wealthy. Americans hold very little store by titles, I understand."

"That's true." Marian turned away from the window to face him. "I suppose now he is ill, possibly dying, and thinks to clear up matters he has neglected. Should I be gratified that he has chosen now to interfere in our lives?"

"Perhaps he is childless and means to make you heir to all his wealth," Reginald responded maliciously. "Do you wish to wait before pawning your necklace?"

Marian's eyes widened as she remembered their earlier conversation. "The necklace! It's a family heirloom. Do you think he means to ask for it back?"

"You mean it is not yours to sell?" Reginald gave her a shocked look.

"It is." Marian set her chin stubbornly. "My father gave it to my mother. It was not on the inventory of entailments or my mother would never have taken it with her. It is ours to do with as we wish."

"Then perhaps you will wish to wait to sell it until after you discover if he means to make you any monetary gifts. Dying men sometimes like to salve their consciences."

She heard the cynicism in his voice and chose to ignore it. "He is more likely meaning to make my life miserable in some manner or another, but you are right. I cannot pawn the necklace until I know what this is about. Perhaps he might even lend us the money of his own accord. I would sleep much easier if I knew the necklace was where it belonged."

Reginald lifted his hand as if he were about to touch her, but Lily came hurrying in with the tea tray then, and his arm fell back to his side. Making his excuses, he collected his hat and left.

Oddly enough, Marian felt strangely bereft with his departure.

Reginald jiggled the two boxes in his coat pockets uneasily. He had retrieved the necklace and the copy just after leaving the shop for the day. He knew Darley had the lady occupied for the evening. There would be no good opportunity for returning the jewels to her now. He wished he had a safe in which to deposit them. He'd never had enough valuables for anyone to steal to acquire one.

The elongated boxes were difficult to hide, and he had a thief for a valet. Questioning his sanity, Reginald withdrew the plain box in which rested the copy. As he entered his chamber, he threw it on his dressing table in plain sight. He could not conceivably keep both boxes hidden from his nosy valet, but he might distract him with one long enough to get the other to the lady on the morrow. She would want to take the original with her on her visit to the marquess.

The real necklace in its velvet container he secreted among the belongings already packed in his valise. Upon hearing that his master was invited to visit the manor house of the new Marquess of Effingham, O'Toole had been beside himself with delight. He had begun packing immediately. Reginald wasn't certain whether to be relieved by his valet's behavior, or suspicious. Either the man was happy to be returning to his home, or had no reason to fear returning because he'd never been there. Reginald hadn't quite decided which.

The object of his thoughts came in bearing a stack of laundered shirts, grinning happily as he caught sight of his employer. "You are home. What entertaining jaunt will we take this evening? The Opera? Or will you wish to visit your ladybird before going on an extended journey?"

"O'Toole, you are insolent to an extreme. Just see that I have sufficient clean linen for the morrow and I will take care of myself for this evening." Reginald pulled off his wilting cravat and began to shrug out of his coat.

O'Toole pretended offense. "Everything is all prepared. It is only a matter of knowing where to load it. Surely the curricle will not be sufficient for the journey? Shall I hire a phaeton?"

"I will be traveling with Darley in his landau. There will doubtless be more than adequate room for everything you have managed to pack in every valise and portmanteau in the house. Do not concern yourself."

"You have not told me how long you plan to stay. I have no choice but to be ready for any event," the valet replied huffily, as he helped his employer pull out of the coat. "Your lady will expect you to look your very best."

"She is not my lady, confound it." With his arms freed of the tight coat, Reginald began on his shirt buttons. "She is Darley's lady. I only accompany them out of friendship."

"Lady Marian is much too spirited for a gentleman like Lord Darley," O'Toole replied disapprovingly. "She needs a gentleman with the strength of character of yourself."

Reginald flung the shirt across the room. "I do not intend to marry, O'Toole, and I am certainly not wealthy enough to meet the lady's standards. Now leave off, or you're sacked."

O'Toole hummed happily to himself as he assisted his employer in his ablutions and in preparing for the evening's excursions. Matters were far from perfect, but they were proceeding obligingly. He doubted that he would be rewarded for his outstanding diplomacy, but playing strategist was much more amusing than standing in the pouring rain moving walnut shells and peas around for the entertainment of spectators. Perhaps he should have made a career out of politics.

As soon as Montague left for the evening, O'Toole settled himself at the dressing table where the jewel box had been resting temptingly all evening. He was already familiar with all the jewels in the Montague household, and this box wasn't among them. He snapped open the lid and whistled thoughtfully.

The ruby winked in the lamplight. The diamond setting sparkled. The gold glittered almost as if genuine. O'Toole ran the ornate chain between his fingers. It wouldn't fool an expert, but it would fool just about anybody else. He didn't have to think twice to know where the original came from. The necklace was unforgettable to anyone with any familiarity with jewelry at all. He had admired it more than once on portraits of the late marchionesses of Effingham.

Still whistling quietly, O'Toole replaced the necklace, stood up, and gazed consideringly around the room. Where there was a copy, there was bound to be an original. It might not be here, but he could think of no other reason for his wily employer to leave the fake sitting out.

He started with the partially packed valise.

The Eighth Marquess of Effingham, Earl of Arinmede, Viscount Lawrence, stared at the single candle lighting his neatly ordered and exceedingly dust-laden desk. The heavy, moldering draperies on the windows behind him adequately insulated against night sounds, but they wafted gently every so often in the breeze from the broken windowpanes. The candle flickered against the darkness whenever they did so.

Volumes of books lined the study wall across from the desk. The candlelight occasionally caught a flicker of gold on a binding here and there, but the marquess wasn't overtly aware of it. There was another room just down the immense hall with more volumes than this, a veritable library larger than any he had seen in America other than in cities like New York. He was still rather in awe of the generations of history and knowledge patiently stored within these walls. But it wasn't the past that concerned him at the moment.

Crumpling a hastily scribbled note and flinging it at the faded Turkish carpet covering the floor, he muttered a "Damn Michael to hell and back." Reaching for a brandy decanter, he poured a sizable amount of liquid into a snifter.

He couldn't see the mirror on the side wall that reflected his image as he bent into the candlelight to pick up his glass. The image wouldn't have looked out of place in the portrait gallery above. It reflected a tall, broad-shouldered man with black hair too long at the nape for style, a dark, sun-weathered complexion, and a sharp, aristocratic nose with a slight hump in the middle. Piercing eyes beneath heavy brows added to his brooding appearance. When he turned, the candlelight did not quite catch the fine white scars shattering one side of his face.

The marquess sipped the brandy and damned his own curiosity along with the absent Michael. It had only seemed natural to look up the relatives he had never known once he had finally made his way here. He glanced derisively upward at the ornate ceiling and faded gilded molding above the bookcases that represented "here."

He had only been a boy when he came into the title, and he had not learned of it until the death of his mother. It had taken him years after that to scrape together the funds to arrive in England in some semblance of style. He'd had visions of a rambling stone mansion with servants and tenants and all the things he had remembered hearing about when he had been a child. He should have known an estate that couldn't afford to finance an heir's trip to England wouldn't be worth arriving to claim.

And now Michael was giving him this folderol about the penniless dowager and her daughter as if he were capable of resolving any problems of his unknown relatives. In actuality, he had hoped to locate a rich earl or two on the family tree to hit up for loans on the sentimental basis of saving the family homestead or whatever. A penniless widow wasn't precisely what he had in mind.

He groaned and sank back in the chair. It exuded dust with every movement, but it was one of the few pieces that hadn't been covered by those infernal ghostly linens that were scattered everywhere in the house. He wondered how far it would get him to sell off the moldering furniture. Back to the states, at least.

He ought to wring Michael's neck for this. They had spent the better part of their lives surviving on their wits alone. Why didn't Michael know to leave things as they were? What was he supposed to do, wave his magic wand and open the manor for a house party? Michael was the one with the magic wand. Let him wave it.

That thought relieved the marquess's disgruntled mood. Grinning irreverently at a worn tapestry blowing slightly in the breeze, he lifted his snifter in toast to his own good sense. Let Arinmede Manor welcome guests one final time.

Eleven

When the travelers set out the next morning, Darley's landau carried two valets and an assortment of baggage. The gentlemen chose to ride alongside the carriages, where they could occasionally lean over and converse with the ladies through the windows of the marquess's coach.

The coach was of the old-fashioned kind, with badly sprung wheels and four unmatched hired horses. The driver was taciturn and undemonstrative, occasionally tippling from a flask in his coat pocket as the day wore on. Both Reginald and Darley kept cautious eyes on him.

But Reginald was also distracted by the wealth he was carrying on this journey. He did not like taking the necklace with him, but he'd had no time to find a safer place to deposit it. He would have preferred to return it to the ladies, but the opportunity had not yet arisen. He hoped this evening he could find a moment alone with Lady Marian, when the necklace could be returned.

He hadn't breathed easy on the prior night until he had returned to his chamber and checked to find the duplicate where he had left it and the original safely tucked in his valise. O'Toole had said nary a word about it, which was suspicious in itself, but he had left the ornament alone. Uncomfortable allowing the necklace out of his sight, Reginald had taken the original out of its box and tucked it in his purse before setting out this morning. As a precaution, he carried a pistol in his saddle.

The early morning journey had started out under blue

skies. A spring breeze tossed the heads of jonquils in flower gardens along the way as they entered the country. Bird song filled tree branches covered with new green leaves. The fresh air had made the ladies smile until even the shy Jessica was laughing over some jest of Darley's. Reginald thought perhaps he ought to get out to the country more often.

His gaze strayed to Lady Marian's thinly drawn face framed in the window as she gazed pensively over the fields. She was wearing her yellow bonnet again, and a ribbon curled enticingly against her cheek. She brushed it away impatiently, only to have it fall back again an instant later. She didn't seem to notice.

He tried to follow her gaze, but Darley was on the other side of the carriage, and she was seated with her back to the horses, staring behind them. He didn't think she was seeing the lovely spring day at all, but rather some dark cloud she imagined on the horizon.

Reginald discreetly allowed his mount to nibble at a patch of grass along the roadside while glancing back the way they had come. To his surprise, there *were* clouds on the horizon. If they did not stir the carriages to a faster pace, they would no doubt be caught in a rainstorm.

The blamed woman should have said something. Irritated, Reginald spurred his horse to take up with Darley's. Pointing out the clouds, he got his friend's agreement that a faster pace was needed, and he ordered the driver to spring the horses. The taciturn coachman just gave him a disgruntled look and reached for his flask.

Cursing, Reginald ordered the driver to halt. The driver didn't obey that order any better. All he had succeeded in doing so far was attracting the interest of the ladies. Lady Grace and Jessica seemed oblivious to the consequences of this little spectacle, but Marian had begun to frown in concern. No doubt she meant to reach through the trap door, grab the driver by the coattails, and box his ears if he did not respond to her liking.

He ought to let her do it, but he had been raised to be a gentleman. With a word to Darley, Reginald rode his mount as close to the coach as he dared, reached over and found a handhold on the side, caught his foot on the driver's box, and hauled himself out of the saddle and into the driver's seat. Darley caught his horse and rode back to the trailing landau to tie the horse on behind.

The surly coachman raised his whip as if to strike, but Reginald hadn't spent years sparring with Gentleman Jackson for nothing. Short of laying the bastard flat, he caught the man's arm, pried the whip loose, and grabbed the reins that were falling lax in the struggle. With a muffled curse, the man gave up and curled in the corner of the box with his flask for sustenance.

"Bravo," a soft voice whispered behind him.

Reginald hadn't been aware that the trap door had been opened until then. He cast a quick squint to the face framed there before returning his attention to the horses. He hadn't expected any other than the dark curls and dancing eyes of Lady Marian, and he wasn't disappointed. The lady was a rare handful, and that was God's honest truth.

"How do your mother and sister fare?" Reginald asked quietly over his shoulder as he found the horses' paces and urged them on.

"They think you very odd but have decided you must belong to the Four-in-Hand Club they have heard about. Apparently the club members are capable of odd stunts." Her voice was soft so as not to be overheard by the ladies chattering with Darley through the window.

Reginald made an inelegant noise. "I have better to do than wear hideous waistcoats and waste my time destroying good horses. I trust they will not be too disappointed in my lack of dash."

"I am certain they will be quite delighted if you get us there before that storm breaks. My sister is afraid of storms."

So that was the reason for the pensive look. Well, he should have known better than to expect her to be idly daydreaming of true love. Reginald cracked the whip over the horses' heads. "Close the trap, my lady. These nags aren't much, but I mean to spring them."

The coach pitched forward with a jerk and settled into a rocking rumble as the horses took up their new pace. Mar-

ian turned back to her mother to discover her looking
mildly alarmed. She should have known they were trading
Jessica's fear of storms for her mother's fear of speed. Between the two of them, they had enough timidity for three
ladies. Marian felt quite justified in surrendering any frail-
ity in herself.

"Mr. Montague wishes to arrive before it rains," she said
in pacifying tones.

Lady Grace nodded hesitantly and, clasping her hands in
her lap, refused to look out the window again.

The clouds were directly overhead and the wind had
grown to a gale by the time they reached the crumbling
gates of Arinmede Manor. If there had once been an actual
gate, it was gone now. Only the loosened stones of the
posts remained. Gravel slid from the decaying mortar as the
coach rattled past.

The drive was lined with ancient evergreens that swayed
threateningly in the wind. Marian gazed anxiously out the
window for some glimpse of the house, but it was obscured
by the trees. Lightning crashed overhead, and Jessica gave
a shrill scream and moved closer to her mother.

"Is this how it looked when we lived here?" Marian
asked, eager for any information about the life she had
never known.

"The trees were young then. Your grandfather had them
planted. He had seen the like somewhere in his travels.
They weren't nearly as formidable then."

"Are we close? Did you used to be able to see the house
from here?"

Lady Grace wrapped her arm around her younger daughter as thunder rocked the air around them and the coach
lurched hurriedly in and out of ruts. "The park is extensive,
but you should see it soon enough."

The trees appeared ready to whip from the ground in the
wind and the first drops of rain began to fall as they rolled
from the secluded drive into the curving entrance of the
manor. Marian tried to drink it all in as the coach turned
and the house loomed before them, but there was too much
to see at once.

The manor itself loomed upward in a solid wall of gray

stone. The windows were large and evenly spaced, indicating a house built early in the last century, but both glass and stone were mostly covered in wandering ivy. Brambles that might once have been roses scratched at the bottom rows, and the noise was slightly eerie when heard through the silences between booms of thunder.

The small party waited briefly for some sign of footmen or grooms to come to their aid, but the rapid patter of rain sent Reginald and Darley to ordering their valets into action.

Without waiting for admittance, O'Toole dashed up the steps burdened with several valises, shoved open the massive carved doors, and led the way. Astounded by this impropriety but reluctant to remain in the rain, the ladies hurried to follow.

Marian glanced upward at the grand entrance hall. A skylight several stories above glistened with stained glass and she could imagine the dancing patterns it would send across the marble floor on a sunny day. Vague recollections of lying on the floor and letting the light dance over her simmered somewhere in the back of her mind, and she could almost hear the deep laugh of her father as he found her. Perhaps it was just her overactive imagination.

The walls were of a heavy dark wainscoting, without any of the grace and ornamentation of an Adams interior. There was a certain dignity in their lack of ornamentation that carried through in the formal paintings of Greek gods that provided their only decoration. Marian suspected the long hallway stretching out beyond the foyer led to masculine studies and offices and billiard rooms. Her attention was drawn upward to the graceful curve of the mahogany stair rail.

That was the direction in which O'Toole led them. With still no sign of a servant in sight, the little party could only mill aimlessly in the foyer, watching the rain come down in buckets as the last piece of baggage was carried in. The coaches drove off around the bend to the stables, and still no one came to greet them. Taking the initiative, Reginald grabbed a valise and followed his valet up the stairs.

Lord Darley attempted to prevent Marian from carrying

any of her own luggage, but it seemed the height of silliness to leave everything sitting belowstairs when it was becoming more than obvious that the manor was seriously understaffed. She managed their jewelry and cosmetic cases while Lily carried hatboxes. Even Lady Grace and Jessica picked up an item or two to carry with them as they ascended the magnificent stairs.

Glimpses of the rooms to either side of the hall when they reached the top told the tale of abandonment. Holland covers still hung over the furniture. Spiders scurried into corners and cobwebs dangled from doorways. Desperately, Marian groped for some familiarity in the scene, but there was nothing.

Lady Grace led the way from here, directing the gentlemen to their wing, leading her daughters to the ladies' wing. Lily and the valets scurried between them, arranging boxes and trunks in some semblance of order as the ladies chose two separate chambers and the gentlemen found their own.

Marian found Mr. Montague in the hall when she went in search of one of her boxes, and he allowed her to go through the assortment he carried until she had identified those that belonged to her. He set the stack on an inlaid ebony table covered in dust and rearranged his burden, while thunder roared overhead and the pounding of rain on tile hit the roof.

"Your marquess is more eccentric than I imagined," Reginald muttered as he dusted off his coat sleeve. "There are probably two fortunes in Ming Dynasty china in the sitting room connected to my chamber, but there doesn't seem to be a single servant to see to the fires to keep out the damp. I shudder to imagine how much has been damaged just by neglect."

Marian kept her voice to a whisper as if the walls might have ears. "Have you seen the library? It is utterly immense. I'm afraid to go in it. What if the roof has leaked? The thought of all those volumes ruined makes me shudder."

Montague grinned. "Plan to snatch a few, do you? The

old goat will probably not miss them. Shall we rendezvous there when we are unpacked and see what we can find?"

She gave him a sharp look, uncertain as to how much was said in jest, when Darley came up the stairs with the remains of their baggage.

"I say, this is the strangest house party I have yet to see. Do you think we're the only ones here? I have an odd feeling that we ought to turn around and go back." He had doffed his hat and his lanky dark hair bore the signs of wet weather, falling into his eyes until he impatiently shoved it back. His anxious gaze instantly went to Marian.

Realizing how their whispered conversation might be misconstrued, Reginald stepped out of the shadows and away from the mischievous Lady Marian. The skylight over the foyer provided some illumination for this end of the hall. "O'Toole has gone down to the kitchens to see if he can arouse someone. If nothing else, maybe he can find some candles and fuel. We're likely to get quite damp and dark before long."

Marian picked up her boxes and started toward her end of the hall. "Damp and dark are unpleasant enough, but I am starving. Unless he scares up a cook, I mean to go down and see if the larder is as empty as the rest of this house."

"You must allow me to accompany you when you do, my lady. There could be rogues secreted in these rooms and none would know until they were stumbled upon. If it were not for the weather, I would be in favor of returning to London." Darley set down his own valise and hurried to take Marian's burden.

She gave him an impatient glance but allowed the courtesy. "Mother would be most disappointed. She is taking a sentimental journey through the bed chambers at present, and she means to show me my father's portrait when I am done here. After all, she was once lady of the house. It seems natural that she act the part of hostess again."

Darley glanced at the niches along the halls filled with busts of Greek gods on marble pedestals and shook his head. "It is in serious need of redecoration. These styles went out with the first George, I should think. Perhaps the new marquess wishes to ask your mother's help in renovating this monstrosity."

"Do not let us dream, my lord, we will only be disappointed. Come, if we hurry, we may catch up with her tour."

Reginald watched them go with Marian's words ringing in his ears. Do not let us dream. He gazed up at the particularly ugly portrait of some earlier marquess garbed in the court dress of the sixteenth century. Lousy bastards, all, he decided, to steal a young girl's dreams.

It was a damned good thing he was a practical man. Otherwise, he might be tempted to find the last sorry bastard who had stolen the lady's dreams and beat some sense into him.

The sorry bastard of Montague's thoughts was leaning against a wall, listening to the scurry of footsteps up and down his dust-covered stairway. With a minimum of effort he could listen to their conversations, but the snatches he had heard were enough to make him uncomfortable. Eavesdropping had never been one of his vices.

But his damned curiosity had him watching for the ladies as they explored along the west wing. The building was still in sound repair so far as he had been able to determine. There shouldn't be any danger in their explorations. He just wished to have some glimpse of his only living relations outside his addle-pated brother.

The hidden corridor he occupied hadn't been built for viewing. When he had first discovered it, he had thought some perverted ancestor had enjoyed watching the inhabitants of the various bedrooms off this floor. But he had been unable to locate viewing holes. He had since come to the conclusion that the hidden corridor was there so the master of the house could visit his mistress undetected. It led directly from the master chamber to a prettily decorated room at the far end of what he now knew as the ladies' wing.

He waited outside the door to that room now. It was hidden behind a wardrobe, and he had left the wardrobe door ajar. If they stood in just the right place, he would be able to see them.

He heard their voices. Already he was beginning to separate the sounds and identify them. The placid, assured tones of an older woman was undoubtedly the Lady Grace, his late cousin's wife. The timid, whispery voice of a young girl apparently belonged to Jessica, Lady Grace's daughter by her second marriage. The third voice . . .

The owner of the third voice was standing just where he hoped, at the foot of the portrait that was her father. The eighth Marquess of Effingham leaned back against the wall, arms crossed, and studied his young cousin.

She was just as Michael said. Lawrence blood ran true. Dark curls framed a slim face of no great beauty, but the velvet darkness of her eyes and the rosy flush of her cheeks and the soft exclamation of her lips as she looked up at the portrait painted her in all the character of her ancestors.

The marquess fingered his scarred cheek, a cheek that had once been the same sun-warmed hue as hers. His gaze went to the portrait of the man with those same features. His own father had looked much like that, although he scarcely remembered the man. His memory came from the miniature in the watch that he had inherited from his mother. The resemblance was strong, although his father had apparently tended toward corpulence in his old age. The marquess didn't like thinking of that, because then he would remember how much younger his mother was, and he began to make excuses for her.

Well, now they were here. What in hell was he going to do about it?

To find Michael and thrash him within an inch of his life seemed the only alternative open at the moment.

Twelve

Reginald sat staring morosely at his mud-spattered boots as the air rang with laughter around him. It seemed the ladies of Effingham and Oglethorp were as familiar with kitchens as they were drawing rooms. They were having a grand adventure exploring larders and pantries and wine cellars, sending the maid and valet scattering in search of fuel for the ancient stove and the lanterns hanging from the beams overhead. His own valet had gone missing at the first hint of any work that might besmirch his immaculate cuffs.

Reginald fingered the necklace in his pocket to reassure himself. He had already hidden the copy from his valise in a secret drawer he had located in the desk in his sitting room. Let O'Toole spend his hours searching for that.

His trouble wasn't related to the necklace, however. Reginald grimaced as Darley asked if he had minced the carrots fine enough. The resulting laughter answered the question without need of further explanation. Reginald's trouble was that he was almost beginning to believe that Lady Marian might be the wife for his friend after all.

He didn't know why that should bother him. He should be relieved. Instead of sitting here admiring his boots and tending the fire, he should be on his way back to London to fetch a preacher and a license. Darley's wealth would set the ladies up in comfort and they need no longer worry about a pestilent marquess who hadn't the grace to put in an appearance in his moldering castle.

Perhaps he ought to make one more attempt to make

Darley see the lady's true colors. He couldn't let his friend go into marriage thinking his lady all sweetness and light when she could also be tart as a cold lemonade on a hot summer's day, and swift and sharp as a surgeon's scalpel. Reginald wasn't certain Darley would be as appreciative of these character traits as he ought, but he was smitten enough to accept them if he must. He just needed to have his eyes wide open before he proposed this marriage.

The thought of the scene that must be enacted made him surly. Reginald poked at the fire and announced it ready, then started for the door with the immediate goal of hiding in the library.

"Mr. Montague! You cannot desert us now, unless you are going to fetch that annoying valet of yours. Someone needs to slice the bacon, and these knives seem quite dull." Lady Marian indicated the assortment of cutlery hanging near the cutting board.

Reginald scowled. He wished to say he knew nothing of kitchens or knives, but in reality he did. He would have starved long since if he had not worked out a few of the intricacies of his landlady's kitchen in the days of his misspent youth. He crossed the floor, grabbed a knife, and went in search of the whetstone.

"I do believe Mr. Montague is sulking," Marian said brightly to the room in general. "P'raps we ought to let him sit upstairs and enjoy the must and damp while we wait upon him."

Darley grinned at his friend's rigid back. The scene earlier when he had discovered the lady in earnest and intimate conversation with Montague had left him feeling uncertain, but Marian's teasing tones now reassured him. Ladies did not generally insult gentlemen whose attentions they wished to attract.

"I thought I saw a throne in one room. We could sit Reginald there and fetch a few hounds to lay at his feet. But I think we need game with bones he can gnaw and fling to the dogs. I believe his valet can successfully play the part of fool for his master's entertainment." Darley brandished his knife so his carrots could be inspected again.

Lady Grace swiftly gathered the vegetables and added

them to the pot, ignoring the badinage between the young people. She hummed happily to herself as she stirred the contents of one pot and kept an eye on Jessica, who was managing the egg dish.

"If I am to be crowned lord of this castle, I'll demand better peons than the lot of you, I should say. Insolence will get you horsewhipped." Reginald finished sharpening the knife and slammed the hunk of bacon on the cutting board for slicing.

O'Toole miraculously appeared through the back entrance with two plucked chickens, and the entire company turned to stare. The storm was still rattling the rafters, but the valet didn't appear in the least bit damp. He looked questioningly to his employer.

Reginald gave him a surly glare. "Excellent. We shall have eggs for dinner and fowl for breakfast. You're a trifle late, lad."

Lady Grace gave the young man a gracious smile and relieved him of the hens. "I shall simmer these tonight and we can have them for lunch tomorrow."

Darley looked uneasy. "I think we should leave in the morning. It does not appear as if our host is at home."

"He sent his coach for us," Marian reminded him. "P'raps we ought to instigate a search of the house after we eat. He may be lying ill in a chamber we have not yet discovered."

"Oh!" Jessica let her spoon clatter against the pan. "If he is ill, we should go look for him right now. The poor man could be dying as we speak."

"Unless the 'poor' man is given to doing his own cooking, he is undoubtedly caught by the storm in the village with his servant. He is probably tucked up at the inn keeping his frail old bones warm and dry while cackling at the thought of our arrival."

The hint of sarcasm in Marian's voice drew Darley's questioning look, but then a sound that seemed to echo from the walls made them all jump.

"That sounded like a moan," Jessica whispered, her face growing pale with fright and anxiety as she scanned the dark shadows in the far corners of the kitchen.

"I'd say it sounded more like some dimwitted ghost laughing," Reginald said dourly, then regretted the remark when the timid Oglethorp ladies both went white. Marian, on the other hand, appeared intrigued.

"I could not tell the direction," she said softly, listening for a repetition.

"It was, no doubt, squirrels in the walls. We had them once in our hunting box. The wretched things made all kinds of racket until we chased them out. I'll take a look after we eat." Darley offered the women a reassuring smile.

Lady Grace and Jessica went happily back to their cooking, but Reginald noted Marian gave her suitor a look of irritation. Squirrels did not moan or laugh. Or perhaps it was a groan or chuckle. Whatever it was, it was more human than squirrel, unless one believed in ghosts. Remembering their jests about the missing marquess, Reginald had his own theories on the matter.

He waited until after their impromptu supper—which was quite good considering he had been hungry enough to eat boiled haddock if need be. Then while Darley was lighting the way to the drawing room, Reginald slipped back downstairs to explore.

Minutes later he heard the sound of light footsteps, and he stepped behind a door to hide his candlelight. The thunder had moved away, but he could still hear the rapid patter of rain on the windows. The roads would, in all probability, be impassable on the morrow. He ought to save his explorations for morning.

"Mr. Montague, I know you are in there. Do not try to scare me or I'm likely to set the place on fire with this infernal candle."

At the sound of Marian's voice, Reginald stepped from his hiding place. "I should have known better than to think you'd sit quivering in the drawing room with the others. Do you have no fear of what happens to young ladies who wander about strange places all alone?"

In the candlelight, her upturned oval face seemed smooth and serene. The dark hair pulled back from her brow and dangling in curls about her ears was no more than a shadow in the darkness. Reginald had the insane urge to bend and kiss those parted lips. He wasn't at all certain that wouldn't be the best thing to do for all of them.

"This was my home, sir. Why should I fear it?" she asked before he could move to take action on his thoughts.

Reginald moved to a safer distance, searching for a lamp on the desk. "It hasn't been your home for nearly twenty years, as best as I can determine. Anything can happen in that length of time."

The lamp, when he found it, was freshly filled. Reginald frowned at that, but the sudden flare of light as he lit it removed some of the temptation of darkness. He turned and found her still clinging to her candle. So she wasn't entirely impervious to the perils of darkness.

He reached in his pocket and produced the purse that had bothered him all day. "Here is your necklace. I would rather that you held on to it until you decide what to do about it."

Marian didn't take the offered purse. She looked at it sadly, then turned to examine the book shelves behind her. "I don't think there is any decision to make. It is rather obvious that the marquess is not going to be able to help us save our home. He must be in danger of losing his own from the looks of it. The necklace will have to be pawned."

Reginald frowned at so casually being left in charge of a piece of jewelry worth almost more than he was. He opened the purse to inspect the piece and reassure himself once more of its existence.

The lamp light caught on the brilliant red stone and glittered on the setting of—

Reginald gasped and turned the necklace to the light again. A setting of crystal?

He tried to remain calm. After all, the necklace had been in his possession all day. He had dealt with gems for years and was well aware of when he held the genuine thing. It had been genuine diamonds and rubies he had pocketed this morning. It could not change by magic during the course of a day.

He turned the gem to a better angle. Glass. The ruby was glass.

The strangled sound he made must have been heard

across the room. Marian swung around to face him with curiosity.

"Are you all right? You look a little pale. Perhaps you ought to sit down. I'm certain there must be brandy or something around here. I thought I saw a decanter earlier." She held up her candle in search of the decanter she distinctly remembered seeing on a table when she had explored in here before dinner. It was gone. She blinked in confusion, but Mr. Montague was shaking his head and staring at the necklace with such a terrible look on his face that she forgot her search and hurried to stand beside him. "What is it? What is wrong?"

As if unable to speak, he held out the necklace for her inspection. She saw nothing wrong with it. She fondled the intricate chain, but it felt real to her. She glanced up to his face for explanation. Usually, his cool gray eyes were aloof, and pride made his expression seem stiff and unyielding. Now, there was a terrible panic revealing his true humanity beneath the handsome mask.

"This is the copy," he managed to grind out between clenched teeth. "It is not possible. I put the genuine article in my pocket before we left this morning."

Cold seeped around her heart as Marian gazed at the glittering jewel. "It looks real to me. I don't find this a very funny jest, Mr. Montague."

"It's not in the least funny, I assure you. Come, I left the copy upstairs. If this is the genuine thing, then the copy will still be where I left it."

As the sound of their feet echoed away into the distance, the figure behind the tapestry sighed and fingered the weighty necklace in his pocket. If Michael was right about the worth of this jewel, it would be sufficient to fund the purchase of enough lands to set this estate properly functioning again. He just hadn't realized he was going to cost the ladies their home by stealing it.

Carrying the brandy decanter, the eighth marquess stepped out of his hiding place and settled into his desk chair. He took a healthy swig of the potent liquor and sighed again. Not bad for an old man with frail bones, he chuckled to himself as the brandy burned a trail to his

stomach. That damned young cousin of his was too clever
by half, and she had a sharp tongue to boot. His empty insides growled in complaint. His guests had finished off the
entire delicious meal they had cooked right before his very
eyes. He wondered if ghosts could be credited for eating
chicken legs.

Carrying the decanter and staggering only slightly, he
went in search of the kitchen and the chicken that had been
stewed for the morrow. He didn't know how long his un-
welcome guests would stay, but he would enjoy their cooking while they were here.

As Mr. Montague turned down the hall to the gentlemen's wing, Marian wanted to protest that she couldn't follow him, but she wasn't about to let that necklace out of her
sight, either. She didn't know what kind of trick he meant
to pull, but she was determined to catch him at it. She
couldn't believe a gentleman like Mr. Montague could be
so dishonest as to steal their only source of income, but she
wasn't inclined to trust anybody for very long.

Unheeding of the lady's qualms, Reginald turned into the
chamber at his left and went directly to the spindly-legged
secretary near the fireplace. Setting the lamp down on the
open surface of the desk, he felt around at the back of one
of the drawers until he sprung the catch. Within seconds he
was withdrawing a plain box that should contain the copy.

Marian came up beside him and watched with bated
breath as he snapped open the box. The box of white satin
was empty.

With a soft cry, she swung away and stared out the rain-
spattered window. Reginald followed her with grim sympathy, touching a hand to her shoulder, not knowing how else
to comfort her.

"I will find it, Marian. I have a suspect, and I shall have
it out of him if I must beat him to a pulp to do so. I am only
sorry that I have given you cause to worry."

She didn't even notice that he had addressed her familiarly. She only knew she wanted to lean back into the comfort of his arms and weep. She was tired of being the strong
one. She wanted someone else to help share her burdens,

someone to make things just a little easier for a change. For some odd reason, she had relied on Mr. Montague to be that someone. She should have known it was a mistake to rely on anyone but herself.

She stiffened and pulled away. "I wish to be there when you question him. Who is it? That insolent valet of yours?"

The woman was too damned quick for her own good. Reginald retreated a few feet, removing his hand. "I can understand your concern, but a woman would give him hope of some sympathy. He knows he will receive none from me. Go back to your mother while I track the wretch down."

She would go back to her mother all right, but it wouldn't be to quietly sit before the fire. Straightening her back, she marched out of the room without looking behind her. Reginald had an eerie premonition of what would come next if he didn't act quickly.

Throwing open the door to the antechamber his valet had taken for his own, he yelled, "O'Toole, get yourself in here now or I'm coming after you with a whip!"

The room was terrifyingly empty.

Thirteen

The search for the missing man and jewel in the dark in a strange house on a rainy night had little chance of being successful. The small party eventually returned to the dying fire of the drawing room with nothing to show for their efforts.

Marian felt guilty for telling her mother anything at all. She could simply have produced the fake and allowed her to think all was well. But her first thought had been to find the thief before he could escape, and that had necessitated explaining the necklace's disappearance. Now, they had nothing, neither thief nor necklace, and her mother appeared thoroughly shaken by the experience.

She could still miraculously "discover" the copy, she supposed. That would relieve her mother's mind if not her own. But she could not do it tonight. Everyone was weary to the bone, and no one would believe the discovery directly after such an extensive search. It would have to wait until morning.

Lord Darley hovered sympathetically near her as if he would speak to her alone, but Marian didn't have the heart for his words right now. She had been disappointed too thoroughly this day to give anyone the opportunity to hurt her more. She couldn't bear to be proposed to out of sympathy, and she didn't wish to have him offer her a replacement for her jewel or other such nonsense right now. She might feel differently in the morning when her better sense had time to catch up with her, but right now she was too lost to the dismals to care.

She didn't even have it in her to blame Mr. Montague. He appeared to be as miserable as she over the loss. Unless he was a great actor, he had suffered a terrible blow to his integrity and was not likely to recover until he had redeemed himself. She had seen him furiously striking the walls as if they would speak. No one else knew that he had been the one carrying the necklace, but the knowledge lay unspoken between them like a guilty secret.

She didn't want to have guilty secrets with Mr. Montague. He made her feel quite guilty enough every time he looked at her when she was with Lord Darley. The loss of the necklace made it imperative that the viscount come up to scratch soon, but she couldn't think of how she would do that right now without it looking like pity. She would worry about it in the morning.

Jessica was extremely quiet as they readied themselves for bed. Lily always tended to their mother, so they aided each other now in the unbuttoning and unfastening of their gowns. The room was chilly and damp but not cold, and they made no effort to start a fire. Marian slipped between the covers without questioning her sister, but Jessica wasn't ready to sleep yet.

"Was the necklace worth a very great deal, Marian? Will that poor man be transported when Mr. Montague finds him? Mr. Montague seemed to be in a terrible temper. I would not want to be that poor valet."

"His pride has been hurt, that is all. I daresay I should like to whip the odious man if he is found, but I shan't imagine he will be. Go to sleep; there is nothing more we can do about it."

Jessica snuggled deeper into the pillows, but she continued to toss restlessly. "Mr. Montague is a trifle frightening, is he not? I'm rather afraid of him. Could we go home in the morning?"

"The only one who need be afraid of Mr. Montague is Mr. O'Toole. We'll talk about going home in the morning."

"Lord Darley is such a nice man. I don't understand why he has a friend like Mr. Montague."

Marian didn't bother to answer this nonsense. She was

out of charity with the entire male gender right now. She
didn't wish to speak about them.

As the company gradually drifted off to sleep or continued to stare miserably at the ceiling depending on their
state of mind, the drunken ghost below settled on the library couch and began to snore.

"I tell you, the wretch was here last night. He wouldn't
soil his precious coat by going out in the pouring rain."
Dawn was just breaking over the muddy horizon as Reginald swung his leg over his mount and settled into his saddle.

Darley stood in the stable yard, shaking his head. "You
cannot know which way he went. None of the horses are
missing. He seems to have vanished into thin air. At least
break your fast and let us discuss a sensible course."

"There is no sensible course but murdering the thief. I
mean to find the magistrate and set a hue and cry if nothing
else. He'll not get off easily."

Darley watched his friend ride off before returning to the
house through a side entrance that led in from the stable.
He didn't think the ladies were up and about yet. A little
exploration might be called for, under the circumstances. If
the valet was still here, he might find some clue that would
track him.

Darley carefully scanned the gentlemen's smoking and
billiards room and saw nothing out of place. The lord's
study was a dark little room toward the back of the house,
and he pulled the draperies back to allow in the morning
sun. An antechamber was stacked with generations of estate records, the dust virtually undisturbed for twenty years,
if not more. In the study itself he found a table much like
the one in his father's study. A silver tray held a collection
of crystal glasses and a stopper that still smelled vaguely of
brandy. Darley's eyebrows rose as he sniffed the glass and
looked around for the bottle that it belonged in. His father's
tray always held an ornate decanter. This one also had,
sometime in the very near past.

He found no sign of the decanter that the stopper belonged in, but he could see where the dust on the desk had

recently been disturbed. A trail of what could only be a woman's footsteps marred the dust near the bookcase. One of the ladies must have been in here when they searched last night.

He could not remember any of the ladies coming down-stairs to search, but Darley pushed that thought aside as he continued his examination. The tapestry hanging from one paneled wall seemed to drift slightly in the morning air. He glanced to the broken window beneath the drapery he had pushed back, but no air came through there.

Darley had never prided himself on his intelligence. He had always been a mediocre student with more interest in horses than books. But he did possess a modicum of com-mon sense, and common sense told him that heavy tapes-tries did not normally move without some very good reason. Dragging a chair over to the wall, he stood on it and reached for the wooden rod holding the tapestry up.

"Lord Darley! Whatever are you doing?"

The soft voice nearly startled him into falling from his perch. He glanced down to see the surprised expression on young Miss Oglethorp's face. It occurred to him that if it had been her sister standing there, the expression would have been much more suspicious. He didn't know what made him think of that. He let the rod and tapestry fall to the floor with a dust-exuding thump.

Jessica stepped hastily backward, waving her hand be-fore her face to rid her nose of the particles.

"'Pologize for that, Miss Oglethorp, but the thing weighs a bloody ton. Excuse me. Didn't mean to say that. Slip of the tongue. Hadn't you ought to be with your mother?" Darley climbed down from his chair and nervously dusted his hands on his trousers.

Jessica gave him an innocently questioning glance. "I thought to look for the necklace before anyone got up. Mar-ian scarcely slept all night, and I thought I heard her crying once. Do you think the thief hid behind there?" She nodded to the newly uncovered paneling.

"I thought there might be something behind the wall, leastways. There's a bl—a bad draft coming through. Look, I think there is a crack along here." He ran his hand down the wall, searching it with his fingers. "One of our houses has a place like this where one of the ancestors kept his valuables. There's usually a little dent . . . " He gave a grunt of satisfaction as the wall swung outward.

Jessica gave a little scream of excitement. "Oh, my, you are so clever! Is he in there?"

Feeling just a little proud of himself, Darley explored the recess behind the wall. It wasn't particularly deep, large enough for a man perhaps. And as he suspected, there was a vault in the wall. But the vault was open and empty. He stepped back in disappointment.

"He could have hidden here, I suppose, but there is nothing here now. I wonder how many other hiding places there might be?"

Jessica didn't look in the least downhearted by his failure. Looking at him with gleaming eyes that made him feel ten feet tall, she responded eagerly, "Mother will know! Let us go see if she is up yet."

"I'm afraid he might escape while we are gone. Let me stand at the bottom of the staircase while you run up, just to make certain you are safe. Then I will stand guard in the hall and listen for any suspicious noises."

Neither of them seemed aware that their shyness had disappeared in the excitement of the chase. Jessica obediently ran up the stairs as fast as she could while Darley looked on. When he was certain that she was well on her way to her mother's room, he wandered around the octagon of the entrance foyer, admiring the faint glimmers of color from the skylight while listening for any oddities in sounds.

On the couch in the library, the eighth marquess squeezed his aching eyes closed and pinched his nose to halt the throbbing. If he were not mistaken, his unwanted guests were about to descend upon him en masse unless he acted soon. He had no grand desire to explain himself, particularly when his head felt like an overripe melon. He wasn't certain he could explain himself even if his head was in working order, which it very definitely was not right now. And he had no desire to find himself transported or hung from a gibbet for stealing what rightfully belonged to him.

Stifling a moan as he eased himself upright, the marquess sought a position of safety. If he did not miss his guess, the clank of boots on the marble entrance floor indicated one of the gentlemen patrolled there. He cast a reluctant gaze around the solid library. If there was an escape route here, he had not yet found it.

With a sigh—he was beginning to think he knew why ghosts sighed and moaned—the marquess eased himself from the couch and crossed to the tall window. At least he'd had the sense to pass out on the ground floor. Figuring the dogs would be on his heels in minutes, he shoved upward on the casement and felt it give, but not without a great deal of noise.

By the time Darley raced down the hall and discovered which room had the open window, the phantom intruder was gone.

Cursing vehemently, the viscount threw his boots over the low sill and followed the path of footsteps in the muddy turf. Behind him, he heard Jessica's shouts, followed unmistakably by those of the Lady Marian. His heart quailed at failing that redoubtable lady, and he added speed to his flight.

Inside, Marian quickly located Darley's route. She stuck her head out the window just in time to see him disappear around the house in the direction of the kitchen garden. Not seeing any reason why she should wet her good shoes, she picked up her skirt and raced down the hall in the direction of the kitchen.

She popped out the back door in time to realize there indeed had been hounds in the stables. Darley had evidently released them and they were howling across the distant hillside in search of their prey. The viscount himself was saddling his horse with every intention of following.

He turned to see her standing there as he mounted, and she waved as he rode off. It didn't seem very practical to attempt saddling a carriage horse even if a saddle happened to be lying about. She would have to content herself with waiting for Darley's efforts.

Surely a thief on foot could not long escape a pack of hounds and a man on horseback.

"Did you see him? Is the thief out there?" Behind her, Jessica excitedly wrung her hands. "Isn't Lord Darley just the bravest person you've ever known?"

Marian would wait and pass judgment on that later. What she wanted to know was the precise location of Mr. Montague while all this was going on. It seemed highly suspicious that the noise hadn't aroused him.

But she was left to wonder as her mother and Lily wandered down, followed by Darley's valet. There were fires to be stirred and water to be heated and breakfast to be made. Chasing thieves had become men's work, apparently.

By the time a breakfast of sorts had been put together, Darley was back with two hares and a quail, but no thief. He slung the game sheepishly on a pantry table, set the shotgun against the wall, and cleansed his hands in the basin Jessica brought for him.

"What happened?" she asked eagerly. "Did he dash over a cliff?"

Marian raised her eyebrows slightly at her sister's sudden boldness, but Lord Darley was answering Jessica and not looking in her direction, so she held her tongue.

"The hounds were just out for a romp. They weren't on anybody's trail. I don't know where the thief got to." His disappointment was so evident that no one could chastise him, not even Marian.

"That means he could still be on the grounds," Marian answered thoughtfully. It wouldn't do to worry her mother, but she wished to get her hands on O'Toole and personally wring his neck. She set down her pitcher and casually glanced at the door that Darley had just entered.

"Step one foot further in that direction, Lady Marian, and I will personally haul you back to London so fast your head will spin."

The voice roared from the doorway behind her, and she spun around to glare at Montague. "How dare you speak to me that way!"

Having achieved next to no sleep and spent the past hour attempting to locate some semblance of a magistrate only to be told he was away, Reginald wasn't in any humor for argument. He slapped his hat and riding crop down on a cabinet and glared back. "He's my bloody valet and if anybody goes after him, it will be me. You're a damned sight better off not witnessing his capture."

He strode through the kitchen and out the door, leaving his audience open-mouthed behind him.

Lady Grace was the first to recover her aplomb. Reaching for a heavy frying pan, she said, "He must be a bit peckish without having had breakfast. Jessica, do you think you could find the ingredients for those little muffins we used to make?"

Flushing, not knowing how to excuse his friend's behavior toward her, Darley gave Marian a tight smile and hastily followed in Montague's path. When he was gone, she threw a pewter sugar bowl at the door. She was tired of holding her tongue. One of these days she was going to let them all have it, bound and gift-wrapped.

Fourteen

The men returned some time later, muddy, hungry, covered with straw, and irritated beyond speaking. Lily hurried to pour their tea while Darley's valet relieved them of their filthy coats. Lady Grace attempted to send her daughters out of the room while the gentlemen were in their shirtsleeves, but even quiet Jessica would have none of it. Without waiting to serve in the formality of the dining room, they set plates and cutlery on the trestle table in the kitchen and began setting out the meal while demanding to know what happened.

Darley looked disgusted. "If I did not know better, I'd say there was an army troop out there this morning. After all that rain, there shouldn't have been so many footprints."

Reginald drained his teacup first, then began folding his bacon into his toast. He was all but certain there was more than one person hiding on these grounds. The bootprints looked to be of different sizes to him, and the one appeared to have an incipient hole in the sole. He bit savagely into his toast and ignored the speculations running rampant around him. O'Toole wouldn't be caught dead with a hole in his sole.

"You are being awfully quiet, Mr. Montague. What is your theory?" Marian sipped carefully at her tea. The dark circles beneath her eyes reflected her sleepless night.

He tried not to look at her. Generally, he didn't see women until well into the afternoon, when they were elegantly gowned and coiffed and prepared for the day. Lady Marian had not taken the time to do more than tie her hair back in a ribbon, and its dark waves seemed strangely thick and luxuriant for one so slender. She was gowned only in some frail muslin that apparently had little beneath it to conceal her natural shape. He was having a devil of a time keeping his eyes from straying to discover just how natural that shape was. Instead, he focused on his breakfast.

"I have no theory. The magistrate is not here to order the roads searched. I have sent someone back to London to fetch a Runner, and another with O'Toole's description to the toll keepers. I suggest we search the house one more time in daylight. If your cousin does not put in an appearance soon, I also suggest that the ladies return to town while I remain to deal with the authorities. Short of burning the whole damned manor down, I don't know what else we can do."

"I say, Reginald, your language," Darley reminded him. He threw a worried look to Marian, but she seemed not in the least offended. Jessica was blushing, however. He patted her hand helplessly, and she gave him a shy smile of gratitude.

"We will have to organize the search better this time," Marian suggested. "If the thief is still here, he could just stay one step ahead of us and never be found. We must start at the ground floor and drive him upward until there is no where else for him to escape."

Darley gave her a look of amazement. "That is a capital idea. I wish I had thought of that earlier."

"There are many things we should have thought of earlier. I fear it is too late for any of them now. The thief has gone outside these walls. What reason is there to think that he will return?"

Lady Grace daintily poured another cup of tea. "He will need to eat again sometime," she mentioned calmly. "He has already devoured most of our nuncheon."

They all turned to stare at her. Blithely unaware of her audience's astonishment, she carefully smeared a bit of jam they had found in the larder onto her toast.

"Mama, do you mean to say that the chickens we cooked last night are gone?" Marian asked patiently.

Lady Grace looked up with surprise. "Isn't that what I just said, dear?"

Reginald scraped his chair back and went to investigate

the cold cellar. When he came back, his expression was carefully neutral. "There is naught but the bones of one fowl left. The other is gone entirely."

"Ghosts don't eat, do they?" Jessica asked fearfully.

Reginald didn't bother to give this inanity a reply, but Darley reassured her as Marian set her cup down and stood up.

"I think we need to observe a few precautions. Do you think we could hire some help from the village?" Marian turned to Mr. Montague for an answer.

"I have already looked into that. Most of the men have been hired out for the planting, but there were a couple of old fellows willing to come out for the day. We can station them with the horses. And the innkeeper thought he knew a couple of women who might come out to help for as long as we need them. No one seems to know anything of the marquess's whereabouts, but they're all curious to come look the place over. I suspect we'll have a fair company here shortly."

Both Marian and Montague waited expectantly for some sound from beyond the walls, but only Lady Grace responded.

"I suppose my Gwen has long gone to another household. She used to make the most delicious pastries," she said wistfully.

There was nothing much that could be said to that. The gentlemen went off to see to the horses while the ladies cleared away the remains of their repast. Before they were done, there was the sound of a wagon in the stable yard. Mr. Montague's new employees had arrived.

As Marian watched her mother fall into raptures over a stout old lady who was apparently the amazing Gwen come back for the sake of old times, she took charge of the bevy of young girls come to help out. As Marian set them to scrubbing the kitchen and preparing the game, she marvelled over Montague's audacity. This wasn't even his home, and he was hiring servants. If the marquess actually existed, he must think all this bustle distinctly odd when he returned.

But the new troops were swiftly organized under Mr.

Montague's direction. The men were left to clean the stables and keep guard over the horses. A pistol was left in their care to shoot as warning should anyone attempt to get away. The giggling girls were sent with dusters and mops and brooms into the various downstairs chambers with the instructions not to leave their assigned rooms without permission. If anyone entered their domains, they were to pound their buckets and yell at the top of their lungs, and everyone was to come running.

The rest of the party trudged upward in hopes the thief would attempt to escape the activity below. Reginald stationed Lady Grace at the stairs with a hunting horn and the sewing basket she insisted on. He only hesitated when it came to divide the party to search the two long wings. The ladies could not be sent off by themselves, but it would not only be improper for them to break up into pairs, but the decision as to who would go with whom was beyond his capacity.

Marian caught his dilemma at once. "It seems wasteful, but perhaps we ought all to search each wing together. Mother said she thought there might be a hidden passage on this floor. We will need to be looking for that as well as watching to see no one escapes."

Darley beamed. "Capital idea. If you will allow me?" He offered his arm for her escort.

Forcing herself to smile sweetly instead of impatiently, Marian accepted his arm and proceeded at a stately pace to the first chamber to be searched. The task of searching for a thief or his hiding place was going to be tediously time consuming if she was going to have to do it at this snail's pace, but she needed Lord Darley's approval more than ever. Without that ruby, they would soon have no home to go to when their London lease was done. She bit her lip to hide her anxiety as the others began pounding walls and doors.

Reginald sent her strained expression a look of concern, but his mind was on locating the monster of ingratitude who had stolen his pride and integrity, not to mention his fortune. There wasn't a doubt in his mind that he would have to find some way of repaying Lady Marian for her missing necklace if it should not be found. He just hadn't found any opportunity to tell her so. Perhaps after the noon meal he could separate her from the others long enough to reassure her.

The rattle of a bucket below sent the gentlemen careening down the stairs twice before the maids learned not to knock them with their mops. After the second false alarm, the search began to degenerate into a game of hide-and-seek, with the contents of the manor being "it."

Jessica discovered that some of the wardrobes still contained clothes from an earlier generation. Forgetting her fear of ghosts, she ran from room to room searching out more and more miraculous creations of hoops and petticoats and ostrich feathers.

Darley became engrossed in searching the paneling for more concealed cracks to match his earlier success, and he was soon left behind.

Reginald began mentally cataloguing the value of the artwork and bibelots ornamenting the various chambers and wondering if they could all be included on the entailment inventory.

And Marian discovered a lady's library with first editions and illustrated pages that she had difficulty leaving behind. If there were a thief to be found, he had not begun to steal all the treasures lying around waiting to be taken.

When Reginald discovered her curled in a chair scanning an illustrated version of *Gulliver's Travels*, he threw himself into a matching chair and scowled. "This is not working," he announced.

Marian reluctantly drew herself from the adventures in Lilliput back to the present. She looked around, discovering they were in a sitting room adjoining the bed chamber where her father's portrait hung and there was no one else about. In all propriety, the situation should make her uneasy, but Mr. Montague's harrassed expression did not lead her to believe she was in danger from anything except his temper.

"No, it is not," she agreed. "It is exceedingly boring looking for someone who is so obviously not here. If there is a secret passage, he could have moved half the furniture into it by now and fallen asleep. I had not realized how enormous this place is."

Since the mansion was scarcely half the size of his father's ancestral home, Reginald did not have an adequate reply. He merely sprawled in the chair and continued scowling at her. "I will see that you are repaid for every shilling that the necklace was worth." He hadn't meant to announce the fact so coldly, but it had been on his mind for too long and he wished to be rid of it. He wasn't even certain how he meant to carry out his promise. He might have to give in to his father's wishes and marry an heiress to scrape together that kind of blunt.

Marian simply looked at him with that dark-eyed expression that made Reginald want to haul her into his arms and kiss her until he melted away her false façade.

"That is generous of you, of course," she said slowly, "but entirely unnecessary. I risked the necklace every time I wore it. I risked it by taking it to the jewelers'. You did nothing that I did not ask you to do. You could scarcely have foreseen that it would be stolen."

Yes, he could have. She didn't know he had a thief for valet, but he knew. Reginald wasn't in a mood for arguing with her about it. "I'll speak to your solicitor. We'll make some arrangement. I'll not have you marrying Darley just to pay the bills."

"I don't suppose anyone has ever told you that you are an odious tyrant." Marian closed the book and rose from the chair. She kept her voice pleasant, fearing Lord Darley would enter at any moment.

He drew himself out of his chair and blocked her path. "And you are a sharp-tongued witch. That does not change anything. You will have the funds as soon as I am able to collect them."

He was too close, but to retreat would be a sign of surrender. Marian held her place and glared up at him. She was of an average height and had not ever considered herself small before, but he made her feel helpless. She did not like the sensation at all. It was quite unnerving to have this man glaring down at her as if she were a gnat he could swat. But something in his eyes told her it wasn't swatting that he had in mind. She clenched her fingers into fists and tried not to retreat. "You will remove yourself, sir."

The tension and frustration of the day had been too much

for him. Reginald knew full well the danger of rosy lips and slender curves, even when they were armored with a mind and tongue equal to his own. He could think of no other action other than to reach for her. A brief wish to shake her passed through his mind, but it wasn't Reginald's mind in control now. His fingers clasped her arms and pulled her to him.

Marian felt the harshness of his lips across hers before she fully registered what he meant to do. She was twenty-two years old and could count the number of times she had been kissed on the fingers of one hand, and not one of those times had in any way resembled the ferocity of Montague's kiss. She could taste the experience on his lips, in the way they molded to hers, forcing her to relent and kiss him back. She shuddered as she did just that.

He was hard and warm and his fingers were strong as they held her to him. She feared there would be bruises where his hands held her, but she couldn't bring herself to pull away. Her hands came to rest on his chest, and she realized vaguely that she wasn't wearing gloves. "How improper" murmured through her head, while her mouth grew soft and moist and parted slightly at his insistence.

The sound of Jessica calling her name brought them both abruptly back to the moment. Reginald dropped her arms, and Marian backed away, and they both stared at each other as if lightning had struck between them. Jessica's arrival forced them to turn away.

"Look at this! Do you think I might be introduced at court in this?" She swirled around in a gold velvet cloak with a gold band of ostrich feathers wrapped about her hair.

Marian slid her hand over her cheek, tucking her hair behind her ears, tentatively touching the place where a rough beard had chafed her. She didn't look at Montague as she watched her sister's posturing. "It is rather—" she stumbled for words—"quaint," she managed. Her insides were still shaking. She needed to sit down and recover herself, but she couldn't let him see what he had done to her. She didn't want to appear an inexperienced young miss. She would brush this off as if nothing had ever happened. Nothing *had* happened. It was just the strain they were all under.

"Montague, where the hell are you? Come here, would you? I want you to look at something." Darley stumbled into the room and stopped. Uncertainly, he glanced to his friend's stiff posture, to Jessica's pretty smile of welcome, to Marian's nervous fiddling at her hair. With a shrug, he went back to his original intent. "There's something behind this wall. I just can't find how to get at it."

He crossed the small sitting room and knocked at the far wall. The sound was oddly hollow. "See that? It shouldn't sound like that." He went to another wall and knocked. The resulting sound was more of a thud. "That's the way a solid wall sounds. There's something back there, I tell you."

Marian gratefully turned her attention to this new discovery. She pounded high and low on the wall, getting the same hollow sound as Darley. She tried it on either side of the same wall, with no difference. Reginald left the sitting room and his steps could be heard in the room adjoining. Soon his knock could be heard on the wall on the other side.

"Still hollow!" he called. "And this is the end of the hall. If there's a passage, it can't go any farther."

They all immediately descended on the pretty bedchamber to renew their exploration.

Behind the wall, the marquess unfolded his lengthy frame and crept back the way he had come earlier. It would be a damned nuisance losing his hiding place, but he had other things to think about right now.

Michael had said the Lady Marian was soon to be pledged to the wealthy Lord Darley. From all he could tell, the viscount was the usual pleasant British fool. He had no particular objection to the match. But it hadn't been Darley in that sitting room when all went silent.

The eighth marquess of Effingham had the distinct feeling that his little cousin had just been thoroughly kissed by a man with whom she had moments before been trading insults. And if Michael's information was correct, that "odious tyrant" and cynical aristocrat was little more than a shopkeeper and not the wealthy lord the ladies needed.

It made his head hurt to think about it.

Fifteen

The marquess removed his boots and crept quietly up the servants' stairs to their quarters. He glanced down the bare hallway of closed doors, then decided on the nearest one. Michael wouldn't waste steps going to the end of an empty corridor.

He swung the door open quickly and stepped in, pushing it closed with his heel. Had his gaze been steel, it would have pierced the occupant through the heart.

Instead, the auburn-haired man on the narrow bed merely threw another card in his hat, wriggled his wrist, and flung a coin at the man glaring at him. The marquess caught the coin and shoved it in his pocket without looking at it.

"I ought to wring your neck." The look in his eyes was murderous, enough to make anyone believe he meant to carry out the threat. The scarred cheek twitched furiously as he spoke.

"You'll disturb your guests," the other man replied calmly, gathering his scattered cards with a wave of his hand.

"They've all taken a break for something they're calling 'nuncheon' but which smells very much like roasted game and apple pies. I'm damned well going to starve, thanks to you."

"Tarts. They call them tarts here. Pies contain meat." O'Toole crossed his legs blithely, tailor-fashion. "You could go down and join them. They're only looking for me."

The marquess grabbed a straight-backed chair and straddled it. His expression wasn't any more pleasant. "Fine idea. I'll go down and terrorize the ladies, have the damned hot-headed gentlemen call me out, and spill my blood on foreign soil. What else have I got to do today?"

The irrepressible O'Toole grinned. "You're all cock-a-hoop about nothing, as they say here. Your fair visage ain't nothing to expire over. Lady Marian will no doubt pin you to your chair and interrogate you over hot coals, but the other two will twitter and offer you tea. Scary thought, ain't it?"

The marquess rubbed idly at his mutilated face. "It isn't your Lady Marian I'm wary of, it's that other damned bastard, the stuck-up fellow who looks down his nose all the time. He's already putting two and two together, and it's his cash on the line if the ruby doesn't show up. I heard him offering to pay for it."

O'Toole looked impressed. "I didn't think he had it in him. From all I can tell, he lives pretty modestly by London standards."

The marquess crossed his arms over the back of the chair. "He's arrogant enough to bankrupt himself trying. When all this started, I just thought we'd be removing a bauble no one would miss. Now we're losing ladies their homes and bankrupting noble aristocrats. I don't like it."

"Gavin, your soft heart is showing. Besides, the ladies can't lose their home and Montague lose his blunt both. It's one or the other. Once we sell the necklace and get things righted around here, you can ask the ladies to come stay."

The marquess scowled, drawing the scars into a formidable mask. "It's not going to be that easy. That blasted Marian has all the gall of every Lawrence ever born. She's determined to throw herself away on the viscount and save the family fortune. And I think your friend Montague is likely to tear a few people apart to prevent it. The situation is getting downright nasty out there."

O'Toole gave a fascinated whistle. "And here I thought the British were a cold lot. I'm damned glad Mother had the sense to find someone besides a Lawrence to father me."

The marquess stood up quickly and kicked the chair

aside, bunching his fists as he did so. "Say that again and I'll beat you into a shadow on the wall. You're a Lawrence, just some hideous throwback, that's all. I'd suggest you put that active brain of yours to finding some way out of this mess, or I'm going to have to give the necklace back."

He turned and strode out of the room, leaving his younger brother to grin after him.

His brother, the marquess, wasn't such a bad lot, O'Toole mused to himself. Perhaps Gavin had killed a few men in the latest war between Britain and her former colonies and wouldn't be looked on all that friendly in these parts, but he hadn't bothered to kill his closest living relative yet. Considering the temptation Michael had offered frequently enough, that was saying a good deal about the marquess's character.

"If it doesn't rain again, the roads will be clear enough for the ladies to go back to London. There will be enough light if we hurry." Reginald wiped his hands on his napkin and sat back in his chair as if he were the head of their odd household.

Marian managed a pleasant smile. "We have hired the servants for at least a day's work. We cannot leave them unsupervised."

Reginald gave her a sharp look. "And tomorrow there will be some other excuse not to leave. You will wish to wait for the marquess to be certain he is well, or to make your apologies for intruding, or half a dozen other damned excuses. I say we leave now before anything else happens."

One of the new maids came to clear away the dishes, but Lady Grace spoke as if she were not there. "You really must mind your language, Mr. Montague. I had to remind the squire quite frequently. Single gentlemen often fall into bad habits, you know."

Since this was not at all to the point and misdirected his intentions, Reginald scowled and looked to Darley to pick up the notion again. His friend was so lost in thought that he did not appear to notice there was a conversation going on.

Reginald stifled an exclamation of disgust. The damned

hidden passage had yet to be discovered and explored. He wasn't going to get Darley out of here any time soon, and he had hoped to send the viscount back with the ladies. He could see when he was overruled. He didn't even have to look to Marian to see her triumph.

"I suppose we must search a little longer, then, but we are all leaving here on the morrow. I will speak to the help and see if any wish to stay until then." He waited patiently for Lady Grace to lead the way from the table so he might get about his business. Reginald wasn't accustomed to having ladies in the house, but he remembered his upbringing when it was necessary.

Lady Grace gave him an approving smile and rose from her chair, indicating that her daughters follow. Reginald felt as if he had just been given a motherly pat on the back. He hadn't known any such damned thing since he had been in leading strings, and then it had most likely been from a nursery maid. His mother had seldom noticed his existence when she had been around, and she had left his father when he was little more than a lad. He had scarcely been aware of her existence by the time she died. Motherly pats weren't anything he expected.

Shrugging off the odd feeling caused by that approving smile, Reginald went in search of the old woman who had made herself head of the household servants. Lady Grace would no doubt wish to have the woman's pastries for breakfast on the morrow.

They congregated in the upstairs hall a short time later to resume their search for the passage. Marian had pinned her hair up before the meal, and now she was wearing a more appropriate afternoon gown that concealed most of her figure in loose folds. Now that he had been made aware of her, though, Reginald could not forget the willowy slenderness of her waist nor pretend he did not see the long-legged grace with which she walked. He clenched his teeth and tried to keep his mind on the subject at hand.

"We will need to find the length of the passage and position look-outs all along the way so our thief cannot escape if he is hiding in it."

"There are no doubt stairs to the first floor. We cannot

possibly guard all exits," Marian replied thoughtfully, her gaze following the length of the various halls.

"The house is not old enough to warrant a warren of old passages like some." Darley did not realize he was correcting a lady. He was too lost in this new game to remember that he was actually talking to a female. He, too, was following the length of the hall and determining the passage's possible path. "I think the original owner simply had some eccentric tastes. It would have been costly to build in hidden staircases."

"It does not appear to me as if cost ever deterred any of the Effinghams," Reginald replied cynically, "but I think we can begin with one of us standing here and watching down the hall where we know one end is, and the rest of us starting down at the end of this other hall and working our way around."

They applied themselves more seriously this time, now that they had some evidence that there might actually be a hiding place. Discovering that the hollow wall actually began in the master suite occupying the entire north end of the manor, they quickly examined all the rooms in between to determine that it passed behind all of them, then set about looking for exits. Lady Grace stood at the stairway as before and watched with mild interest, calling encouragement.

Possessing more patience than the others, Darley was the one to discover the door concealed between the fireplace and the windows in the sitting room of the master suite. The ladies came running at his call, and they cheered as the hidden door silently opened. Then they grew silent at the prospect of someone entering that unlit hole.

"I think it might be dangerous," Jessica whispered, standing back from the cold draft of air coming from behind the wall. "I wish you would not go in."

Marian tried not to give her sister an impatient look, but she could tell she was not entirely successful by the flicker of amusement she caught in Mr. Montague's eyes. She managed to hold her tongue, however, and allow the gentlemen to make the decision, not doubting for a moment that they would ignore Jessica's admonitions.

"I think it would be best if we found another exit before exploring the passage," Montague advised.

"We're more apt to find it from within the passage," Darley argued.

"Perhaps we could follow on this side while you explored the other," Marian suggested, attempting to disguise her impatience with this argument. She wished to grab a lantern and descend into the darkness right now to see if it harbored a despicable thief. "You could knock on the walls as you go and we would answer as to which room you're nearest."

This suggestion was eventually adopted, with Darley being given the honor of exploring the passage, since he had discovered the door. Both gentlemen carried pistols but neither thought there would be need of them. The thief was no doubt long gone.

Montague guarded the doors into the hall while Jessica and Marian rushed in and out of the chambers communicating with Darley behind the walls. If the thief left the passage by some route and attempted to leave by way of the hall, Reginald meant to catch him.

By the time they reached the final sitting room at the end of the east hall, everyone was thoroughly disappointed. Darley had reported no hidden treasures, not even a skeleton or an old sword behind the walls, and still no other exits had been found. When he thumped against the final length of the wall and the sound came from within the wardrobe, even Montague joined them in searching for the door.

It was scarcely a minute's work from there to discover the latch that unfastened the door, and Darley stepped out. He dusted himself off as he stepped from the wardrobe, but there wasn't the amount of webs and dust that could be expected from a long-deserted passage. He exchanged glances with Reginald but didn't say anything aloud in order to protect the ladies. The passage must have been used recently.

Marian caught the glance and tried to interpret it, but her mother rushed in and exclaimed excitedly over the hidden door, examining it front and back while rattling off conjectures on its purpose. The gentlemen could very well guess the purpose, but they didn't mention the possibility to the dowager. For all they knew, her late husband could have kept a mistress in this room.

Marian waited for her mother to quit prattling before asking, "How could Mr. O'Toole have known about this passage?"

Reginald managed to look uncomfortable. "He claimed to have worked for the old marquess. I wasn't certain whether to believe him or not. I suppose I should have believed him."

Lady Grace looked surprised. "He did not look old enough to work for George. George has been dead nearly twenty years, after all. Mr. O'Toole couldn't have been more than a child then. I should think I would have remembered him."

Silence reigned momentarily. Montague was the first to break it. "Is it possible he may have worked for the new marquess?"

Everyone turned to Lady Grace, who shrugged her delicate shoulders. "It is possible, but I have been told he has been here only a very short while. He is an American, you know. They had to go back to the heirs of the fifth marquess to find a descendant." It had been her failure to provide a son that had resulted in that search. She had never been bitter about being turned from her husband's home upon his death. She had only been upset about the brief amount of time she had been given to do her duty.

"O'Toole didn't sound American," Montague said more to himself than any other.

"I can't think of any good English servant speaking as he did," Marian reminded him. "He was above all insulting. I cannot understand why you engaged him in the first place."

As of this moment, neither could Reginald. Darley, however, interrupted his thoughts.

"O'Toole insulted you?" he asked with a hint of outrage.

That had let the cat out of the bag. Marian bit her tongue and glanced helplessly at Mr. Montague. She could not very well explain the contretemps that had led her to exchange words with his valet.

Reginald gave her a closed look from beneath his lashes and lazily explained, "He also acted as my groom. I asked him to take the ladies to some lecture or another and they had a difference of opinion. He was appropriately dealt with for the incident."

The question was quickly dropped as Marian swept from the room declaring as she went, "I have had enough of this nonsense. I think it is time we searched the third floor. Who is to guard the stairs?"

By the time they reached the servants' quarters, O'Toole, his hat, and his cards had vanished. All that remained in his place was the carcass of one chicken.

With frustration and disappointment, the small party searched the remaining rooms, pounded all the walls, and wished the valet to the devil. When their search was complete, they were tired, filthy, irritable, and hungry. It didn't take a second request when Lady Grace called them down to wash for dinner. The ladies went one way, and the gentlemen, the other.

Feeling thoroughly wretched, Marian discarded her filthy gown as soon as she entered her chamber and quickly washed herself off in the bowl provided. The ruby was lost, Darley had not proposed, and the elusive marquess was obviously bankrupt. The entire journey had been a complete disaster. She did not see how matters could get any worse.

She did her very best not to even think about Mr. Montague's kiss. If she allowed herself such an indulgence, she would lose sight of all her goals. She could not be swayed from her purpose by a kiss that made her soul ache.

She closed her eyes and tried not to remember Mr. Montague's hands upon her, nor the firm feel of his chest beneath her palms, nor how it felt to be held so close while a man's mouth devoured hers. It would not do at all to think these things.

But the moment she saw his tall, elegantly garbed form standing in the hall waiting to escort them into the salon, her heart began to pound, and she greatly feared he would hear the commotion it was making. She refused his arm, tilting her chin proudly as she entered the salon without his aid.

Sixteen

Reginald sipped at the claret some enterprising person had found in the wine cellar and watched, disgruntled, as Marian turned her rapt attention to Darley's repetition of the day's adventures. She was hanging on to every one of his friend's words as if they were pearls of wisdom, when even Reginald was forced to admit they were little more than self-serving paeans to himself. He knew Darley's faults intimately and had never been irritated with them before, but was now.

She was staging this show for his benefit, Reginald knew. She was simpering like an idiot to show him she and Darley would suit beautifully. After that kiss today, he damned well knew otherwise, but he was at a loss as to how to prevent the inevitable. Darley was so thoroughly blinded by her act that the viscount would be calling on the marquess to make his offer right now if the dratted man could be found.

Reginald would have to appeal to the lady herself. She knew precisely what she was doing. She wasn't blinded by anything but her damned need to save her family. She could let Darley off the hook gently, if she chose. He would have to force her to so choose.

He bided his time. The ladies rose and left the gentlemen to their claret. Darley eagerly followed them shortly afterward. Reginald finished his wine, then found his way to the library instead of joining the others. It would drive Marian crazy not knowing where he was or what he was up to. He was beginning to understand her nature very well. And she understood his. She would look for him here first.

He wasn't disappointed. When Marian arrived, she carried a candle and a book she had borrowed earlier from the shelves. They both knew it was highly improper to meet like this, but it was rather difficult not to be in each other's pockets all the time when the party was so small. No one would suspect collusion except the parties themselves.

She didn't even bother to act surprised when she found him examining the shelves. "Most of the selections are quite boring," she informed him.

Reginald tried not to turn and look at her, but the temptation was too strong. She had dressed for dinner in an appropriately low-cut gown that had kept him on the edge of his seat all evening. He had dined for years with ladies wearing less and had only given them a second glance when attracting attention had clearly been their purpose. He had also seen ladies with more assets to display than this one. He could see no earthly reason why he should suddenly be so fascinated with a woman who held him in contempt, but his gaze wandered unerringly to the soft swell of ivory breasts in candlelight. Since he still held an open book in his hand, he hoped she would think his eyes were on it.

He forced his gaze to lift to her face. She was watching him with suspicion, but she really was too innocent to know what he was thinking. Reginald wondered what it would be like to teach her the power of her femininity, but he had a strange reluctance to teach her something she would only use on others.

He answered politely, "Boring, perhaps, but some are quite valuable. This one, for example. There is only one other known copy in existence." He held out the book for her perusal.

It was in Greek. She looked at it with disappointment. "It is in very poor condition."

"The entire library will be in very poor condition if changes are not wrought soon. There is damp in the walls, and without fires in the winter, I daresay the pages are becoming very brittle. I have a mind to seek your cousin out and make a bid for the collection." Except that he would

have no money with which to make a bid once he repaid
the ladies the cost of their necklace. Reginald kept that to
himself.

"Obviously, it would do better in the hands of someone
prepared to take care of it, but I should think you would
find very few buyers for as large a collection as this. Did
you think to acquire it all for yourself?"

She had the mind of a shopkeeper. Reginald tried to remember his purpose here. "That is not to the point. I have
decided we must return to town in the morning. I will begin
transferring funds to your man of business as soon as the
banks open. I know you did not wish to sell the necklace,
but I think it can be arranged so that your mother believes
the copy is the real thing. Once you have the worth of the
necklace, you need not worry about funds for quite some
while. I can advise you on how to invest them, if you wish.
They should bring in more than adequate income for as
long as you like and even provide dowries, if that is your
wish. You need not go fishing for wealthy husbands any
longer."

There had been ample opportunity for Marian to consider
his earlier offer, but her answer had not changed. As much
as she craved the excuse he offered, she could not accept it.
Pride would not allow her to take such an immense sum
from any gentleman, and certainly not from this one. She
shook her head vehemently. "No, I cannot accept that. You
cannot be made to pay for a favor that I asked of you. I
know you think me a vulgar fortune-hunter, but please do
not insult me in this way."

Furious, Reginald slammed the book back on the shelf.
"I am offering you and your sister an opportunity to seek
affection instead of wealth. I would not have my friend suffer for your greed. Obviously, Darley is worth a great deal
more than your necklace and he is titled, as well. Are you
so greedy that you would make his life miserable in return
for what he can do for you?"

"I have no intention of making his life miserable!" Marian's voice raised an octave, and she glared at him. "He
likes me, even if you do not. Why can you not see that he is
happy and leave him be?"

"He is not happy!" Reginald roared. "He has a harpy of a mother and two for sisters. They tell him what to do night and day, and he is too good a fellow to say them nay. You will only add to his long list of nags and make his life hell. I will do everything within my power to prevent that happening!"

"Is that why you are forever tempting my temper? Do you think to expose me as a shrew and make him take a disgust of me? How very considerate a friend you are! Did you hope he would come upon us when you kissed me today? Is that what that was all about? I have wondered, you know, but I am not a complete fool."

She was practically standing beneath his chin, daring him to admit the truth, and he could not admit it even to himself. Without a single coherent, logical thought, Reginald halted her tongue by putting his arms around her and clamping his mouth to hers.

He felt her start of surprise. Her hands pushed ineffectively at his arms. But her mouth was an unwilling victim that he tortured unmercifully until he felt her surrender. He would teach her there were more pleasant things to do with her tongue than wield it in anger.

Reginald had not meant things to go so far, but once she was in his arms, he could not seem to set her aside. Her lips learned his lessons quickly, eagerly. Her hands began to cling to his arms rather than push. She resisted the persuasion of his tongue at first, but as her breaths came rapidly, she could no longer fight him. He felt the shock of his invasion ripple through her, and it drew him closer to taste more. He had never experienced a woman as innocent as this one. The pleasure of her response was greater than he could ever have imagined. He craved more, and his hand slid naturally up her waist, to the curve of her breast that had tempted him all evening.

She sighed against his mouth. Her breath was sweet and intoxicating, and Reginald pressed his hand upward that last little inch until his thumb rubbed the pebbly crest of her breast beneath layers of thin cloth. The jolt of shock rushing through her at his touch caused an equal throbbing in his loins, and he could not have separated himself from her now had he wanted. He pressed his kiss deeper and thrummed her sensitive nipple carefully, until she was melting in his hands. She had no defenses against him, and he wanted it that way.

The little capped sleeve slid easily from her shoulder. He knew just where to find the ties of her chemise. Reginald lifted her breast from its concealment just as he lifted her from the floor to bring her to the leather couch behind him. Marian clutched desperately at his neck as she lost her toehold to reality, but she sank gratefully into his lap when he sat down and wrapped her in his arms. If her head was spinning as much as his, they both needed to sit down.

The lamplight was dim, but Reginald used its small illumination to admire the breast he had freed from confinement. His fingers smoothed the skin and played a tune upon the crest that had her wriggling with small cries against his already aroused flesh. It was time to put a stop to this, he knew, but not without one more kiss. He could not remember when he had acquired more pleasure by the simplest of sight and touches. He could not release the moment completely just yet.

That was his mistake. Had he set her aside then, allowed her to whip him with her tongue, no one would have intruded. But the protracted silence after the earlier explosion had aroused too much curiosity. Unfortunately, Reginald's mind wasn't on anyone but Marian at the moment.

A small hand grabbed Darley's arm as he clenched his fist and prepared to enter the library. He had only the dim light of one lamp to shatter his illusions, but he had heard enough of the earlier argument to understand what was happening behind that chair back now. The hand closing around his arm caught him by surprise.

He looked down into the terrified expression of Miss Oglethorp. The hall was much better lit than the library, and light danced off her golden curls as she turned a pleading gaze to him.

"Please, don't," she whispered. "It is all my fault. I was supposed to be the one to make a great match, but I have been much too timid. Marian means only to take care of me."

That was an extremely odd way of looking at what was happening in there. Darley couldn't see the other couple in the distance very well, but it hadn't precisely looked like a wrestling match when Montague had lifted the lady from her feet. He needed to move quickly, but he couldn't just ignore Miss Oglethorp's pleas. Her timidity had caused him to overlook her more than once, but in these last days he had come to understand and respect her a little better. One did not completely ignore a lady's requests.

"I am not blaming Marian. I blame Montague. Go back to your mother. We will be there directly," he whispered, trying to keep one eye on what was happening in the library.

"But you heard what they said. Let me go in there. Marian never meant to hurt anybody, I know it."

Her voice was breathless and hushed and Darley wished he could shove her aside, but she was the only voice of reason in a vacuum of pain. He was having difficulty sorting his feelings out. His very best friend was making love to the woman he wished to marry—in order to protect him. He wanted to kill them both, but he wanted to weep for the loss of what he thought he'd had. He was being torn in two, but violence presently had the upper hand. He could cry when he was done with them.

But he could do nothing in front of Jessica. "I will do nothing to harm your sister. It is Montague I mean to kill. He has done this deliberately."

A look of alarm flashed across her face. "You cannot! You will have to leave the country. Please, do not. We will think of something. There must be some other way."

"Before he ruins your sister completely? I think not," But a plan was already forming in his head, one that almost made him chuckle if he were not hurting so badly. Montague had never wished to marry. His friend had frequently pronounced he had no desire to have his independence crippled by a woman. He was just about to have his words thrown in his face.

To Darley's surprise, just as he pushed his way past Jessica and stepped into the room, an unfamiliar voice spoke from the distant wall by the fireplace. Both figures on the couch leapt apart at the sound.

"I thought perhaps I ought to put in an appearance so you could make your offer before the fact instead of after," the strange voice said dryly.

All eyes turned to the far shadows where a tall, lanky male figure leaned against a shelf, twirling the large world globe at his fingertips.

Reginald recovered first, leaning over Marian and adjusting the sleeve of her gown discreetly, returning her to the couch while keeping his eye on the stranger. He felt her shivering uncontrollably, and he kept his arm around her, even though his own heart was pounding madly—more from nervousness than fear. The situation looked very bad.

"I don't believe we have been introduced," he answered coldly, refraining from using so much as a "sir" to this stranger who had walked in on them like this.

The man gave the globe one last twirl and stepped forward to light a lamp on a desk. The flare of fire gave a twisted shadow to his face, and Marian gasped and sank farther into his arms. Reginald held her protectively while knowing his best choice was to put all the distance in the room between them.

The light of this new lamp flickered over a tall form garbed in a loose coat without tails, trousers that did not pull taut over his legs, and a pair of boots that looked as if they had seen better decades. Nonetheless, he stood there in perfect arrogance, arms crossed over his broad chest, as if he were the marquess himself.

Marian gasped as her gaze reached the shadows of his face. He *was* the marquess himself. The face was almost exactly the same as the man in the portrait that was her father, only her father would have been nearing fifty now and this man could scarcely be thirty, the same age as the man in the portrait twenty years ago.

A twisted version of a smile crooked his lips as he watched Marian's recognition. "Very good, little cousin. I have been admiring your intelligence, although I have cause to doubt it under current circumstances. The man you are clinging to is a rascal who needs to be shown how to behave." He bent his head in Montague's direction. "I believe your customs here are similar to ours, but as I have no friends in this country, I request that we dispense with seconds. Would you prefer pistols or swords?"

The gasps from the doorway behind them had Marian and Montague swiveling their heads in a different direction. With a reassuring pat, Reginald stood up and faced this new audience.

Darley finally broke free from Jessica's grasp and marched into the room, his face a mask of anger. "If anyone challenges the bastard, it will be me. Marian, leave the room, and take your sister with you."

Jessica darted between the two men and placed her hands on her hips. "Stop it. This is silly."

As an argument, it left much to be desired, but as a deterrent, her action worked. Darley halted, and Marian had time to recover herself sufficiently to rise, although she kept her arms wrapped around herself as if fearing she would shatter at any moment.

Although sensing her approach, Montague kept his eyes on Darley. "It would be better if you went to your room, Lady Marian. I'm quite capable of dealing with this."

"No doubt," she said dryly behind him. "But entertainment here has been lacking until now. I do not wish to leave just when it is becoming interesting."

Reginald wanted to laugh. He could almost see her expression as she spoke. He might be fighting for his life within hours, but Marian's irreverent tones made it all seem quite reasonable. He just feared his laughter would stir Darley to greater lengths.

The man behind him had no such fears. The marquess's chuckle came closer as he walked up to this little tableau. "I am beginning to think I like my little cousin too much to saddle her with a loose screw like you, Montague. Where I come from, we don't always wait until dawn to level these things out. There's a set of pistols over the mantel. Let's just check them out now, shall we?"

"Who in hell are you?" Unaccustomed to being ignored quite so obviously, Darley shoved Jessica behind him. He would have done the same with Marian could he have reached her, but she was currently standing between Montague and the stranger, glaring at them both.

"Lord Darley, I believe I ought to introduce you to my cousin, the Marquess of Effingham. Unfortunately, I cannot give you his name since he has not seen fit to introduce himself to his family, but I think we could settle on something obvious, like Bumble-headed Ninnyhammer."

Marian's scathing tone brought another smile to the stranger's face. He made a slight bow to the surprised company, "Gavin Arinmede Lawrence, Eighth Marquess of Effingham and all that other rot, at your service, sirs." He straightened, and his smile was gone. "And now you will all get out of here while I straighten out this ruffian."

He grabbed Reginald by the coat collar, jerked him backward, and slammed a fist into his jaw.

Seventeen

A s dramatic action, the punch was quite credible, Marian decided as she shook off Darley's hand. But Montague wasn't completely cooperative. Instead of staggering backward and falling when the marquess released his collar, Reginald lunged forward, slammed his fist into her cousin's abdomen, and sent his attacker into the bookshelves. Marian was forced to sidestep hurriedly.

She would have been forced to leave just to remove Jessica from danger had not Reginald immediately stepped back, dusted himself off, and halted the fight before it really started. Taking his cue from the Englishman, the American marquess straightened and shoved his hands in his pockets.

"Not bad from a spineless womanizer. Shall we move on to pistols now?"

Marian lost her patience. "That is quite enough! You have no right to come in here after twenty years and make claims to a family you have never bothered to know. I am quite capable of looking after myself, and I will thank you not to interfere. For my mother's sake, I ask that we be allowed to remain the night. We will be gone in the morning and you need not concern yourself over us any more."

For the proper dramatic exit, she ought to grab Jessica's arm and sweep out of the room, but drama and intelligence weren't always related. Marian knew better than to leave until she had the promise of the men that this would go no further. From their resounding silence, she could see that she had more work to do.

The marquess lifted a mocking eyebrow. "You may stay the night. Now get out of here so we may continue our conversation in private."

"Conversation? Is that what you call it in America? Your drawing rooms must be *vastly* amusing of an evening." Unable to rely on any of the gentlemen at the moment, Marian glanced over her shoulder to her sister. "Jessica, can you climb up over that mantel and retrieve the pistols? Then we can leave the gentlemen to their 'conversation'." She drawled the last word in imitation of the marquess.

As Jessica obediently drew a heavy Jacobean chair toward the mantel, Darley stepped back into the picture. "This has gone entirely too far. Jessica, leave that chair alone before you hurt yourself. Sir," he glanced at the marquess, "the insult has been to the lady I wish to marry. It is my place to call Montague out."

Reginald gave a gutteral groan, threw up his hands, and crossed the library to pull Jessica down from her precarious perch. She had apparently decided her sister had the right of it, and he wasn't one to argue in this case. She squealed when he lifted her down to the floor, but she made no protest as he reached for the pistols and put them in her hands.

"Take them to your mother. And take your damned sister with you, if you can. I promise not to kill anybody if you do."

Marian noted Montague was speaking to her sister but not to her. That was a pretty kettle of fish after what he had done, but she wasn't going to quibble with his tactics for the moment. She just wanted the situation defused and her questions answered.

She turned to the damnable marquess. He really didn't seem particularly angry. In actuality, she thought he was laughing at all of them. His eyebrows quirked as he caught her gaze, and he waited to hear what she had to say next. Marian wondered if her father had been that annoying. She shouldn't wonder that her mother would have wished him to an early grave, if so.

"I think you should present yourself to my mother, sir. She has been most apprehensive of this visit. We'll promise not to tell her you've been lurking in the woodwork if you'll promise to behave."

He grinned, a wide grin that went from ear to ear, although drawn up badly at one corner because of his scars. He looked to the other men to see if they were as appreciative of her challenge as he was. Lord Darley still seemed furious and perhaps a bit confused. Montague shrugged his shoulders as he came back across the room, escorting Jessica and her tightly clenched pistols.

"She'll jaw you to death if you don't," Reginald informed him coolly.

The marquess stopped smiling. His hand went to the scarred side of his face. "I'll not upset the lady unduly. It would be better if I remained an invalid outside this room. If you ladies will excuse us, I think we gentlemen can settle things amicably without you." He took a firm grip on Marian's arm and pushed her toward the door.

She grabbed a bookshelf and refused to go farther. "Unhand me, at once, sir! There is nothing to be 'settled' that does not concern me."

Reginald stood back out of the way, crossing his arms and looking to the appalled viscount for action. "Well, old friend, there's the woman you wish to make wife. Control her, if you will."

When the marquess attempted to pry Marian's hands from the bookshelf, she stamped on his toes and smacked his hands, then darted out of his way. Hands defiantly on her hips, she glared at all three men. "I don't need any of you!"

She swung around and walked out the door—right into her mother's arms.

All three men cringed at the polite, lady-like tones coming from the hall. "Why, whatever is going on here, Marian? I do hope it is proper. You are looking flushed, dear."

The marquess was already trying to blend in with the bookshelves when Lady Grace sailed into the library. She went pale at the sight of Jessica attempting to hide the pistols behind her back, and accusing blue eyes circled the room. When they came upon the stranger hiding in the shadows, she straightened and headed straight for him.

She frowned as he made a polite bow. "You are undoubtedly a Lawrence, sir, even the scars cannot hide it. If you are anything like that reprehensible old man who was your grandfather, I can see why you might try to disguise yourself, but it won't do. Introduce yourself, and explain all this faradiddle at once."

Jessica and Marian stared at their mother with awe. They had never seen the Marchioness of Effingham in action. The Lady Grace had always been a fey, pampered lady who smiled indulgently and allowed her husband to make the decisions. Squire Oglethorp had reveled in his role and indulged her slightest wish. She had never, ever lifted her voice to anyone. They couldn't believe what they were hearing now.

Unaware of the lady's true nature, the marquess hastened to do as bid, introducing himself formally and making a polite—if slightly rusty—bow over her hand. When she seemed undaunted by his scarred visage, he relaxed visibly.

"Matters are at a pretty pass, madam, and I cannot promise to rectify them any time soon, but I wish you to know that you and your daughters are always welcome in this house. It is more yours than it will ever be mine."

"Very well said. We will discuss 'matters, 'as you style them, in the morning. This has been a very trying day. I suggest that we all retire now." With an imperial wave, she gestured for her daughters to follow her from the room.

Marian hung back long enough to give Reginald a steely look that he could interpret any way he liked.

He preferred to interpret it as a challenge. He waited until the ladies were gone before boldly turning to the marquess with the accusation that had just leapt to mind. "Circumstances require that I offer to wed Marian, but if you will just return the necklace, Effingham, I think we can all get out of this relatively unscathed."

Reginald dodged Darley's furious punch, walked past the stunned marquess, and helped himself to the nearly empty brandy decanter on the far table.

The marquess glanced to the hapless viscount. "Back home, someone would have put a bullet between his eyes long ago."

"That's what being civilized does for us," Darley answered grumpily. "One cannot live on an island for long and not try to get along with the other inhabitants or we would kill each other off."

The marquess chuckled. "I like you, Darley. Or do I call you 'my lord' or some other such nonsense? I haven't quite got the hang of this title business yet."

The viscount looked vaguely irritated as he continued staring at Reginald, who was now pouring two other glasses of brandy. "You rank higher than me. You can call me anything you damned well wish. 'Cousin-in-law' was what I had in mind."

Gavin Lawrence shook his head. "That won't do, and we both know it. I like you too much to give you to my cousin. She'll make life hell for you. We Lawrences are a stubborn, arrogant lot. What about the other one? Miss Jessica? She seems to be quite attractive, and obedient, I noticed, much more so than her sister."

Darley sent him a look of loathing. "Affections cannot be manipulated so easily. Miss Oglethorp is entirely too young to know her mind yet."

Reginald returned carrying the brandy. "Then begin your assault in the morning and teach her. I wager she'll come around soon enough. Once she knows her mother and sister are taken care of, Marian will be free to find someone more suited to her temperament."

Darley scowled and took a deep drink of the brandy offered. "That's bloody rot." He set the glass aside. "And if I cannot have her, you must offer for her. After what we all witnessed here tonight, there is no better solution."

The marquess sipped his brandy slowly and allowed Reginald to speak first.

"There are a thousand better solutions. I do not have the wealth she requires. You know perfectly well why I cannot offer for her. She is the daughter of a bloody marquess, for heaven's sake! She could pursue Devonshire if she wished."

The marquess cleared his throat, distracting the attention of the two combatants. "I think the lady has made her choice, and Mr. Montague has sealed his fate by encourag-

ing her. I'll have your offer now, Montague, or your head at
dawn."

Reginald drained his glass and set it aside, turning to
glare at Marian's cousin. "She'll refuse me, and rightly so.
You would do better to inspect my background before offering Lady Marian as a sacrifice to your American morals.
We can keep what happened here to ourselves. There is no
need for it to be mentioned elsewhere." The muscle over
his jaw tightened. "And if you'll persuade that thieving
valet of yours to return the necklace, she will have all the
dowry she needs to attract a suitor more worthy to her station."

The marquess shrugged beneath his loosely tailored coat.
"Even if I knew where the necklace was, it belongs to the
estate and not to Lady Marian. And I have thoroughly in-
vestigated your circumstances, Montague. That shop of
yours is doing quite well. You have paid off a monstrous
debt in a few short years. You are in a position to keep my
cousin quite comfortably."

The two Englishmen stared at the American as if he had
grown two horns and a tail. Reginald's face had turned
pale, and his jaw tightened until it seemed immovable. Darley was the first to recover.

"That is privileged information, sir. You should not have
access to it. But since you do, you must surely see why
Reginald cannot marry Lady Marian. She would be appalled to discover he is a shopkeeper. As much as I would
like to see him brought to justice, we must consider the
lady's position."

The marquess no longer looked amused. "What a
damned bunch of hypocrites! I suppose you would have the
timid Jessica marry this arrogant bastard because she is the
daughter of a country squire and more suited to a shopkeeper? You all have bats in your belfries." He turned to
Reginald. "I'll have your offer or your head. Which will it
be?"

Stiffly, Reginald nodded his head once. "Your permission to ask the Lady Marian for her hand, sir?"

The marquess grinned broadly again and slapped him on
the back. "Well done! We'll discuss the settlements in the

morning after you pop the question to her." He turned hopefully to Darley. "I don't suppose you'll want to take the other one, would you? I can see that Lady Grace is kept off your hands."

Darley looked glum. "I'm not much of one for the ladies. Marian's the only one as has ever listened to me. I'll wait for her answer to Reginald's proposal."

Reginald cursed and wished there were more brandy. For Marian's sake, he needed to persuade her not to accept his offer. For Darley's sake, he needed to persuade her that she must accept his offer.

What a bloody rotten fix he found himself in now.

Hearing Jessica's breathing even into that of sleep, Marian climbed out of bed and went to the window. A light rain had started to fall again, and she could see very little through the darkness other than the row of evergreens swaying on the lawn. She would have seen very little more had the moon been shining brightly. Her mind was elsewhere than the front park of the manor.

Her thoughts were on the way Reginald Montague had kissed her. Worse yet, they were on the way he had touched her. Her breast burned through her heavy nightgown with just the memory of what he had done. She should be red with shame and embarrassment, but it was curiosity that held her firmly in its clutches. She wanted to know more of those kinds of touches. She had a vague notion that they led to the forbidden, but she had been certain what had happened tonight *was* the forbidden. She could not imagine what could be more dangerous and shameful than what she had already done.

She was not a silly young miss. She knew Montague would have to offer for her. She did not know why he had done what he had if he had not meant to offer for her, but she knew that hadn't been his intention. Reginald Montague was not one to marry where he must. But she hadn't thought him one to toy with innocent misses either. She was beginning to suspect that there was a great deal more to the gentleman that she did not know, but she would find out the hard way if she must marry him.

She wrapped her arms around herself and tried to keep from shuddering. When she had thought of marrying Darley, it had only been the wealth and comfort that he could offer that she had considered openly. She had chosen a gentle man who did not drink heavily and would not be abusive, because even in the country she had seen what could happen to wives if they did not marry the proper sort of man. But she had not thought beyond that.

Her mind was feverishly thinking beyond that now. She was quite certain that what Reginald Montague had done to her in the library this evening had more than a little to do with what happened between husbands and wives. She had not really given the physical act of marriage any thought at all. No one had mentioned it to her at any time. It was not a topic that was discussed among gentlewomen, particularly unmarried ones. She had received vague impressions from her reading that men did something to women that eventually caused them to bear children. Even though she had lived in the country, she had never quite learned the process by which hens had chickens or cats had kittens. The squire had kept them very protected, after all. She just hadn't realized how protected until confronted with her own ignorance.

Surely what she and Mr. Montague had done would not lead to children. That did not make any sense that she could see. The sensations that she had felt then, the ones she felt now, left her to believe there was something more, something that might have happened had they not been interrupted. She ought to be hideously frightened, but she was terribly curious instead. She wanted to know where those sensations led.

And she could not apply them to Lord Darley. Try as hard as she might, she could not imagine kissing Lord Darley and feeling the way she felt now. Perhaps that wasn't necessary when one was married. Perhaps she need only let him do what he wished with her and everything would be quite as she had expected it to be. But that wasn't enough any longer. She needed to know what she would be missing.

That thought frightened her as no other had. She couldn't

find out what she would be missing without ruining herself. She would have to marry Mr. Montague to find out where his kisses led.

It would serve him right if she accepted his offer. Lord Darley would never offer for her now. She could never accept Mr. Montague's cash for the lost necklace. She and her family would have to return penniless to the farm and pray for some means of finding the money to pay the debts. Unless she married Montague.

Marian felt as if her insides were on fire as she considered that notion. Flickers of flames danced in places she could not even think about. And she had yet to consider Montague's wrath at being forced unwillingly into marriage.

She closed her eyes and leaned her fevered brow against the cool pane of glass and prayed that he would not murder her in her sleep.

Eighteen

"Lady Grace, if I might, I would like to speak with Lady Marian in the salon," Reginald said stiffly upon finding the ladies leaving the breakfast room. There was no sign of the ephemeral marquess. It was as if he had never been. Reginald knew better.

Lady Grace made a slight nod and departed in the direction of her chambers, leaving Marian to stand awkwardly in the hall, avoiding his look. Reginald caught her arm and steered her firmly toward the salon that had recently been draped in Holland covers. A watery sunshine came through the newly cleaned windows to illuminate the stately, old-fashioned furniture.

He dropped her arm once they were in the room. She still would not face him. Her back was stiff and uncompromising, but the thin muslin did not disguise the soft swell of her hips and derrière. Reginald did not often find himself admiring the posterior portions of a lady, but knowing how close he was to possessing the right to touch her, he could not help himself—and the thought was making the rest of his thinking fuzzy.

Reginald tried to raise his mind to a more serious level, but Marian chose that moment to walk toward the window. The sunlight filtered right through that bit of gauze and muslin, revealing a clear outline of what lay beneath, and his thoughts fell in tatters once again. Just last night he'd had the opportunity to learn some of the soft swells of flesh he saw silhouetted there now. He found himself mentally stripping the clothes from her back.

Appalled, Reginald closed his eyes and tried to recover his thoughts. Women never had this effect on him. He had a satisfactory mistress who relieved his physical needs in quite creative ways. He never bothered thinking about her when he wasn't in her arms. Outside of that relationship, he found ladies to be boring, on the whole. They were selfish, uneducated, small-minded, and generally did not find much pleasure in physical pursuits. He had no need to think about them. Why then, was he unable to keep his physical cravings and his mental faculties off the female in the window?

There was only one solution. He must have this over and done with at once. He'd never imagined proposing marriage. He had no easily prepared speech. He just knew his duty and had some notion of how the woman he spoke to would think. He tried to combine the two in some modicum of rationality.

"Lady Marian, I know I am not the grand match that you had imagined, but I can keep you comfortably and I think we would suit very well. If you think you might return my affections, I hope you might do me the honor of accepting my suit."

Marian heard the stiffness in his voice. He looked very well this morning, even if his cravat wasn't stiff or his waistcoat buttoned. She didn't need to turn around to see how his light-colored eyes watched her from a carved visage that could have been made of wood for all one could detect emotion in it. He didn't wish to marry her. He had made that very clear despite his words.

"I'm appreciative of the honor you do me." She had practiced the words all morning. She didn't mean them to be malicious, but when she sensed he relaxed in relief behind her, she knew she had not chosen wisely. He thought she was about to turn him away.

Marian forced herself to turn and face him. That was the least she could do, show him the same courage he was showing her. She thought she could almost see a look of genuine affection in his eyes. She was about to destroy that quickly enough.

"I'm also appreciative of the fact that you offer because

you must. That is not the way I would start out married life. Perhaps we could have a long betrothal?"

To give him credit, he did not look horribly floored by her reply. He recovered rapidly, although as she had expected, the gleam in his eye disappeared. He made a formal nod of agreement, seemed to debate the proper procedure involved in declaring his delight, and evidently decided on the obvious. He drew her into his arms and kissed her.

It wasn't quite the same as before. It was a very controlled kiss, one of possession and decision, as if once he had decided she was his, he meant to mark her. He succeeded. Marian could still feel the handprints on her back when he stepped away.

"I shall have the announcement made as soon as we return to London. You have made me a very happy man, my lady."

Marian gave him a look of annoyance. "No, I haven't. We haven't bothered in polite deceit with each other before. I see no reason to start now. You had to offer for me, and under the circumstances, I could see no choice but to accept. I am conscious of the favor you do me, and I will try very hard not to interfere in your life. In return, I trust you will not expect a great deal of me. I suspect the less we see each other, the happier we will be."

Reginald managed a small smile. "If your wretched cousin is listening through the walls again, he will undoubtedly choke on his laughter right now. Do you care to give him more to amuse him?"

"I do not see what is so amusing. I would have been happily married to Lord Darley had you not interfered. I would have the funds to pay my mother's debts had your valet not made off with my necklace. As it is, I have no other alternative but to return penniless to the country and watch our home be auctioned off. I find no amusement in those circumstances. I am doing what I must, just as you are. I was hoping we could come to some amicable agreement. If I am mistaken, please tell me."

His face went cold and tight. "I am not in the least interested in a modern marriage. If I am to be saddled with a wife, it will be to a wife who belongs to me alone. You will find among my other disagreeable habits, I tend to be very possessive of what little I own."

Marian scowled and returned to the window. "You do not own me, nor will you ever. I am prepared to respect you, even to obey you if your commands are rational, but I am not prepared to turn myself into a doorstop for your convenience."

Reginald felt his fingers curling into fists and wondered how often he would wish to feel them around her throat. "I am not asking you to be a doorstop. I am asking you to be my wife. *My* wife, not anyone else's. That means even if you find yourself enamored of some other exquisite, that you remain loyal to me. Is that clear enough?"

Marian turned to face him again, her expression one of surprise. "I am not exactly certain. What precisely am I suppose to do with some other 'exquisite' if I find myself enamored of him? Run off to Gretna Green? Since I will be married to you, that hardly seems feasible."

Stunned, Reginald took a moment to gather thoughts that had just been blasted to the four winds. She was an intelligent woman. He knew that. She was twenty-two years of age and well-read. Of course, she had not lived in the sophisticated world of society, but surely even in the country. . .

Nothing was certain when it came to Lady Marian Lawrence. She seemed genuinely curious. Reginald raked his hand through his hair and tried to imagine explaining what he had thought her capable of doing when she in all probability did not even know what he meant to do to her once they were wed. He didn't think even his versatile tongue could explain. He shook his head in surrender.

"Never mind. We will have this conversation after we have been married for a while. Just be warned that I will not share you with another man."

A gleam of enlightenment reached her eyes. Reginald would have been relieved had he not been distracted once again by the sight of her silhouette in the sunlight. He would have to put shades on all his windows if he meant to remain a sane man. He was beginning to think a long betrothal would not be a wise idea.

"Did you really think I was capable of kissing another man? Or doing what we did last night?" Her cheeks burned as she asked this, but Marian was determined to keep this relationship on an honest basis. That was the least she could do for him after all these weeks of deceit. She was almost relieved that it was over.

Reginald didn't need to be reminded of what they had done last night. His mind couldn't go beyond that at the moment. He took a tentative step in her direction, his hands itching to reach for the breasts so temptingly displayed beneath that flimsy material. "I am not the only man in the world who knows how to kiss," he responded dryly. It was a wonder she did not see the direction of his gaze and run for shelter.

Instead, she stepped forward until he need only lift his hand to have her. "Kissing with other men isn't nearly as pleasant as kissing with you," she murmured.

He couldn't help it. She had wide lips, lips really too wide for her face, but he could imagine a dozen things she could do with those lips, all of them pleasant. They were moist and red as summer strawberries. Tasting them was absolutely required.

This time, the kiss was not nearly so controlled as earlier. Reginald collected her in his arms, pressed her tight against his length, and took her mouth with an intensity that had them both fevered in seconds. Their tongues were already discovering the places remembered from prior explorations when the salon door exploded open.

"Dammit, Montague! Can you not keep your hands off her until the vows are said? I will recommend to the Lady Grace that an early date be set." Darley stopped behind a carved mahogany chair and curled his fingers around the back.

Reginald gently returned the lady to her feet. His eyes didn't stray from her as he answered his friend. "I was just thinking the same myself. How about you, my dear? Shall we make this a short betrothal?"

She looked up at him with alarm. "We scarcely know each other," she whispered.

Reginald shrugged. "We'll learn quicker once we're

married. I think we'd best take the news to your mother, then set about our departure. I'll not be content until I have my back to this place."

The harsh, arrogant Montague was back, but his hand was still wrapped around hers, and his grip was tender. Marian contemplated this contradiction as she allowed him to drag her from the room. She was terrified of having bound herself to a man who held half the world in contempt, but some other part of her, some hidden private part of her, craved to know his affection. She hoped with time that the hidden part would overcome the terrified part.

They found Lady Grace in her sitting room, sharing tea with the scar-faced marquess. The other man stood when they entered the room, then returned to his seat when Marian was seated.

"May I extend my felicitations?" he asked, raising his brow.

Reginald ignored him, turning to Lady Grace instead. "Lady Marian has consented to take my hand in marriage, madam. I hope we have your approval."

Marian's mother looked to her daughter to confirm that everything was as it should be and, reassured by the stunned look she found there, she smiled pleasantly. "Of course, Mr. Montague. Marian has ever had a mind of her own. I would not think to question it at this late date."

"Then with your permission, madam, I would like us to return to town after nuncheon. We would both prefer to make this a short betrothal, and there are things I must do in preparation."

The marquess intruded at this point. "I don't see the hurry. The ladies have only just arrived and I am just beginning to make their acquaintance."

Reginald gave him an impatient look. "And you are enjoying the service at the expense of myself and Darley. You have the ruby now. Pay for the servants yourself. We will be leaving this afternoon."

"The ruby?" Lady Grace looked up expectantly. "Has it been found? I certainly hope so. Marian's father meant it to be part of her dowry."

The marquess bowed politely in her direction. "We have

yet to discuss the settlements, my lady. The ruby, however, wherever it is, is part of the estate."

Lady Grace blinked in surprise. "No. No, I am quite certain it is not. I would never have taken it otherwise. George gave it to me quite explicitly when Marian was born, saying it was mine until our daughter wed. But the point is moot, is it not? The necklace is gone. I am sorry, for I could have wished Marian to have something of her own when she went into marriage."

The marquess appeared to be losing his patience. "I could have wished the same, my lady, but the point is that the entailment inventory lists all prior jewelry. It is quite obvious from the portraits in the gallery that the necklace has been in the family for a long period of time. A valuable piece like that would go a long way toward restoring this estate. You would be assured a home for a lifetime were I to turn this into a profitable estate again."

Montague quietly interfered in the escalating argument. He had seen the look now on Lady Grace's face on her daughter before. He did not wish to hear what would come next. "That necklace would save Lady Grace's home and give her an income for life. There are more valuables in this blasted mausoleum than she could collect in a lifetime. Sell some of them if you are in need of funds."

The marquess turned him a wary look. "I think we need to leave the ladies alone. They will have no interest in our discussion of business and settlements. If you will excuse us?" He stood up and bowed to the dowager.

Marian wondered what would happen if she told them both to take a flying leap off the nearest cliff. She had as much interest in settlements as they did. It was her life they were dictating. Since it was quite obvious that her cousin could not provide anything for her, she had hoped that Montague might be persuaded to settle an allowance on her. She wasn't at all certain that the American would even think about that. He must, or there would be nothing for her mother and sister if he decided to abandon the estate and return home.

Montague must have seen the rebellion in her eyes. He

caught her hand, raised it to his lips, and murmured "Trust me," before releasing her.

It was the first command he had given her. They were fatal last words if she had ever heard them, but she had promised to try to obey.

Marian looked resigned as she watched them depart. She had promised to trust a man who had lost her only valuable and who had seduced her away from his best friend. What was the phrase Darley had told her the American had used? She had "bats in her belfry."

Darley had retired to the stable to nurse his aching heart. He hadn't really believed Reginald would do this to him, but he had seen the way Lady Marian had looked at his friend after she had been so thoroughly kissed. There wasn't any way he could pretend she was anything else but enamored of a man who was by all accounts a good deal more dashing and handsome than Darley could ever hope to be. He would have to go in and wish her well as soon as he could force his tongue around the words.

Perhaps it wasn't his heart that had been hurt so much as his pride. He had thought he had caught a rare diamond, and he had been feeling very good about himself. There were other wealthier and better looking gentlemen out there who Marian could have set her cap for, but she had chosen him. She had listened to his ramblings with interest, and had made him feel respected and important. Now he supposed that had all been a ploy to win him.

He sighed and kicked the dirty straw. The place needed a good groom. He'd like to get his hands on that valet of Montague's. He had a feeling the scamp was somehow behind all this. He'd like to throttle the thief.

Blaming someone else for his problems wouldn't solve them, however. His mother had been expecting a wedding any day. He was going to have to go back and tell her it was off. He'd rather go to Scotland and throw himself into a loch than tell her that. He had been prepared to marry Marian despite her indifference rather than face his mother without a bride. Now he didn't know what he was going to do.

He heard a cooing sound from one of the far stalls. Frowning, Darley shoved the barn doors open until a ray of sunlight cut through the center of darkness. A pigeon ought to let itself out, he thought, but there was no flutter of wings.

He followed the path of sunlight deeper into the barn. The cooing noise had become soft murmurs. Indistinct at first, they became clearer as he approached the last stall. A smile tipped his lips slightly as he leaned over the gate.

A fair-haired enchantress sat curled upon the straw, stroking a lap full of furry, playful kittens, completely oblivious to the streaks of dirt on her cheeks or the appearance of her gown as the kittens attempted to climb it. She was talking contentedly to the animals, a good deal more contentedly than he had ever heard her speak in public.

Darley cleared his throat nervously. She was beautiful and he was not. One of the reasons he had dared speak to Marian had been because she looked so much like himself. But Miss Oglethorp was the kind of shining blonde that he had never hoped to attain. But then, he had never seen a diamond of the first water sitting in a bed of straw with a lap full of kittens, either.

She gave a start of surprise at the sound he made, then looked around to see him. With a small, shy smile, she glanced back to her kittens. "Lord Darley, the marquess said I might have whichever one I wished, but how can one possibly choose? They all seem so perfect to me."

Thinking very much that there might be a moral in that dilemma somewhere, Darley crouched down beside her and picked up the tiniest, ugliest kitten clinging to her hem. "I would choose this one."

She glanced at him in surprise. "Would you? Why?"

He curled the kitten in his hand next to his lapel and listened to it purr. "Because he's the one most in need of loving."

Nineteen

hat fellow Montague says the paintings are just beginning to gather value, that they'll increase in worth every year, and that the Ming vases—whatever in hell they are—are worth a fortune already. He seems to think there is a goldmine in damned gewgaws around here, if we can figure which aren't on the inventory. Do you think he really knows his stuff?"

Michael juggled three silver spoons and watched them whirl and catapult back and forth before making them disappear. He seemed more interested in his practice than in his brother. "I followed him to his shop once," he said offhandedly, pulling the spoons from various places amidst his attire. He was currently occupying the butler's quarters on the lower floor, since there was no butler. "It was packed with shiny, valuable looking things, and he was doing a steady trade. He's made his blunt knowing something."

"You're beginning to talk like a bloody damned Englishman," the marquess muttered, straddling an uncomfortable chair.

"I talk like the people around me. It's one of the tricks of the trade." Michael calmly began juggling the spoons again, only this time there were four.

"I wish you'd juggle us out of this one. Montague is convinced we have the necklace and that he can get out of marrying our cousin if we'll just return it. I don't like this business of playing lord of the manor. I want them all to just go back where they came from and leave me to the business of righting this place."

Michael shrugged and one of the spoons fell to the bed covers. He quickly scooped it up and returned it to the circle of whirling silverware. "You wanted a family, now we have one. It won't hurt to have a wealthy cousin-in-law who knows how to pawn off the family valuables, either. From what I see, he and the lady deserve each other. Our cousin could out-Lawrence you if she tried. Once she's set her mind to something, we would probably have to put a bullet through her head to stop her. Marriage to Montague is very definitely the right step. And I like your idea about the viscount and the shy one. Just think, one day we could have an earl in the family. You being a fancy marquess and all, we'll be rubbing shoulders with the whole bloody aristocracy."

The "fancy marquess" rubbed his scarred cheek and scowled. "You'll more likely be in jail if Montague has anything to say about it. How do you plan to show your face again if we don't return that blasted necklace? We could have the lawyers fight over it and make it legal."

Michael grimaced and caught the spoons in one hand. "The only ones who would profit then would be the lawyers. I'm not much for moving in society, anyway. Maybe I'll abscond to the states and sell the necklace there."

"You'll bloody well stay here and help me out for a change. We're not street beggars anymore. Give back the necklace and figure out some way of getting yourself back in circulation. I'm going to start selling off anything not on the inventory."

Gavin removed himself from the chair and stalked toward the door, leaving his red-headed brother multiplying spoons and producing forks.

"I must return to London, Marian. If you and your family wish to stay here, that is your choice, but I cannot. Among other things, I must see that your man of business has the funds to pay those notes you owe. If you will give me his direction, I will make that one of my first tasks."

Marian felt a sinking sensation in the pit of her stomach as she turned to look at the man she meant to marry. Reginald's words made it all too clear that he had already come to think of her as his responsibility, and he meant to deal with her problems alone, without need of her help. She wasn't certain she liked that idea at all. It made her feel like a schoolgirl again. Or was it the idea of belonging to this man that she didn't like?

"I cannot ask that of you," she murmured, staring down at the faded carpet at her feet. "I will sell the rest of the squire's library. It is his home we are attempting to save. It only seems fair."

The only person who would give her a fair price for the books was him, but Montague refrained from reminding her of that. She thought him a collector, and that Jacobs had purchased the last manuscript. She didn't know he would have to turn around and sell her precious library to make a profit so they could live. He would not be able to explain if he bought her library and then she couldn't find it in his home when he brought her there. This was beginning to get too complicated for words. He needed to keep things simple.

"That is a trifle foolish," he reminded her. "You could not get what you deserved out of those books unless I bought them. Wouldn't it be simpler if I just paid the debt and we kept the books in my library?"

Marian appeared taken aback by the notion, but then her eyes began to gleam as she understood. Reginald felt the full force of her smile as it fell on him, and he felt oddly warm inside, odd because it was not the heat of desire but something else entirely.

"Then it would be a fair exchange of sorts, would it not? Except that I still get to keep the books but you are out the money." She puzzled over that. "I still feel as if you are coming out on the wrong end."

Reginald smiled and tilted her chin until she looked at him again. "I will not only have the pleasure of sharing ownership of your books, but I will be getting my sister and mother-in-law out of my hair. It will be much better if they have a house of their own to go to. Mine is none too large, and I would prefer to have my wife to myself. I don't feel slighted in the least."

Marian's cheeks burned under the warmth of his gaze. He was scarcely touching her, yet he was doing that to her again—making her feel all hot and wiggly inside. The notion of marriage to this man was looming larger and larger, like some giant obstacle she must cross. She tried not to gulp as she stood still beneath his hold.

"I don't suppose my cousin was able to make much of a settlement on you. All I seem to be bringing to this marriage is my family. Do you think I might be of some use to you in some manner? I know how to run a household, but that seems scarcely enough."

Reginald shook his head and brushed his thumb across her lips. "You really don't know, do you?" He brushed his lips where his thumb had been, and she quivered slightly. He raised his head again, and a flicker of amusement reached his eyes. "I can see where you might save me from one of my extravagances. I'll let you know if I can think of any others."

Reginald remembered that wide-eyed dewy look well after he was down the road. Lady Marian Lawrence would definitely save him his most expensive indulgence—his mistress, Madelyn. Reginald didn't think he would have any trouble adapting to this one pleasure of having a wife. Lady Marian had his blood racing hotter than any opera actress he'd ever seen, and he wasn't adverse to teaching her what a mistress ought to know. Perhaps other men thought ladies were only for getting an heir. Perhaps other ladies thought they only must do their duty to get an heir. He was of a different mind, and he thought Lady Marian might be the same. If he must marry, he was glad that it was to someone he could bed as readily as his mistress.

Reginald sighed as he thought of Madelyn. She was going to throw a tantrum when he gave her her congé. He was going to have to give her a very expensive gift to ease the parting. That would have to be the first thing he did upon returning to London. He didn't wish to imagine what would happen should Marian discover he kept a mistress.

Theirs was going to be a difficult enough marriage as it was.

If marriage there must be. He was still more than certain that the marquess and O'Toole were working together to hide the necklace. Perhaps the first thing he ought to do when he returned to town was to visit the dealers he knew so well to determine if anyone had tried to sell the ruby. He'd have them nab the thief if he showed up anywhere in London. Once the necklace was back in his hands, he might have the power to release Marian from this vow they were neither willing to take.

Of course, if he were released from his betrothal after he had disposed of Madelyn, he would have to go to the trouble of finding another mistress. That would be a damnable nuisance. At the moment, he had little enough interest in Madelyn. He definitely couldn't summon much interest in finding someone new. He was much more interested in having Marian.

At that startling thought, Reginald spurred his horse to a gallop and rode into London in a brown study unconducive to communication of any sort. The idea that he might possibly prefer marrying Marian to taking a mistress was a bite he was having great difficulty swallowing.

"Lord Darley! I thought you had left for town with Mr. Montague." Marian entered the dining room and found the viscount already there, conversing with her mother and sister. The marquess was again nowhere to be found.

Darley looked up with a small frown between his eyes. "I am not presently speaking to the cad. Besides, we have not yet found the necklace, and I am convinced it and that blasted valet are still about. I mean to do more exploring, and I don't think you ladies ought to be left unprotected while a thief is still on the grounds."

Neither Lady Grace nor Jessica objected to the fallacy in this explanation, but Marian couldn't refrain from reminding him. "Our cousin is about somewhere. We aren't entirely unprotected."

Darley scowled as he pulled out a chair for her. "He's as much a rascal as that valet. I don't trust him."

Marian looked to the walls and waited vainly for the

choked laughter she was certain she had heard more than once. Perhaps she was imagining things. After all, they had only found one passage behind the walls, and that was in the other wing.

"We thank you for your care, sir," Lady Grace murmured when it became obvious that Marian would not. "You have been more than gracious under the circumstances."

Darley took his seat and threw a brief glance to Jessica, catching a shy smile on her face before she returned her gaze to her plate. She was too young, he decided for the millionth time that day. But then, so was he. A man shouldn't have to think about marriage until he was thirty-five, not for another good six years. But in six years, Jessica would surely be snatched up by someone bolder than he, and he would be back to looking at simpering misses half his age.

Dash it all, there was no escape from this marriage trap. Morosely, he examined the plate of food he had chosen and wished he had followed Reginald. It had all been much simpler when Lady Marian was leading the way.

Marian was set upon doing just that now. Wielding her fork, she mentioned casually, "I am sensible of the fact that you wish to come to know our new cousin better, Mother, but as we could not cancel our gowns with the modiste, we are due back for fittings shortly. That is, unless you have decided we should not go to the ball?"

She was perfectly aware that now that her mother and sister were back in the country, they were not disposed to readily return to town. Their brief fling had been more than adequate to satisfy their curiosity and craving for company. But the problems that had sent them to town in the first place had not been adequately resolved, and they could not be while remaining on this bankrupt estate. Since Marian had failed to make a triumphant marriage, it was now Jessica's fate to find a husband of her own. That couldn't be done while chasing ghosts in the walls.

Besides, Marian was not yet ready to trust Montague out of her sight. He could have gone haring off to town with the necklace in his pocket for all she knew. She didn't think he would, but she had learned not to trust so easily these last weeks. If they were truly to be married, it would be better to be seen together after the announcement. It probably wouldn't do to let him gallivant around London behaving as if he were still unattached. If she must marry Montague, then she meant it to be a very real marriage.

"Uh-oh, Marian's got that look in her eyes," Jessica whispered in an aside to Darley. "That means we might as well agree now or she will never let it go."

Caught by surprise by this admission, Darley looked up in time to see the resigned look on Lady Grace's face and the determined one on Marian's. He was beginning to understand who ran this family. He felt a little quiver of relief at the thought of Reginald instead of himself running up against this stubborn determination every day of his life. He ought to be ashamed of the thought, but he wasn't.

"I suppose you are right, dear. Perhaps we could persuade the marquess to accompany us. He really must be introduced to society."

The elusive nobleman appeared as if summoned by the sound of his name. He strode into the room in rolled up shirt-sleeves with the smell of the stable still on him, and when the ladies didn't appear to take offense, he pulled out a chair and made himself at home.

"This marquess doesn't need any such thing," he said as if he had been included in the conversation all along. He watched with interest as a maid hurried to pour tea in his cup. He would have preferred something stronger, but he was thirsty enough not to argue. He drained the cup while dishes were passed to him so he might fill his plate. "I have enough on my hands without having to meet a bunch of gussied-up snobs."

"They're not all snobs, dear," Lady Grace said as she wrinkled her nose in thought. "But they can be frightfully judgmental, I suppose. It would be better if you could appear in the proper clothes. Perhaps Lord Darley and Mr. Montague could help you there."

Gavin glanced up to see if she were serious, then looked to his young cousin to see how she was taking this monstrous suggestion. Marian was fighting a smile and hiding behind her teacup. At least she had the sense to understand that his clothes were the least of his worries. He rubbed his cheek unconsciously and returned to eating.

"Personally, I think Lord Effingham is much more effective as a phantom," Marian murmured with some amusement. "We could host house parties and insist that the guests must bring their own servants and food as the price of admission. All we need do is go back to London and gossip about our Gothic visit with missing jewels and haunted passages and ghosts, and all society will wish to visit for the excitement, hoping they will be the first to see the phantom marquess. It would be as diverting as Vauxhall. We could charge admission, I'm certain."

"Obviously, you are in dire need of entertainment, Lady Marian," Gavin growled. "Shall I wear a black cape and lurk in shadows to keep the company thrilled?"

"Ohh, please don't," Jessica hastened to answer. "That would be much too frightening. I don't like masquerades. At least, I think I don't. I have never been to one, actually, but lurking in shadows sounds most unpleasant."

Marian almost giggled and hastily sipped her soup as Lord Darley leaned over to pat her sister's hand and reassure her no one would lurk in any shadows when he was around. She looked up and caught her cousin's eye. There was a glint of something there that made her quickly look back to Jessica and then to Darley. Her eyes widened as she noticed the slight flush on her sister's cheeks.

When she looked back to the marquess, he was calmly devouring his food.

How odd. She had the distinct impression that the marquess was feeling very satisfied with himself about something, and that something seemed to have to do with the new color in her sister's cheeks.

Twenty

Reginald cursed as he struggled into his coat without the help of the wretched O'Toole. He had too quickly grown accustomed to the services of a valet, a result of his own expensive upbringing, he realized. He trusted Marian's taste didn't tend to be as expensive as his own or between them they would be in dire trouble quickly.

That was a ridiculous thing to think, and showed the unstable state of his mind lately. He wished he had a well-furnished town house, an elegant carriage, and an unlimited budget for fancy gowns for her, but he knew only too well the limits of his means. Had this been a love match, he might have felt more comfortable with that knowledge. As it was, he feared he was going to be a dreadful disappointment to a woman who had hoped to marry money.

This train of thought led back to the blasted necklace. He had agreed to settle a comfortable allowance on Marian for her own use, but the amount would be much more comfortable should the necklace be found and sold. He was quite aware that Marian would use her allowance to provide for her family, and that if the necklace came to her, she would sell it without a qualm to help them. He had no objections to that if the necklace rightfully belonged to her. The damned marquess could obtain his funds elsewhere.

But first he had to find the necklace, which meant finding O'Toole. So far, his search of London's dealers had yielded nothing. He hoped the man wasn't foolish enough to go elsewhere to sell the thing. He'd never get half the price anywhere else but London. But then, O'Toole might fear getting caught if he tried to sell it in London and prefer to take a lesser price. Reginald would gladly give him the difference for the opportunity to wring his neck.

Deciding his coat was as straight as it was going to get, he checked his image in the mirror, gave his cravat one last tuck, and picked up his hat and stick on the way out the door. The announcement of his impending marriage had appeared in the newssheets just today. He needed to play the part of happy fellow as he made the rounds of his clubs tonight.

Reginald found himself wishing for Darley's company after the first round of congratulations. The betting had been running heavily in the viscount's favor of late, and there were those who were looking at Reginald with suspicion and a trace of disapproval. His intention never to marry had been widely known. Suddenly announcing a betrothal to a woman without a shilling who had been known to favor Darley was causing gossip in all corners. Only Darley would appreciate the subtleties of this quagmire.

Reginald suffered through the first round of drinks with what he considered to be great aplomb. Offers to take Madelyn off his hands he referred to the female in question. She had thrown a rather valuable crystal vase at his head when he gave her notice. He didn't think she would take any of his suggestions when it came to her next lover. He also didn't believe Marian would be properly appreciative of the sacrifices he was making for her. All things considering, he was feeling particularly put upon.

It wasn't until he walked into White's and found his brother waiting for him that he knew the evening was going to plummet from low to lower.

Charles, Viscount Witham, gestured an invitation with his port glass. "Thought you'd be around this evening. Sit, Reggie. Tell me what you've been doing with yourself lately."

It was bloody unlikely that he would tell his family precisely what he had been doing, but Reginald knew the reference was to the announcement in the paper. It was just his luck that Charles had trotted out of his country home across the breadth of England just in time to read that announcement. Reginald took the seat and the glass offered.

"Don't play sly with me, Charley. You saw the paper, else you'd not be here. If you want to meet her, you'll have to travel up to Hertfordshire to Effingham's Gothic relic. You'll need to bring your own servants, though. He's not got a penny to squander on one." There, that ought to tell his brother everything he wished to know without getting too personal with Marian's history. Reginald disliked talking about her behind her back. He preferred that she be by his side while he introduced her to his family. That was another thought that caught him by surprise, and he took a hefty swallow of his wine.

"You could have had any heiress in the kingdom, yet you settled for a penniless bluestocking? I had not thought you a romantic, brother mine."

Older than Reginald by some five years, Charles did not have the same dramatic looks as his younger brother. His hair, always thin and of a lighter color, had begun to recede slightly. He wasn't quite so tall nor as athletically built as Reginald, but there was a quiet handsomeness in the way he held himself that marked him of a superior nature. His speech was no different. Refined and elegant, he did not raise his voice or even use sarcasm. His question hit its mark all the same.

Reginald tried not to wince. "Where did you hear that she was a bluestocking?" was the only reply that he could make.

Charles smiled slightly. "I left my card at the lady's house, of course. It was the only proper thing to do. While I was doing so, my groom had a long chat with hers. Seems the lady enjoys Hatchards and museums and scientific as well as literary lectures. I cannot think of another soul in our circle who is half so well educated."

Reginald wondered if there was enough wine in the bottle to get him through this night. He didn't think so. Perhaps he ought to go back to Hertfordshire. He enjoyed being roasted by Marian a great deal more than by his peers. That was probably because he could spend most of the time imagining other uses for her tongue and wondering

how best to win her into his arms. Her tongue might be tart,
but by Jove, the rest of her was as sweet as any he had ever
sampled.

His thoughts were interrupted by a laugh from across the
table.

"Smitten good, are you? You aren't even listening to me.
I didn't think I'd live to see the day when the mighty Reginald was brought down by a pretty face. I'm itching to meet
the lady. When will she be back in town?"

Reginald shrugged. "Devonshire's ball is in two days'
time. I daresay she'll return for that." He struggled with his
conscience, wondering how much he ought to say to
Charles. His brother knew him too well to believe he had
actually fallen for any woman, bluestocking, penniless, or
not. But he found it difficult mentioning the actual circumstances of his unplanned betrothal. Charles didn't seem to
be questioning too hard yet. Perhaps it could be glossed
over.

"If she's not an heiress, how do you intend to support
her? I find it hard to believe Effingham even permitted your
addresses."

That was cutting to the bone. Reginald grimaced and
filled his glass. "You'll have to meet Effingham to understand. He's an American and a recluse. He's inherited a de-
teriorating estate and no funds. I imagine he's simply
interested in seeing that he doesn't have any relatives encroaching on what little he does have."

Charles made an uncommunicative grunt. "So you have
seen the man. I wondered. The town is agog with rumors,
you realize. No one was even certain he existed."

"He exists, all right." He was the reason for this damned
marriage, but Reginald didn't say that aloud. There was another thing or three he held against the marquess. "As I said,
he's American. He doesn't know our ways and isn't much
interested in learning, apparently. He's been badly scarred,
by a rapier it appears. I imagine he was in the war. He has a
military bent to him. Combined with the fact that he hasn't a
shilling for entertaining, I can understand why he stays out
of society."

"Then I suppose it will be up to us to introduce the lady

and your betrothal. Harriet has been wishing to come in for the Season, but she's breeding again and I didn't wish her to travel. I suppose the weather has improved enough the roads shouldn't be too difficult for her now."

Reginald gave his brother a sour look. "Congratulations. You mentioned nothing of the blessed event when I was there last month. Starting your own dynasty, are you?"

Charles shrugged carelessly, but there was a gleam of pride in his eyes. "She says she wants a pack of 'em. Damned inconvenient, if you ask me, but I can't think of any way to stop her. She'd kill me if I set up a mistress."

Suddenly imagining Marian growing round with his child, Reginald reached for his glass again. He'd never given children a thought. The idea made him weak in the knees now. Had Marian given any thought to carrying his child? Of course, she had. Women always thought of these things. They had to. They were the ones who had to bear the burden. By agreeing to marry him, she agreed to bear his children. Devil take it, but his lust was aroused at just the thought. He was going to turn into one randy bounder before this was over.

"Lost you again, didn't I?" Charles inquired genially. "I can remember before I married Harriet, I went around with a third leg for months. Hits you like that sometimes. Never thought it would hit *you* though. You always come across as a deuced cold fellow, little brother. I still haven't figured out how you've set yourself up so well without father's help. He swears it's that racing stable of yours, but I've watched the odds. You can't make a living that way."

Reginald sighed. It always came around to that. He'd burn in hell before he'd tell his family he was a shopkeeper. He wasn't certain how he was going to tell Marian either, but he was still having a hard time dealing with even the idea of Marian. He took another swallow of wine.

"The stable takes care of itself. I've been lucky. You may tell father not to worry. We won't come begging at his doorstep. I've set aside funds for Marian's welfare in case anything happens to me. If we could just find her damned necklace, she'd have an additional income to fall back on, but the thief's been too clever for me." Reginald glared at his wine glass. The port must be stronger than he had thought for him to blurt that out. He seldom mentioned anything that troubled him to anyone, and he had a good head for wine. He'd better leave the rest of the blasted bottle alone.

Charles refilled his glass. "Necklace? The lady's jewels have been stolen? Why didn't she call Bow Street?"

Now he was in for it. Cautiously, Reginald outlined the bare details of the theft, leaving out the reasons for the copy but including his suspicions about his valet and the marquess. Charles appeared fascinated.

"So, you end up offering for the lady to make up for the loss of her dowry, eh? Very noble of you."

Reginald slammed his glass down. "No, I did not. I offered to reimburse her for the necklace. That is neither here nor there. I am marrying Marian because she is all that I could ever ask in a wife. We will rub along very well together." He found himself believing this quite thoroughly. Maybe he ought to stock up on a case of this port. He glared at the glass again. He hated port.

Charles sat back, satisfied. "Just wanted to make certain you weren't doing something foolish that we could get you out of before any permanent damage was done. Marriage is a lifetime sentence, Reggie. You don't want to go into it with your eyes closed. Didn't think you'd do anything bumble-headed, but where women are concerned, men can be damned blind. Father will tell you that. He's been worried you'd do something foolish if the tide started going against you. I knew he'd want me to ask. Maybe we ought to settle the cost of that necklace on her as a betrothal gift since you feel responsible for its theft. Seems to me there ought to be a few other baubles in the vault that she might wear, too. Harriet is fair and can't wear the colored things."

His head was beginning to feel rather light. Reginald found himself nodding foolishly, thinking how well Marian would look in the family jewels. He didn't think even his father possessed a ruby to match the one lost, but Marian wouldn't mind that. He'd like her to know that her husband's family wasn't impoverished, even if her husband was. He wanted her to feel like she would be taken care of in any event, unlike her mother. He was glad Charley was an understanding sort. Reginald closed his eyes and tried to remember the path of his thoughts, but they had gone wandering.

Charles laughed. "Think it's time we took you home, old boy. You never were much of a port drinker. Bet you had a bottle of brandy before you even got here. Never mix your alcohol, that's what I always say."

Reginald allowed himself to be pulled from the chair and led home like a drunken schoolboy. He felt like a drunken schoolboy. He was about to be married and he had never before given the state of marriage a thought. He could be a father by this time next year, and he'd known the potential mother for all of four weeks, at best. His mind flickered from images of Marian lying naked in his bed, to children screaming up and down the stairs, to chattering women in his parlor. He was about to be very, very sick.

Charles held his head as his younger brother cast up his accounts in the gutter, then hired a hack to take them the rest of the way home.

The viscount wasn't in the least surprised when an auburn-haired servant ran down the stairs of Reginald's town house to help carry his master in. The surprise came when Reginald looked up to see who it was, gave a cry of rage, and launched into the smaller man with two fists. It wasn't like Reginald to take advantage of his greater size.

It took two nightwatchmen and the secretary, Jasper, as well as the viscount to pry Reginald off the man now identified as his valet. Charles nodded approvingly as Jasper paid off the watch and closed the door firmly behind them. These things were better kept in the family.

Reginald continued to glare at the man lying on the parquet floor, holding a handkerchief to his nose and bleeding from cracked lips. "Where in hell is it, you miserable excuse of a lying, thieving . . . "

He seemed on the edge of launching himself at the smaller man again, and Jasper and Charles grabbed his arms.

The man on the floor gasped for breath as he answered. "A man can't visit his dear old parents for two days without being treated like a mangy dog. That's what I get for falling onto sad days. My father always told me never to lower myself to begging. Lord knows, I tried to hold myself proud, but a man can only stand so much, you know. Here I've turned your wardrobe into a thing of beauty, a thing to be admired by Brummell himself, and what do I get in return, I ask? He wrinkles his linens and muddies his boots and comes home with his coats covered in filth, then complains to me about it. I'll not have it anymore. I'll go back to begging in the streets before I do this again. I'll—"

Charles kicked him lightly in the ribs. "Shut up, you wretch." He looked at Reginald, who appeared little the worse for wear although a trifle wild-eyed. Charles kept a firm grip on his brother's arm. "I suppose you're going to tell me this is the valet who made off with the necklace?"

"Damned right, and I'm going to beat every miserable little diamond out of him if I have to bring them out through his nose." Reginald launched himself forward, only to be jerked back again by two firm holds.

The man on the floor sat up, dabbing daintily at his nose, which did not seem to be in serious disrepair. "Now I'm accused of being a thief, I suppose. Damned suspicious lot, you are. I just went to visit the old folks. They live right there in the village. Had a little too much of the hair of the dog, you know, and they put me up for the night. Had to make my way back here alone when I found I'd been left behind. Not the way a man ought to act to his personal servant, if you ask me, but then, no one ever asks me."

"Rightly so," Charles said sourly. "You talk too damned much. My brother says you absconded with a lady's necklace. Unless you want to end up in Newgate, you'd better put that fast tongue to better uses."

O'Toole made a show of dragging himself from the floor and scraping a low bow. "My pardon, your lordship. I didn't recognize your worthy self." He grabbed the handkerchief to his nose again to keep a fresh spurt of blood from staining his shirt. "I do not steal necklaces, my lord. They are not at all suitable for my attire." The words came muffled through the cloth. "I may occasionally borrow a shirt stud or two, but I always return them. And I have never so much as touched a watch. I can assure you, I have no necklace on me."

Reginald made a threatening noise and Charles was tempted to allow him to go for the fellow's throat. It would do the rascal good to turn purple for a while, but it wouldn't solve the puzzle of the lady's necklace. The viscount lifted an eyebrow at the somewhat bewildered secretary. The man had obviously been in his bed when the commotion erupted. He had trousers pulled on backward over his nightshirt.

"You'd best call the watch back. Let him try his tongue in Newgate for a while, then maybe he'll be a little more forthcoming."

The valet shuddered visibly. "No, no, sirs, please do not do that to me. I am innocent. I am a cherished only child. I would never survive such a place. If you are looking for a necklace, perhaps you want the one I found in Mr. Montague's coat pocket when I cleaned it. Blue fustian of the finest quality, and he brought it home covered in filth. Cobwebs! I have never seen the like in all my born days. There's no accounting for what the aristocracy will do."

Reginald went still. His eyes were murderous as he glared at his valet. "O'Toole, produce that necklace at once!"

O'Toole looked at him with green-eyed innocence. "Why, it is on your desk just as it was before we left, sir. I'm sure I wouldn't know what to do with anything so valuable as that. It seemed odd to me, sir, but I'm not one to question my betters."

Reginald was halfway up the stairs before the last of these declarations was out of his valet's mouth.

Twenty-one

T hat the genuine article?" Charles asked, watching his brother hold the stones to the lamplight and examine them thoroughly.

Reginald made a dissatisfied noise and reached in his desk for his glass to better examine the stones. "It is the original," he agreed coldly.

"Then what is the problem? Admit you made a mistake, give the poor fellow a bonus, and return the necklace to your lady." Charles watched with bewilderment as his younger brother scowled. Reginald had been stubborn and independent as a boy, but he had always readily admitted his mistakes.

"The five largest diamonds are paste. The bastard's had them replaced." Reginald set his glass back in the drawer and clenched the necklace as if he would murder it.

Charles whistled. "We'd best call the watch, then. He'll remember where they are once he's spent a night in Newgate."

Reginald frowned thoughtfully. "No, let him think we're fooled. He could have hidden those stones anywhere. He could have sold them already. We have no proof of anything. I still firmly believe he's working with Effingham. I want to catch him at it."

"I don't know how you plan to do that." Puzzled, Charles looked at the necklace for himself. He could see no difference between the glittering bits.

Feeling quite weary and more than out of sorts, Reginald made a gesture of dismissal. "I don't know yet either, but I will find a way. Take the damned thing with you. I'll not give the scoundrel another chance at it." He rubbed his hand over his eyes. "Wait. I'll have to take it back to Marian." He had cost her the advantageous marriage with Darley; he would not take away her only other alternative. He wondered if she would use the return of the necklace to call off their betrothal. His head ached too much to think about the other aches that thought engendered.

Charles slid the necklace into his pocket. "I'll be around to get you tomorrow. We'll go to see the ladies together. If they are going to the ball, they will be back then. It always takes ladies days to prepare for an occasion like that."

Not Marian, Reginald knew, but he didn't say it aloud. He wanted to say that Marian was different. Marian didn't waste time primping and painting and adorning herself and deciding between this ribbon and that. Marian would be plotting to wring O'Toole's neck or to sell the Effingham library or to find her sister a husband. Marian wasn't like any other lady he knew, but Charles wouldn't appreciate her finer qualities. Reginald kept them to himself, as he kept his own secrets.

He just nodded in agreement and watched his brother leave with the necklace in his pocket.

He didn't even have to yell for O'Toole before the ever-efficient valet appeared to help him off with his coat. At least the thieving bastard had the sense to hold his tongue.

When the butler came up to inform Marian that Mr. Montague and Lord Witham were below, she almost panicked—not because she couldn't remember any Lord Witham, but because she feared Mr. Montague had come to beg out of their betrothal. Having had a day or two to reconsider, he might have realized what a bad arrangement he had made.

Surely he wouldn't do anything like that in front of another man. A Lord somebody-or-another wouldn't be a solicitor. Reginald had just brought a friend to lend him support since he and Darley were no longer speaking. She would have to find some way to repair that damage.

Since Jessica and Lady Grace were still recuperating

from their journey, Marian called Lily to act as chaperone and waited nervously for the gentlemen. Her gaze went instantly to Mr. Montague when he entered. He looked splendid in his chocolate-brown frock coat and fawn trousers with his Hessians polished to a high shine, but there was a smudge of color under his eyes and a crease upon his brow that spoke of an uneasy night. She felt her heart lurch when he bent over her hand.

"You do not look as if you slept well, sir," she murmured quietly, for his ears alone, as he straightened.

A trace of a familiar wicked smile touched his lips. "I thought only of you while you were gone."

That was the Montague she knew. With a slight blush staining her cheeks, Marian jerked her hand away and turned her interest to his guest. He was very distinguished looking, and there was a trace of something familiar in his face. She tried not to stare too boldly.

"Lady Marian, may I introduce my brother, Charles? Charles, my betrothed."

Of course, she had forgotten. Mr. Montague was the son of an earl, but not the heir. It stood to reason that he had an older brother. She just hadn't considered his family, since he seldom spoke of them. She tried not to bite her lip as the viscount bowed over her hand. He really was quite formidably dignified. She felt like a schoolroom miss.

"My pleasure, sir," she managed to murmur, wishing her mother were here to help. Darley was a viscount, but he hadn't made her nervous as this man did. For all that mattered, her cousin was a marquess, but he didn't have the kind of presence that demanded respect and dignity. Marian sent a helpless look to Mr. Montague.

Reginald took a seat beside her and propped his arm along the back of the sofa as if he belonged here and as if she belonged to him. Which she did, she admitted uneasily to herself. She had given him every right to think of her as his. He crossed one booted leg over the other and watched his brother settle into a chair across from them. Marian very much thought her betrothed was hiding a grin that probably deserved an elbow to the ribs, but she played the demure miss as well as she could.

"I'm glad to have this opportunity to meet some of Mr. Montague's family, sir. He speaks of you often." She kept her eyes modestly on the rug between them.

Charles leisurely lifted a doubting gaze in his brother's direction. "Why do I find that hard to believe? Reggie would prefer to believe that we don't exist except when it pleases him."

Reginald caressed a curl at the back of Marian's neck and leaned toward her familiarly. "Hadn't you ought to call me by name now, my dear? We would not wish to give my brother the wrong impression."

He was laughing at her, she could tell. He knew she was putting on the same act for his brother as she had these past weeks for all society. She really ought to open her mouth and let out all those things she really wished to say, but she wouldn't jeopardize her chances another time. She didn't wish his family to take offense at her and talk him out of this marriage. And he knew it, the dastardly toad.

She turned a sweetly admiring smile in his direction. "I didn't wish your brother to think me too familiar, Reginald. I am sure Lord Witham is much too proper to behave as you do."

Charles chuckled. "I think I am beginning to see the attraction, Reggie. All these years you've been cleverly ripping people to pieces in front of their faces without their ever knowing, and now you've found a female with as much wit as you. You needn't be polite for my sake, Lady Marian. The rogue needs to be taken down a peg or two, and that's a fact."

Marian turned a real smile to her guest. "Would you care for some tea, my lord? We could discuss your brother's faults over scones, if you'd like." With a nod, she sent Lily to fetch the tray.

Reginald growled softly near her ear at the insult and tugged on the curl in his possession, but when the maid was gone, his voice was pleasant. "We have a surprise for you, my dear. Charles, the necklace, if you will."

Marian looked up in surprise as the viscount stood and presented her with a velvet pouch. He seemed to be watching her curiously, but she forgot that as she opened the pouch and saw the glitter of her ruby. She gave a cry of delight and drew the necklace through her fingers. "My mother's necklace! You have found it. Where? Did you catch the thief?" She turned excitedly to Reginald.

He smiled at her excitement, admiring the way it made her eyes dance. He also liked the way she automatically assumed he was the one responsible for returning the jewel, even though it was his brother who had presented it to her. He could do worse than Lady Marian Lawrence, Reginald decided. If one had to have a wife, it ought to be one who believed in one's worth.

His smile disappeared as he answered. "O'Toole returned last night with some story about finding it in my coat pocket. You and I know that the necklace in my pocket was the copy, but I have no proof of his guilt." He hesitated, wondering if he ought to mention the missing diamonds. If the marquess was involved, it would disturb family relations. But if she discovered they were fakes, she might blame him for the theft. He glanced to Charles for advice.

Charles shook his head. "We have no way of knowing who was responsible for the theft. You'd best give the lady the whole truth. Since the necklace was in your hands at the time, I think we can safely offer to replace the missing pieces."

Marian looked questioningly back and forth to the two men.

Reginald was the one to explain about the missing diamonds and O'Toole's wild explanations of his whereabouts. Marian looked at the necklace again but could see no difference in it, but then, she couldn't tell the fake from the original, either. She slid the jewel back into its pouch and closed it.

"Perhaps, if my cousin is responsible, we should say nothing to Mama. It does not hurt to share a little of what we have. He was not greedy. He gave us back the most valuable part." She looked to the viscount. "I really don't think it's necessary to replace anything. The necklace was to be part of my dowry. It seems foolish for Reginald to have to replace what would have been his anyway."

Charles gave her an approving look. "The family is bound to do something in honor of your betrothal. You and Reginald may decide how you wish it settled. In the meantime, we will wish to have a dinner and perhaps some dancing in your honor. When my wife arrives, I will have her call so the two of you may make the arrangements." He rose as if to depart.

"You have not had your tea, sir. Would you not care to stay to refresh yourself?"

Charles sent his brother a quick glance. "I have another engagement, but I suspect Reggie might stay for a scone or two. I trust your maid will be prompt if I leave now? I wouldn't wish to leave you alone with him for long, not the way he's looking at you right now."

Marian looked up at Reginald in surprise but didn't see anything there that hadn't been there before. Charles chuckled and walked out, leaving the two lovers to work it out between themselves.

"You are learning very quickly, my dear. I might come to miss hearing your brutally honest truths, but I suppose the sugar-coated kind will go farther in keeping harmony among family." Reginald leaned over and touched his lips to hers.

Marian hadn't been prepared for that. She had little or no experience with men. She couldn't tell what they were thinking from one minute to the next. She particularly couldn't tell what this one was thinking because he kept everything hidden behind a stoic façade that would give credit to a marble statue. But his mouth had no resemblance to marble at all. She gave a sigh of contentment as his lips slowly administered to hers.

A tingle of excitement was just beginning to build when the rattle of a tray outside the door forced them back to a more respectable distance. Marian heard Mr. Montague—Reginald—give a frustrated moan as he sat back, and she stole a peek at his expression. He wasn't exactly looking cold at the moment.

Lady Grace followed the tray in. She looked as if she had only just arisen and had dressed only because they had guests instead of remaining in her usual dishabille until she had been served her morning chocolate. She hid a yawn behind a discreet hand, and smiled at Mr. Montague.

"You are early, sir. Eagerness in a suitor is recommended. I understand I have missed your brother?"

Reginald rose from the sofa to bow over the lady's hand and to escort her to a chair. He took his place beside Marian again but refrained from his more possessive pose of earlier. "There will be time for you to meet all my family shortly. My sister-in-law will be arriving soon, and no doubt my father will accompany her. I trust your journey was not too uncomfortable?"

"No, the weather was fine. The hours were long, however." She dismissed the maid and poured the tea.

Marian leaned forward and laid the velvet pouch upon the tray. "Mama, Mr. Montague has found our necklace. It was apparently only lost instead of stolen."

Reginald showed no emotion at this version of the story. He sipped his tea and watched Lady Grace exclaim over the return of her one piece of jewelry. It was more than obvious that the necklace's only value to the lady was in its memories.

He tilted a look at the demure miss beside him. They needed to talk. "Is it too early to ask you for a drive in the park? I thought we might stop by a jeweler and choose a betrothal gift, since I failed to have one available earlier."

Marian sent him a look of surprise from beneath her lashes, but she answered calmly enough. "The park would be lovely. Mama, would it be all right?"

Lady Grace dismissed them with a wave of her hand.

When they were within Reginald's curricle—without O'Toole as groom—Marian turned a questioning glance to her betrothed's suddenly grim expression.

"There is some other problem that you have failed to mention?" she asked, trying to ignore the annoying feeling of unease roiling in her stomach. He had played the part of attentive suitor much too well. She feared now was the time he pulled the rug from under her feet.

"I placed the announcement of our betrothal in the papers before the necklace was returned. All of London knows of our plans to wed. Now that you have your necklace back and don't need me any more, I would appreciate it if you waited a while to change your mind about our marriage. I have no wish to be a laughingstock."

Marian gaped at him in surprise. "Are you hoping that I will end our betrothal?"

Grimly, Montague smacked the whip over the horse's heads and turned them through the park gates. "That's plain speaking. I suppose I deserve that. This honesty business becomes a trifle difficult, doesn't it?"

Marian sat back against the squabs and stared out at the lovely green of the trees. Her expression didn't reveal any appreciation of the scenery. "The necklace was ever only a temporary measure. I must marry so my mother need not worry about my support for years to come. If you are truly opposed to this marriage, then we must end the betrothal now and pray that no word of our . . . indiscretion . . . leaks out. We can only afford this one Season. I will need to find another suitor before it ends."

Montague gave her a hard stare, but she didn't meet his gaze. "I only wished to give you the opportunity to end the betrothal if that was what you wished. I have not changed my mind in the least." He sent the horses into a trot that had pedestrians dodging to the grass.

Marian clutched her gloved hands in her lap. He was only doing the honorable thing. She ought to release him from his promise after all he had done for her. That was evidently what he had expected. She closed her eyes and tried to force the words to her tongue, but they wouldn't come.

She wanted to marry Reginald Montague.

Twenty-two

They did not appear the affectionate couple searching for a betrothal gift when they entered the jeweler's. Montague stiffly surveyed the cases until he found a display of brooches. Marian slowly followed in his footsteps and stood behind him as he examined the available wares. When he dismissed the selection and turned to the rings, she remained where she was, looking wistfully at the brooches. This was not at all what she had in mind for a peaceful marriage.

"This one is quite pretty," she said softly, trying to diffuse some of his anger. "It is like the ivory one we once saw. It would look very well on several of my morning gowns."

Reginald gave it a second look and turned away. "I wish to give you something you will wear when we go out together, not something no one will ever see."

Marian's shoulders drooped. She was tired of fighting. She had chosen her course; she must stay with it. She just wished she had chosen an easier one. Reginald Montague was going to be a hard man to please.

She glanced around at the rings. He had the tray with the most expensive selections, and she shuddered at the waste of wealth displayed there. She turned to a more modest display and pointed out a small gold band with a single garnet. "Something like this is very elegant."

He scarcely gave it a second glance. "Society would think me a niggardly fellow to give you something so small."

With an exclamation of disgust, Marian gave up. She had offered all the compromise she could. If he was determined to stand on his end and never move toward the middle, there was little she could do about it. She turned around and stalked out.

"Damn." Reginald turned to the startled jeweler. "Give me the ivory brooch and the garnet ring." His gaze caught on a display of necklaces, lighting on a delicately contrived design of emerald and diamonds—one that would suit his betrothed's subtle tastes and his own preferences. "And have that delivered to this address." He passed the man his card and the address and gathered up the jeweler's boxes the clerk had produced. The name on the card was scarcely needed to cause the man to nod respectfully. He knew Reginald Montague on sight.

He had spent far more than he had meant to, yet she had asked for far less. He must be out of his mind, Reginald fumed, as he looked up and down the street to find his runaway bride. Had she asked for garish diamonds, he would have laughed and bought her garnets. So she had asked for garnets and he had bought her diamonds. He was quite simply losing whatever control he might ever have maintained.

He found her gazing in the bay window of "Aristotle's Antiquities," and he groaned. Whyever had he brought her to this street when there were jewelers all over town?

"I wonder if he has sold my manuscript?" she asked calmly as he hurried to catch up with her. "He doesn't display his books."

"The covers fade and dry out in sunlight. The crystal and the gems look much better in the windows. Collectors know to ask for the books." He produced the box with the brooch. "You have excellent taste, you know. The artisan who carved this is very talented."

She opened the box and gave the contents a look of surprise. She touched the gently unfolding rose carved in ivory. "Thank you," she murmured in a choked voice. There were tears in her eyes when she finally looked up to him.

Reginald felt a jerk of some unwanted emotion at the sight. He wanted to drag her off the street and kiss away those sparkling crystals, and at the same time, his stomach clenched as he realized what a bastard he'd been. All she had wanted was this simple gift, something meaningful between them. And all he had wanted was to show off his latest acquisition. Gad, but he was a rotten bounder.

Sheepishly, he pulled the box from his other pocket. "Your ruby will outshine it by a mile, but I do want you to wear something that shows you belong to me. I've already told you I'm a very possessive fellow."

Marian clenched the box with the ring in her fingers and searched his face. "I am trying very hard not to make this too difficult for you, Reginald. If I were a better person, I suppose I would release you from your promise, but I'm a coward. I'm afraid I will never find anyone else I like so well. Is that terribly wrong of me?"

Instead of answering, he slid the ring from its satin bed, removed her glove, and tried it on her finger. "It's a little loose. Shall I have it adjusted?"

Her fingers curled possessively around the tiny band. "No, I do not want to take it off. I shall just have to grow into it."

Finally, he smiled, a gentle smile that did not look comfortable on his harsh features. "Not growing romantical on me, are you, my sweet? I'm not very good at that kind of thing, you know. I'm still trying to think of something to say in response to knowing you like me. I had thought you held me in great contempt."

"And so I ought." She pulled her hand out of his grasp and carefully donned her glove. "You think me foolish and romantical and probably wish me to the devil, when I know very well that I will make you a very good wife. If I did not think that, I would never agree to this marriage. And since everyone has made it plain that you are not inclined to be attached to any woman at all, I feel quite certain I am not hurting your chances of finding lasting affection. I'm not at all certain that you are capable of lasting affection. I will settle for respect."

Amusement danced in his eyes as Reginald offered her his arm. "You already have that, my lady. I can think of no other woman in the world who could have managed an offer from me. We will discover some way to make this arrangement work."

Arrangement. Marian kept her sigh to herself. It would have been very nice if she could expect tender looks and soft words more often, but she supposed she ought to be content that he had at least attempted them when presenting her with his betrothal gifts. It was not as if they had a love-match. They had an arrangement.

She tried not to scowl. He made her sound like a bunch of flowers.

"Oh my, Marian, you look so dashing! I wish I could hope for some of your flair someday." Jessica looked wistfully at her sister's image in the mirror as she straightened the sash at Marian's waist.

Marian studied her image critically. Lily had swept her dark hair up in a dazzling array of smooth waves and loose curls entwined with a ribbon made of threads of gold. The ribbon complimented the ornate gold tussie mussie that had arrived bearing three tiny wine-red rosebuds from Reginald which she now wore pinned on the ivory sash at her waist. She had chosen a gown of paper-thin ivory silk with a net of fine gold for her first appearance at a ducal ball, knowing it would accent her one piece of jewelry, the ruby necklace.

However, the low bodice of the gown left such a vast expanse of flesh exposed, Marian feared no one would even notice the necklace. The gowns Lily had made for her had always been modest. This one that the modiste had made exposed more than she thought remotely decent. Marian flushed at the thought of Reginald looking at her there, as he couldn't help but do. The stays the modiste had insisted on pushed her up so that he could scarcely miss the display.

"Dashing" was scarcely the word Marian would have chosen to describe the result, but Jessica was always polite. She could scarcely say "lovely," for Marian didn't have the face for that. Her lips were naturally red and her eyes were too dark and her skin closer to tawny than creamy. She might be called "striking." She would never be called lovely.

But right now Marian felt quite indecent. Surreptitiously, she pulled at the tiny bodice, but it was made to fit snugly just where it was. She wiggled her shoulders to see if the tiny sleeves would cover more, but she succeeded only in dislodging her flowers. Jessica helped her put them back, and Marian surrendered. Maybe she would feel better if she didn't look at herself.

She turned her critical gaze on Jessica. Her sister was everything that a lady should be. Her gown was more modest, as was fitting for a young girl. She was more slender than Marian, and the little flounce of pale-blue silk adorning her snow-white bodice flattered her young curves. A slight train of the pale blue flowed down her back, enhancing her tiny waist and slight stature. With her golden hair and blue eyes, she looked a fairy princess from a storybook, and Marian hugged her fiercely.

"You are beautiful, Jessie. All the men will fall at your feet. Even the duke will have to ask for introductions. Just remember to keep smiling and nod at everything a man says, and you will do wonderfully."

Jessica's smile faltered. "Lord Darley is the only gentleman who has asked if I will be attending. Do you think he will ask me to dance? I would hate to be a wallflower all evening."

"You will dance every dance except the ones you choose to sit out. I am sure of it. Let us see how mama is doing."

If nothing else, Jessica would dance every dance because all society was consumed with curiosity about the marquess and about Marian's and Montague's marriage announcement and they would descend on anyone with information, but Marian didn't intend to say that. She was learning to hold her tongue very well. If curiosity is what it took to make society see what a lovely person Jessica was, then so be it.

They arrived at the residence of the Duke of Devonshire in a crush of other carriages, all of them more elegant than their own. Again, Marian had to wonder why they had received their invitations, but the cards were duly accepted at the door and they were issued inside with the usual announcement just as if they were the duchesses or marchionesses around them. A "Lady Grace" and a "Lady Marian" among the Countesses of This and That was scarcely to be noticed, but several heads did turn as they descended into the ballroom.

Several of Lady Grace's friends hurried to offer their congratulations on the impending nuptials. One or two of Marian's erstwhile suitors came to jest that she had not given them sufficient time and to sign her card for dances. Lord Darley hurried to attend them before his mother could sail up and offer reproaches for taking a lesser man. To show he suffered no harm, he took one of Marian's waltzes, then put his name down for two of Jessica's dances. She was immediately radiant, and the brilliance of her smile attracted several other young men to sign her card. Darley scowled at them all, and continued to stand with the ladies as the room began to fill.

It was almost time for the first dance, and Marian began to watch the newcomers nervously. She had saved the first dance for Reginald, but he had yet to make an appearance. Of course, in that crush of carriages outside, he could be stuck halfway down the street.

When the footman finally announced Charles, Viscount Witham, and Mr. Reginald Montague, Marian gulped a sigh of relief and distracted several young men in the immediate vicinity. Unaware of the direction of their interest, she watched eagerly as Reginald descended into the ballroom. She knew the exact moment he found her, even though a smile never crossed his face. Her heart pounded a little fiercer as he set a straight path in her direction. Others must have been watching, too. It seemed as if the path opened through the crowd between them.

The music was already starting when he reached them. He must have said something appropriate to Lady Grace, and Lord Witham no doubt made some greeting also, but Marian heard nothing. She only felt the heat of Reginald's gaze and the crush of his hand around hers as he led her to the dance floor without even asking.

The opening dance was a quadrille, as was the custom. It left little opportunity for more than an occasional comment, but Marian was aware of Montague's gaze following her throughout the steps, never once leaving her despite the formation of the dancers. She was beginning to wonder if her clothes had suddenly become transparent, but only in the eyes of her betrothed. No one else seemed to pay her any extreme attention. She felt the color rising between her breasts, but she met his stare as calmly as she could.

When the dance ended, Reginald did not immediately return her to her mother as was proper. He pulled her to one side, out of the crush, and touched the flowers at her waist. "I had not thought about where you would wear them, but if I had seen that gown, I would have thought of nothing else. I can see a more appropriate gift would be a jewel that would dangle here." His gaze dropped to the place he had in mind.

Marian blushed deeper. "You are being unseemly," she whispered, but not in protest. His words and his looks were making her tingle like his kisses had earlier. She was much too aware of what the gown did not cover.

"That damned gown is unseemly," he muttered hoarsely. "Haven't you a shawl or something you might use to cover it up?"

She stiffened. "It is no more unseemly than the ones the other ladies are wearing. I had it made by a very fashionable modiste. I thought you would be pleased to see me rigged out properly."

"I'd be pleased if I were the only man in the room. I can feel them all breathing down my neck right now, just waiting for me to get out of the way so they can see you. I don't like sharing." He grabbed her dance card and glanced over it, then deliberately threw it into a potted palm.

He held out his hand. "I will take you back to your mother and explain that I do not intend to share you this evening. She may inform your disappointed suitors."

Bemused, Marian allowed Reginald to drag her back in the direction of her family. She wasn't at all certain how to take his reaction to her gown. She had hoped he would find her attractive. Did he consider her shameless instead? And what right did he have to throw away her dance card? She liked dancing. She wanted to kick and protest, but she was all too conscious of the eyes watching them. Lord Witham was still standing with her mother.

"I believe I see a scene approaching," the viscount murmured as they watched the couple emerge from the potted palms. Marian's growing rebellion was not easily hidden. The black look on Reginald's face was the real surprise. His brother never openly expressed any emotion.

"Oh dear, I hope Marian has not been too hasty. Sometimes she is not overly cautious with her words." Lady Grace twisted her gloved hands and glanced toward her younger daughter to make certain she was safely in Darley's care and out of hearing before returning her attention to the approaching storm.

Witham looked amused at his companion's understatement. He was more than certain that Lady Marian had a way with words that rivaled his brothers's. He didn't think words were the problem here. He glanced at the young lady's revealing gown and bit back a smile. She had hidden herself very well indeed the morning he had met her. Reginald was undoubtedly in a state of agony Charles could not wish on any man, but the viscount wasn't about to try to explain that to Lady Grace or her daughter.

"Madam, if you will, explain to Lady Marian's other partners that I do not intend to allow my betrothed out of my sight this evening. Unless they wish to dance with me, they will have to find other partners for their dances." Reginald spoke stiffly, keeping his eyes correctly on the woman to whom he was speaking rather than the irate one behind him.

Charles chuckled as the stunned Lady Grace sought an appropriate reply. "Don't suppose it is the necklace that has you distracted, is it, little brother? When did you say you meant to set the date?"

Marian tried to shake off Reginald's imprisoning hand. "Never, if I have aught to say about it. He is being beastly unreasonable."

Reginald pulled her up beside him and glared down at her. "Next time, I will go with you to the modiste. I'll not have my wife . . . " A frown formed between his eyes as he bent his head closer over her and stared quizzically and quite immodestly at her bosom.

Marian raised her free hand to push him away, but Charles caught it with a warning shake of his head. He gave a discreet cough. "Reggie, you are going at it a little too far."

Reginald caught Marian's necklace between his fingers and lifted it enough to catch the light from a bracket of candles on the wall. The duke had chosen not to use gaslights, which would blacken his new wall hangings, and the room was entirely illuminated by smoking candles and discreetly placed lamps. It made for a romantic setting, but not good lighting.

Reginald dropped the necklace and frowned at Marian. "I did not bring that back with me. I left it at Arinmede. Why did you choose to wear it tonight?"

Marian stared at him. "Are you all about in your head? You brought this to me just yesterday."

Reginald's jaw muscles went grim and taut as he raised his gaze to his brother. "He's done it again. That miserable cur has done it again. This time, when I get my hands on him . . . " He turned away and started toward the stairs, his fingers clenched into fists.

Although Lady Grace had no clue to what was going on, Marian and Charles exchanged worried glances. While Charles made hasty excuses to her mother, Marian raced after Reginald.

If her necklace had been stolen again, she meant to slit the thief's throat personally and save Reginald the trouble.

Twenty-three

Charles caught up to Marian in a few quick steps. Catching her arm, he tried to halt her progress toward the door. "You cannot go with him. We are making a scene. Smile and go find your next partner. Reggie and I will take care of this."

Marian gave a blinding smile, patted his coat sleeve lovingly, picked up the skirt of her gown, and continued on up the steps. Heads turned as she passed, and hands went up to cover whispers. The duke himself departed the reception line and stopped to inquire if anything was wrong. Marian offered him the same blinding smile and hurried on.

Charles murmured something about a sudden illness in the family and ran after her. He wasn't a man who often cursed, but a few pithy phrases were coming to mind.

Marian caught up to Reginald at the door, where he had summoned his brother's carriage. He scarcely noticed her arrival. Charles had brought him, but Reginald was wishing he'd had O'Toole drive. He wanted his hands around the valet's neck right now.

"I'm going with you," Marian announced beside him.

He wasn't going to take the time to argue. The carriage came around, and he was already running down the steps to claim it. Marian ran after him, and Reginald remembered his manners in time to practically throw her in. He leaped in after her, and Charles had to grab the door and propel himself inside before he was left behind.

"This is insane, both of you. Lady Marian's reputation will be ruined. You cannot go about chasing criminals in the middle of the night. It is not done. I'll call Bow Street. They'll take care of the character until we can get to him. The two of you need to get back in there and settle the gossip."

"You may return Lady Marian and settle the gossip. I intend to wring the necklace out of O'Toole's throat. He has played me for a fool one too many times."

Marian scarcely noticed the luxury of the viscount's velvet-lined carriage. She caught Reginald's hand between her own and wound her fingers between his, needing the reassurance of his touch. "I don't understand. How could he have switched them? I have kept the necklace on me since you brought it back."

Reginald shot her a quick gaze, his mind instantly imagining that string of jewels resting between her breasts as she slept and beneath her gowns as she went through the day. He almost choked on the mental image he summoned. If it hadn't been for his rage at O'Toole and the presence of his brother . . .

He jerked his thoughts back to the moment. "O'Toole was still in the hall when you went down last night?" He turned to Charles with the question.

The viscount considered the question. "Yes. He was leaning against the newel post holding a handkerchief to his nose while Jasper kept him under guard. Then you yelled for him to come up."

"I suppose he brushed past you as you left." Reginald sounded resigned.

"As a matter of fact, I believe he did. I thought he was weak and staggering slightly. He isn't a large man, you know. Your assault no doubt caused him some pain."

"Balderdash." Reginald would have sat back and crossed his arms over his chest, but Marian's fingers were soundly entwined with his. He squeezed her hand instead. "He picked your pocket. He must have found the copy and brought it with him. Damn, but what did he hope to accomplish?"

"He either hoped that once you returned the original to me you would not notice it again, or he meant to give himself a little extra time to escape England." Marian frowned.

"I'm not so certain that he is working with my cousin, Reginald. I truly believe Lord Effingham must have made him bring back the necklace."

"Then Lord Effingham can make him produce it again. I mean to bind and gag the monster of ingratitude and deliver him to your cousin's doorstep." After I strangle him, Reginald added to himself. It wouldn't do to allow the lady to know the extent of his rage. It was entirely a matter of personal pride now. No man—particularly a skinny, red-haired valet—was going to get the better of him.

The journey through damp city streets was a short one. They rode it in relative silence, each with their own separate thoughts. Reginald worried over what he would do should O'Toole not be where he left him. Marian prayed there would be no violence. And Charles tried to conceive a scheme to stop the scandal before it started. None of them had any great hope of being successful.

Reginald was out the door and ordering Marian to stay where she was before the carriage wheels scarcely stopped rolling. Marian was on his heels before Charles could halt her. With a resigned look, the viscount leisurely strode after them, reviewing the fastest sources for obtaining a special license. Ladies other than wives simply did not follow gentlemen into their homes. He would have to remember to impress that upon his own daughters as they grew up.

Jasper came out of his employer's downstairs study when the front door slammed open. The secretary struggled for some semblance of stoicism as his employer—rigged out in evening breeches and frock coat—dashed up the stairs as if his heels were on fire. He rubbed his eyes in disbelief as a goddess in frail silk and gold netting ran after him. But when the dignified viscount trailed in, shrugged, and followed them up the stairs, Jasper turned around and went back to the study where a decanter of brandy always waited.

By the time Marian located Reginald's bedchamber, Reginald had his valet by the throat and dangling a foot off the floor. O'Toole appeared in danger of turning a virulent purple, which didn't go at all well with his reddish auburn hair.

"Reginald, you will never discover anything if you kill him," Marian said prosaically. "I don't suppose you have any rope or anything we can use to tie him up?"

The valet made a strangling noise and gazed at her wildly.

Charles strolled into the room in time to hear Marian's question. He chuckled at the valet's panicky look. "I believe in the colonies they call it 'stringing' him up, my lady. One binds a rope around the thief's neck and flings it over the branch of a tree. The result is quite as satisfactory as a gibbet, I believe."

Marian gave him a curious look but responded instantly to Reginald's order.

"Take the sheets off the bed. They'll do. I'll mummify him."

O'Toole gasped for breath as he was lowered into a chair and his arms jerked behind the chair back. "I trust I get a bonus for playing these kinds of games, my lords," he protested mildly.

"Oh, certainly, O'Toole." Reginald pulled the sheet Marian handed him around the valet's chest and knotted it firmly in back. "Give me the other, Marian. I'll bind his feet too." To O'Toole, he responded, "Transportation to Australia sounds a sufficient bonus to me, unless you prefer a brief sojourn with the Navy. I understand Americans are a little peeved with our treatment of seamen, but you do seem to fit in quite well over here. I'm sure you'd enjoy the sea air."

"I'm not much of a sailor, sir. I'll forego the pleasure, if you don't mind. If you could explain the goal of this game, sir, I might play it a little better."

"The goal?" Reginald appeared to consider this as he jerked the second sheet around the chair and his valet's legs and bound them all together securely. "The goal, my good man, is to teach you not to play with things that don't belong to you. The faster you return the lady's necklace, the sooner you may expect to be released, although I don't promise you will enjoy your freedom anytime in the near future."

"That being the case, sir, I would rather decline the game. I don't have need of any bonus at the moment."

Reginald smiled grimly as he checked his handiwork. "You're a cool customer, I'll give you that, O'Toole." He turned to Charles. "I say we send Jasper for the marquess. Tell him we have his servant here and mean to hand him over to the authorities if the necklace doesn't appear within the next twenty-four hours. Does that seem reasonable to you?"

Marian frowned. "What if Mr. O'Toole doesn't work for my cousin?"

Reginald shrugged. "Then he had better come up with the necklace's whereabouts on his own, hadn't he?" He brushed off his hands and started for the door.

"Wait a minute!" O'Toole called after him.

Reginald turned and lifted a quizzical brow.

O'Toole glanced to Marian. "The lady's wearing the necklace. What is it I'm supposed to produce?"

Reginald smiled coldly. "The genuine one. Good-night, O'Toole."

He walked out, leaving the valet cursing and struggling against the sheets. Marian and Charles hurried to follow him.

Downstairs, Reginald gave orders to his secretary to search out the marquess, and a servant was sent to find the watch to keep a guard on the house. Satisfied that all was done that could be, Reginald turned to Marian with a frown.

"Well, now that we have scandalized the entire *ton* all at once, what should we do for an encore? Do you wish to return to the ball?"

"Are you going to let me dance?" she demanded.

"Of course." Reginald caught her hand and pulled her toward the door. "With me only, unless you mean to change that gown."

"I will not change my gown. I paid a fortune for this gown. I mean to wear it every chance I get." Marian hurried down the steps after him.

"Then resign yourself to dancing with me for the rest of your life. I have no intention of watching grown men drool over you as they guide you around the dance floor." Reginald held out his hand to assist her into the waiting carriage.

Marian ignored it and climbed in by herself. "Only children drool. And if there are only children at these affairs, I have no wish to attend them."

Behind them, Charles rolled his eyes and pulled out his watch. He wished Harriet was here. He needed to hear a few sensible words to keep him steady and on course, else he was likely to say something he shouldn't. He wondered if he had ever been so young as to bicker like this when what he actually meant to do was to haul the young lady in his arms and kiss her mouth shut.

Reginald was struggling with just that urge even though Marian went silent once Charles entered the carriage. The heady scent of the roses he had given her drifted around him, combining with the softer scent of the lemon juice she must have used on her tresses for this occasion. He wanted to bury his face in her hair and pull her against him and forget everything but the joy of making her his. He knew he had gone beyond rationality but he no longer cared. What was done was done, and he meant to make the best of it. He was quite certain that bedding Marian would be the best thing that had ever happened to him.

Reginald gave a grimace of distaste as the carriage returned to Devonshire House. His thoughts were far from the glittering panoply of guests inside. He wondered if Marian felt the same. He sensed her reluctance as he helped her out.

Charles was the one to break their silence. "We will have to enter together so it is known that the lady was not alone with you all this time. I told Devonshire there was a sudden illness. Perhaps the lady's maid?"

"You had best give the truth to Marian's mother. Their maid is a veritable part of the family. She would be concerned if you tell her the lie." Reginald's voice had returned to the cold and impersonal as he escorted Marian into the house.

"I trust you are prepared to marry quickly, then. Lady Grace will not look kindly on this escapade, even with my accompaniment."

Marian gripped Reginald's arm tighter and gave his taut features a look of concern. "I'm sorry. I only wished to keep you from doing something you would regret later."

Reginald managed a grim smile as he glanced down at her. "You will be the one who is sorry for ever having anything to do with me. And I shan't tell you that you succeeded in your quest; it will only lead to more impetuousness on your part. But I fully intended to strangle O'Toole."

Marian gave him an uncertain smile as they made their way up to the ballroom. She wasn't entirely certain of all the innuendoes behind his words. Reginald was capable of many layers of communicating. What was she going to regret and why? Was he sorry that she had prevented him from strangling his valet? Was he prone to acts of violence when enraged? Should she return with him after the ball to prevent him from murdering the poor man?

The prospect of marrying a murderer kept Marian so bemused as they entered the ballroom that she was scarcely aware of the heads turning at their entrance. She smiled politely at the duke as he came forward to express his concern, allowed Lord Witham to make their explanations, and asked to be led to the ladies' retiring room so she might repair herself. She needed time to gather her courage before facing the crowd again. Or facing Reginald. She wasn't certain which.

When she came out, only Reginald waited for her. His brother must have headed off her mother and sister and their questions. She couldn't read the expression in his eyes as he watched her approach, but remembering his opinion of her gown, she felt certain he was looking at her bosom. She lowered her gaze and tried not to blush.

"I thought you might like some punch and then a stroll on the balcony before returning to the ballroom. It is quite stifling in there." Reginald took her hand on his arm and led her properly toward the refreshment room.

"It can't be proper to stroll on the balcony," she murmured as he produced a cup of punch for each of them. "Haven't we created enough scandal for one evening?"

"We might as well start out as we mean to go on. Since we have already announced our betrothal, they will just think we are overly romantic. Of course, everyone will be counting the months until our first child is born, but that is common enough."

Marian gave him a scandalized look, but Reginald's expression was quite calm as he led her toward the doors to the outside. Their first child? She had barely thought as far

as their wedding day, and he was already considering children. The notion sent a fascinating thrill through her as she
stepped out into the coolness of the evening.

"I don't wish to be thought fast," she protested as the
door closed behind them. "It leads gentlemen to assume
things that aren't proper."

Reginald snorted. "That gown leads them to assume a
great many things that aren't proper. I think I'll lock you in
the house when we are married."

"I am growing tired of this argument," Marian answered
peevishly. "I have excellent taste and this gown is no worse
than any other I have seen tonight. If you really mean to be
a possessive tyrant, I will rethink this betrothal at once."

Reginald pulled her firmly into his arms. "Too late. The
deed is done. Neither of our families will allow us to cry
off now. You sealed your fate tonight, my dear. Try not to
protest too vigorously as we march up the aisle."

His mouth closed over hers before she could even begin
her protests.

Marian began to remember why she wanted this marriage. She liked the possessiveness of Reginald's mouth on
hers, the heat of him as he claimed her, the thrill of his
hands as they held her. There were other things she liked
and admired about this man also, but they escaped her
when he held her like this, as did everything else. Her
hands slid to his shoulders and clung there as their mouths
came together with intoxicating fires. She was entirely too
aware of his hard body as he pressed her against him.

They were neither of them aware of their audience until a
dark figure lounging against a far rail asserted himself.

"And here I thought it was my dramatic cape that you
wished to admire, cousin. When are you going to learn to
keep away from this mongrel fellow?"

The caped figure stepped into the patterns of light from
the ballroom window. A hood hid his face in shadow, and
only a glimmer of white linen could be seen through the
folds of cloth as he propped his arms akimbo on his hips. But
neither Marian or Reginald had any doubts as to his identity.

The Marquess of Effingham had come to London.

Twenty-four

Reginald gently but firmly put Marian behind him. "Relation or no, I am growing tired of your intrusion into what is none of your affair. Unless you have come to return Marian's necklace and the missing diamonds, you would do better to make yourself scarce."

Behind him, Marian gasped. Reginald felt her moving to interfere, but he stopped her with his arm, keeping her at a safe distance from the American.

Hidden behind the folds of his cape, the marquess's expression couldn't readily be determined, but there was a hint of amusement in his voice as he replied. "You have a very good eye. The diamonds were needed. They will be replaced as soon as I can generate a flow of cash from the estate. In truth, I did not think the ladies would miss them until I was able to replace them. So you have caught me out in this. But I sent Michael back with the necklace. I still believe it to be mine, but I could not wish to unduly upset the ladies. Michael is generally obedient to a direct order. Is that not the necklace my cousin is wearing?"

Marian's fingers gently closed around Reginald's arm. He liked the feel of them there, and he didn't protest when she stepped to his side. Somehow, the fact that she clung to him was reassuring.

"That is the copy that your blasted valet ferreted from its hiding place. Undoubtedly he thought to rob us both. He returned the original to my keeping, then replaced it before it reached Marian's hands, probably thinking I would not notice it once she was wearing it." Reginald didn't mention that he almost hadn't, distracted as he had been by Marian's more natural assets.

The marquess gave a sigh of exasperation. "I will wring his neck this time. I have warned him often enough that his light fingers were going to get him into trouble. You are only half-right. Michael won't steal from me. He has a warped sense of justice developed over years I won't bore you by describing. He is probably waiting to see if you will discover the switch, and if you don't, he will feel quite comfortable in returning the original to me. His loyalty is commendable, even if his morals aren't. I will see that the necklace is returned."

"Oh dear, do you think we ought—" Marian's question was interrupted by the arrival of the duke and Reginald's brother. The plight of the valet was momentarily forgotten as the two new arrivals discovered the cloaked figure in the shadows.

"Ahh, you are chaperoned. Lady Grace was growing concerned." The duke sent Marian and Reginald a laughing glance, then turned his attention back to the man in the shadows. "Have I had the pleasure?"

"Effingham. I believe your invitation was open?" The voice behind the hood was gruff.

Delight crossed the young duke's face. "Effingham! I should have known you would be here to look out for your cousin's interests. I don't suppose you have time to discuss those artifacts you mentioned in your letters? Or if we could meet at my club tomorrow . . . ?"

Charles grimaced and turned to the young couple he had come seeking. "The two of you had better make an appearance in the ballroom before the gossips have you half way to Scotland. Lady Grace is beginning to lose that beautiful patience of hers."

"Oh, but we must tell the marquess—"

Reginald caught Marian's arm. "We don't need to tell the marquess anything. He hasn't proven he can be trusted any more than his valet." He started moving toward the ballroom doors.

Unimpeded by the British etiquette of dealing with a duke, the marquess abruptly ended his conversation to step in front of them, halting their progress. "Why is it I get the impression the lady has been trying to tell me something?"

"Because the lady is of a more pleasant temperament than I am. Considering the scolds she is capable of giving, I never thought to say that, but the truth will out. If you will excuse us, the lady has yet to dance with me this evening." Reginald started around the caped figure blocking his way.

Charles coughed discreetly behind them. "I say, Reggie, you might at least make a proper introduction before you leave me out here."

Reginald scowled. "Gavin Lawrence, Marquess of Effingham; Charles Montague, Viscount Witham. Now, if you'll excuse us—"

Since the marquess was again moving to block their escape, Charles tried to smooth the social waters. "Effingham! I was hoping we would have a chance to meet before the nuptials. Where are you staying? I would like to pay my addresses on the morrow, if I could."

There was a note of harassment in the American's voice as he tried to fend off a duke and a viscount determined to do their duties while keeping an eye on the young couple who looked decidedly guilty of something. "I'm only here for the evening to look in on my cousin. Marian, if you would, I'd like to have a word with you."

Marian sent Reginald a questioning look. Pleased that she turned to him for his opinion rather than giving in to her cousin, Reginald managed an almost conciliatory reply. "He will come to no harm where he is. I will hand him over to your cousin as soon as I have the necklace in my hands again, I promise."

The duke and the viscount looked vaguely bemused when the marquess grabbed for Reginald's cravat at this seemingly irrelevant comment.

"Where is he, Montague? What have you done to him? He's not much of a brother, but he's the only one I've got. I'll deal with him, not you."

Reginald caught the man's wrists at his throat and twisted. A popping noise of bone rubbing bone forced the marquess to jerk from his captor's grasp and curl his hands into a fist. Before he could throw the punch, the duke and Charles caught his arms.

"Reginald is a damned stubborn independent bastard. If hitting him would do any good, I would have done so long ago, but it only makes him worse," Charles spoke consolingly, holding the marquess's arm in a firm grip. "Lady Marian, if you would, please tell your cousin what he wants to know before someone gets hurt."

"You always did play dirty, brother mine. It's unfair to ask my betrothed to go against my wishes. It puts her in a damned awkward position, and you know it." Reginald straightened his cravat and glared at the hooded figure still prepared to attack him once unrestrained. "I didn't realize the wretch was your brother. He doesn't exactly have the family resemblance."

The marquess relaxed somewhat warily at this reasonable tone. "Fortunately for him, he resembles our mother instead of the damned dark hot-tempered Lawrences. Excuse me, Marian, you are the exception that makes the rule. It is good to know that the blood runs to beauty in the ladies of the family. Now, what have you done with Michael?"

Thoroughly unsettled that she had still another cousin, one who was a thief and a valet, Marian glanced quickly to Reginald for reassurance. At his nod, she admitted, "We tied him up until Reginald could get back to him."

The marquess uttered a curse that Marian had never heard before, shook off his captors' hands, and started for the ballroom door. "Tied him up! Damnation, the house will no doubt be in flames, or flying off on the wings of pigeons before I get there. Tied him up!" He continued muttering and cursing as he threw open the doors and plowed his way through the glittering company, his black cloak flapping behind him.

The sight of this Gothic phantom striding through the room, muttering madly, sent the ladies shrieking and gentlemen backing out of his way. The marquess seemed completely unaware of the chaos erupting around him. Still hooded, he stalked through the room, trailing the duke and the others behind him.

As it became apparent that Reginald and Marian meant to follow in his path, Charles hastened to intervene. "I'll go with him. You two stay here. You've caused enough scandal for one evening. Someone has to stay and explain this scene to the satisfaction of the gossips."

He gestured, and they became aware of the staring faces all around them. Lady Grace was attempting to get through the crowd to her daughter, Jessica and Darley were waiting hesitantly near the steps for some signal to indicate what they should do, and the rest of the guests were whispering and staring at the caped phantom now striding briskly up the stairs to the exit.

Reginald gave a resigned grimace. "Hurry, then. Don't let him out of your sight until you have the necklace in hand. Jasper will help you."

Charles turned quickly on his heels and rushed after the departing marquess, giving a word of explanation to the duke as he left.

Marian just clung to Reginald's hand and shook her head. "It's not worth it. None of this is worth it. I could wish I had never set eyes on the thing. His brother?" She turned incredulous eyes to her escort.

He ought to be frustrated by his inability to follow the action, but Reginald found himself staring down into her bewildered face and wishing they were back out on the balcony again. As people began to cluster around them with a dozen questions, the musicians struck up a waltz. He squeezed Marian's fingers between his own. "My dance, I believe?"

Eyes widening, Marian glanced around them. Her family and Darley had nearly caught up with them. Lady Jersey was already patting her on the shoulder and offering to lead her to a retiring room to recover. Lady Agatha had caught Reginald's right arm and was pelting him with questions. Several of both of their acquaintances were adding their observations as to the identity of the mysterious cloaked figure, the ladies admiring his physique while the men protested his rudeness and speculated about his dangerousness. And Reginald wanted to dance?

That sounded fine to her. She slid her fingers around his arm. "Lead on, MacDuff," she purposely misquoted.

" 'And damned be him that first cries, "Hold, enough!" ' " Reginald murmured as he steered her unapologetically through the curious crowd.

Thrilled beyond speaking that he knew the reference, Marian merely floated into his arms when Reginald held them out at the dance floor. Gaze fastened on his face, she scarcely cared where her feet were as he guided them skillfully into the crowd. The knowledge that she had actually found a man who knew Shakespeare held her rapt as he swirled her in circles around the room. Eventually, however, she became aware of the heat of Reginald's hand at her back and the warmth of the gaze he was returning, and she began to blush.

"I didn't mean to stare," she murmured helplessly.

"That's quite all right, as long as you are not staring at a piece of grape between my teeth."

"I cannot imagine you ever having a piece of grape between your teeth."

His eyes danced. "Straw, then. Braying jackasses most likely keep straw between their teeth."

Marian's lips twitched with the effort to hold her smile. "You will never forgive me for that, will you?"

"Ummm, maybe in a thousand years, give or take a hundred or so. Do you think once we are married my life might return to some order again, or is it your intention for us always to live amidst chaos?"

Marian felt a nervous palpitation of the heart at the way Reginald was looking at her. She still had not quite grasped the reality of marrying this man. They scarcely knew each other. Yet she knew the pressing intimacy of his mouth against hers, and the way it made her feel, and she could think of no other man with whom she would share it. Shortly, they could be sharing their meals together, living in the same house . . . she blushed when she came to the idea of sleeping in the same bed together. Surely not.

"I would like to know what thought led to that charming bit of color in your cheeks, but perhaps I am better off not knowing. The dance has ended. Do you think if we stand here like this long enough, they will take pity on us and begin another?"

She was still in Reginald's arms in the middle of the dance floor while all others around them broke up to return to their various places among the guests. Marian discreetly stepped from his embrace and tried not to stare at him again.

"We had best go back to my mother. We have no doubt made a sufficient spectacle of ourselves for one night."

"I have never had any particular desire to attract attention, but I find myself caring little if we do. Darley is heading this way and I mean to tell him no if he thinks to draw you away from me." Reginald held her hand firmly clasped in his.

"What has come over you?" Unable to help herself, Marian turned her gaze back up to Reginald's starkly handsome face. The determined jut of his jaw made her heart leap. The stiffly arrogant man she had first met was rapidly becoming someone she liked and understood much too well.

Reginald had the grace to return her an uncertain smile. "I don't know. I think it must be that gown. I have this strange urge to ask your mother for a bill of sale so I might take you home with me."

Marian didn't know whether to laugh or scold at this reluctantly given admission. Darley's arrival interfered with either.

"I have been nominated to drag the pair of you off the dance floor before you can make utter cakes of yourselves. You would be doing me a great favor if you can make some show of complying to my authoritative orders."

Reginald quickly masked a look of frustration and irritation and, offering his arm, escorted Marian in the direction of her mother. "How are we to ever come to know each other if we cannot be left alone for even two minutes?" he asked rhetorically, for no one bothered to explain.

"Lady Grace can be quite a tartar when she gets her dander up. You're about to be raked over the coals, or I miss my guess," Darley said genially.

"Perhaps I ought to go see how Charles is faring," Reginald mused as they drew closer to the lady in question.

"Craven," Marian murmured as they came to stand in front of her mother. She wished she could bottle the look that Reginald gave her in return. It contained a confused frustration that she thought never to see in him and would no doubt never see again. It was good to know there were a few things that the lofty Reginald Montague could not deal with entirely on his own.

"Mama, did you know that the marquess has a brother, and that he has been serving as Reginald's valet all this time?" A direct attack usually served to divert Lady Grace's intentions.

Surprise lifted her eyebrows, but Lady Grace still maintained a frosty look as she kept her gaze on her daughter's betrothed. "Then we shall have to invite him to the wedding, I suppose. You are not planning a long betrothal, I trust?"

"I don't think there will be any difficulty obtaining a special license, my lady. I would like Marian to meet the rest of my family, of course, but you may set the date at any time you wish," Reginald answered a trifle stiffly.

"Very good. I think the first of the month will suit. We would not wish anyone to think there is need for haste."

Before Lady Grace could say more, she was distracted by a cry from her younger daughter. Jessica was looking to the entrance, where a small crowd of people gathered. Many of the guests had drifted off to the supper table since the musicians had retired, but a few stragglers like themselves had found some new entertainment.

"He had a dove, Mama. It flew away. Did you see it?" Delighted by the show, Jessica was already drifting in the direction of this new distraction.

Marian looked to see what her sister saw, but she could only discern a small crowd of people laughing and watching something in their center. Taller than she and better able to see above heads, Reginald was frowning slightly at whatever spectacle was there. She tugged on his hand. "What is it?"

Offering an arm to Lady Grace while Darley hurried after Jessica, Reginald led them toward the stairs and the lingering company. Perhaps the duke had arranged some form of entertainment for the supper break. Marian was in no hurry to join the crowd at the banqueting tables. She hurried to keep up with Reginald.

His frown deepened as they drew closer, and he made no apologies as he pushed his way through the onlookers. Marian clung to his arm rather than be left behind. She was beginning to think perhaps this wasn't some innocent entertainment after all, judging just by Reginald's frown. She scanned the crowd for the source of their interest.

A man in black beaver hat and tails similar to those of all the male guests stood at ease near a pillar pulling a string of colorful scarves from his coat pocket. At Marian's approach, he smiled broadly, swept off his hat, and bowed low. When he stood upright again, his hand held a bouquet of flowers he held out to her.

Astonished, Marian looked up to see his face before accepting the offering. His smile widened with her eyes.

Michael O'Toole, the valet. Her cousin.

Twenty-five

Marian clutched the bouquet of flowers and laid a restraining hand on Reginald's arm. She didn't know how Mr. O'Toole had escaped the bonds holding him. There hadn't been time for the marquess and Charles to free him. But he was her cousin, and he hadn't run away when given the opportunity. The marquess had said Michael had his own sense of justice, and something told her that this particular cousin could not be judged by ordinary standards. She waited to see what he would do next.

Casually elegant in his formal clothes, O'Toole—as she knew him—leaned against the pillar, put his hand in a pocket suspiciously large for evening wear, and produced a second bouquet of flowers. He handed them gently to Jessica instead of flourishing them, as if aware that any extravagant gestures would frighten her. Jessica made a coo of delight and eagerly shared the gift with the ladies around her.

While part of the crowd was distracted with Jessica and her prize, O'Toole straightened, opened his coat as if to look for something inside, and a flock of doves suddenly took wing all around them, sending the majority of the onlookers stepping backward and out of the way. Under cover of this commotion, O'Toole bowed to Lady Grace, reached into her elaborately coiffed hair, and came away with a tiny enameled box which he held out for her.

Lady Grace released Reginald's arm to accept the gift wonderingly, patting her hair as if to ascertain there were no further surprises to be found there. Pleased with the box itself, she made no haste to look for the opening. O'Toole solved the problem for her, snapping his fingers with a quick wave that caused the box to pop open.

By this time, the crowd was drifting back, and they gaped and tittered while Lady Grace drew out a delicate necklace of pale sapphires. Or at least, Marian thought they were sapphires. They could have been paste and she wouldn't know, but she couldn't be so rude as to question a gift. Her mother smiled as if they were a treasure of diamonds, and that was all that mattered. O'Toole bent gracefully and kissed the lady's hand when she thanked him.

With a wink at Marian, he swung away from her and back to the completely amazed Jessica. Marian didn't dare take her eyes off him to look at Reginald to see how he was taking this. The son of an earl might not appreciate having a street magician for cousin-in-law, but even Reginald would have to admit that Mr. O'Toole was a rather elegant magician. Also, a light-fingered one, she would have to remember. Her eyes narrowed as he reached for Darley's pockets.

Darley, too, was suspicious of the move, and he attempted to step out of O'Toole's reach. Ostrich and peacock feathers suddenly began erupting from the coiffures and pockets of the ladies and gentlemen all around him, and poor Darley was caught up in the excitement and the crush as the guests laughed and grabbed for the frivolous favors. Before the viscount could escape, O'Toole produced a box from behind Darley's ear, and Darley was protesting and grabbing for the prize.

"It was intended for the lady, was it not?" O'Toole asked smoothly, bowing and presenting it to Jessica.

"Not yet, you idiot!" Darley vehemently protested, but his gaze was anxious as Jessica took the tiny box in her fingers.

When she looked up to him and offered to give the box back, Darley shook his head. "I meant to wait and do it proper," he said stiffly. He sent an uncertain look to Marian and Reginald, then returned his attention to Jessica. "I found it in a shop, and I knew it was perfect for you, and I realized I very much wanted you to have it." He swallowed uneasily as Jessica gazed up at him with wide blue eyes.

O'Toole was busily distracting the crowd with gold watches appearing in ladies' bosoms and silver coins in gentlemen's ears.

Relieved that he was no longer the center of attention, Darley said softly, "I know I cannot properly give it to a lady who is not my wife, but I thought . . . If you would think about it . . . I mean, I can wait until you are ready . . . "

Astonished but evidently pleased, Jessica opened the box. Nestled in the satin was a delicate ring in the shape of a silver rose with a beautifully cut diamond in its center. Not much of a talker at the best of times, Jessica could only stare wordlessly at the ring, then back to Darley until tears rimmed her eyes. Her lips tried to form the words, but nothing came out, and Darley hastened to reassure her.

"You don't have to say anything, Miss Oglethorp. Just keep it until you're ready." Darley closed his hand around the one holding the ring. He threw an anxious look back at Reginald. "I only just bought the damned thing. How'd he know I had it?"

As if sensing he was being discussed behind his back, O'Toole turned around, planted a white gardenia behind Jessica's ear to bring her quivering lip to a smile, and finally turned his attention to Reginald.

Marian noted that Jessica and Darley continued to hold hands while they watched to see what the irrepressible O'Toole would do next. She dared a hasty glance to Reginald's face, but his expression was imperturbable as he met his former valet's look. The gleam in her cousin's eyes was more than mischievous, and Marian felt a nervous quiver or two of her own. She remembered quite clearly the marquess's admonitions about flying houses. At this moment, she was more than convinced that Michael O'Toole could float the ballroom off the ground if he desired.

"The lady's necklace is too easy," O'Toole murmured, idly producing a few coins from nowhere and juggling them back and forth while looking Reginald up and down.

"She wears it now. Perhaps one more suitable to her tastes?" he asked, as if to himself.

Reginald glanced hastily to Marian's throat. The ruby glittered in the light of the branch of candles on the pillar. He was momentarily distracted by the creamy hills rising around it, but he blinked and focused his attention on the jewel. It looked decidedly real in this light. A flush of pink was beginning to color the skin beneath the jewel, and Reginald reluctantly looked away from this fascinating display. He turned his attention back to O'Toole in time to see the man juggle a necklace along with the coins in his hands.

A slow rage began to rise as Reginald recognized the delicately fashioned emerald necklace he had purchased for Marian's wedding gift. He had locked the piece up in his desk drawer as soon as it had arrived. If the blasted thief had stolen the stones from this . . .

O'Toole grinned as if reading his mind. With a wave of his hands, the coins disappeared and the necklace once more lay in the box in which it had arrived. He bowed and presented it to Marian. "Your betrothed is as deceptive an illusion as I am, but his gift to you is the genuine article. He thinks to disguise the real gift with these jewels, but I think you are wise enough to discover the truth. Please accept my apologies for any distress I have caused you, my lady." He sent Reginald a wicked look. "But I don't apologize for any I have caused your betrothed. Keep him on a short rope, cuz." He turned quickly back to the amusement of the crowd.

Marian glanced uncertainly from the lovely emeralds in her hands to Reginald's stoic expression. "Are they yours?" She held the box reluctantly out to him. In the general run of things, she wasn't enamored with jewelry, but this was the most exquisitely wrought confection she had ever laid eyes on. She couldn't help a second longing glance to the glittering stones.

Reginald's expression relaxed slightly. "I had meant to give them to you on our wedding day. I wanted you to have something of your own, and not the family heirlooms. Does it suit?"

Marian's eyes widened as she lowered her hand and allowed herself the pleasure of examining the necklace with more care. "It's a piece of art," she murmured, fascinated by the play of light on the stones. "I never thought jewlery could be so beautiful."

"It can never be more beautiful than your eyes right now. I have been foolish to think my collections were all the beauty I need." Reginald closed the box in her hand, forcing her to look up to him.

Marian didn't have time to interpret the look in his eyes, only to know that it disturbed a tidal wave of sorts in her insides before an explosion of noise behind them distracted their attention.

Puffs of smoke rose upward from the center of the crowd, and an exotic scent vaguely like that of the gardenia Jessica had been given filled the air. Reginald closed Marian firmly in his embrace, pulling her back against him as the crowd stepped away in cries of astonishment. All eyes searched in vain for the elegantly garbed magician who had stood there just moments before. He had vanished into thin air.

Reginald growled in disbelief and would have moved to search the area had not still another sight caught his eye. Closing his fingers firmly around the hand in which Marian clutched her necklace, he glanced to a figure just being announced at the entrance. He stiffened and adjusted Marian to a more proper position at his side.

Shaken by O'Toole's disappearance, Marian gazed up at Reginald, questioning this sudden placement. Her gaze followed his to the entrance, and she sucked in a sharp breath.

The man standing at the top of the stairs had the same proudly erect stance and arrogant features as the man at her side, only aged by years Reginald had not yet lived. Studied closer, the features were perhaps not the same. The older man's nose was sharper and longer, his mouth thinner, but the resemblance was there just the same. Marian shivered slightly in anticipation of the scene to come. There wasn't a doubt in her mind that the new arrival was the Earl of Mellon, Reginald's father.

"Damn," Reginald muttered under his breath. "Between

us, we seem to have an overabundance of relations to entertain the crowd tonight."

Marian began to giggle, probably more with nervous
hysteria than amusement. "If he pulls flowers out of his
coat, I shall faint immediately."

"So shall I," Reginald answered grimly.

Apparently locating his prey, the earl steered a straight
course toward his younger son. With whispers of scandal,
the crowd moved out of his path. Not one among them regretted missing their suppers for this fascinating entertainment.

The Earl of Mellon came to a halt before the unlucky
pair. Marian gripped her bouquet and her necklace nervously, but he dismissed her with a glance. He reserved his
glare for Reginald.

"You will explain the chaos I found on your doorstep
when I came to call."

Reginald remained icily aloof. "Good evening, sir. It is a
pleasure to see you again, too."

The earl scowled. "Don't give me that lie. You'd rather I
disappeared like that other scoundrel just did. I'll make the
lady's acquaintance, if you will, and then I will know what
is going on. Not only is Devonshire's ballroom overrun
with pigeons and silly idiots and smoke, but your place is
teeming with females of ill repute and a rather noisy melee
of mongrels. It seems all of London has gone mad, and I
would know if it is contagious."

Marian began to giggle again. She couldn't help it. It was
all much too improbable. Reginald looked as if he would
choke. The earl—despite his harsh face—seemed fairly
mazed. And she could almost hear Michael O'Toole's
laughter ringing from the rafters. The Phantom and the Magician: her father's family would soon set all London on its
ears.

Lady Grace finally appeared at their side, and as Reginald struggled with all the introductions, the earl's face
softened somewhat. He bowed low over the lady's hand
when all was said and done.

"Grace, it has been a thousand years. How is it we have
not met in all that time?"

Marian's mother smiled thoughtfully. "We neither of us were much for society, sir. It is good to see you again."

Marian and Reginald watched in astonishment as their respective parents exchanged light badinage about her name and his title and an old argument over who should be called what. Shaking his head in astonishment, Reginald gently eased Marian away from the reunion.

"I'm not in any hurry to return home and discover the chaos my father complains about. With any luck, Charley and your cousin will set the house back to rights without my help. Do you think we might retreat to the balcony and learn to know each other a little better?"

Reginald's eyes gleamed knowingly as he looked down at her, and Marian tried not to blush. She had a good idea of what he considered getting to "know" her, but they were betrothed. Wasn't she obliged to obey his wishes?

She glanced up at him through a curtain of lashes. "Are you certain that is wise? What if we take each other into dislike before the wedding?"

"My lady, at the moment I am trying to calculate how I can put your whole damned family on the market and sell them as rare objects. But you, I would keep. Come along, I would see what I have won by my immeasurable patience."

Marian nearly ran to keep up with him as he dragged her through the ballroom rapidly filling with guests returning from supper. "Patience?" she inquired indignantly. "I have not seen you exude one iota of that virtue at any time. You have yet to win anything, sir."

Reginald swung open the door and pulled her out, closing it firmly behind him, shutting out the noise and the people and the music. Dragging her from the light, he circled her waist with his arms. "Then I have my task cut out for me, don't I? Where shall I start?"

Before she could offer any of the opinions so obviously ready to burst from her lips, Reginald leaned over and caught them with his mouth.

It was the best way in the world to silence her, and he enjoyed it immensely.

Twenty-six

The sun sparkled against the bay windows of the shops as they strolled past. Marian was aware of the bustle of people around them, of the expensive fashions and laughing chatter of the society she was coming to know. She liked the smell of meat pies coming from the stalls on the street corner. She enjoyed the variety of objects displayed for her perusal in the windows. But most of all, she loved walking beside this proud man who made heads turn whether he was frowning or laughing.

He was frowning now, and she quailed a bit inside at the expression. He had arrived this afternoon quite unexpectedly, made her excuses to her family, and appropriated her company without asking her permission. She had much rather be in Reginald's company than her mother's, but she was still rather uncertain of his moods. These past weeks had been a whirlwind of activity from which they had stolen every possible moment for themselves, but there still hadn't been enough time. The wedding was only a week away, and the only time they'd had alone together had been measured in minutes of every day.

Reginald hadn't said he loved her, but Marian had never expected that. He'd given her beautiful compliments, and that had been much more than she had anticipated. He had taught her passion with their stolen kisses, and she had no fear of their wedding night. Her betrothed had been more than gentle, more than she had ever dared hope, while still conveying his very real desire for her. She lay in bed at night with her heart thumping in longing for his presence beside her. No, she was more than ready to be his wife. That wasn't the reason for her qualms today.

Her qualms had more to do with Reginald's dangerous quiet since he had swept her from the house. He no longer had a groom to ride behind them in the curricle, and they had been used to talking incessantly and holding hands when they traveled together. There had been none of that today. He had merely driven them to this street, handed the reins of his horses to some street urchin he seemed familiar with, and handed her down to the cobblestones. His grim expression was beginning to frighten her.

Refusing to admit to fear, Marian exclaimed in delight at the display in the windows of Aristotle's Emporium. "Look, Reginald! It looks just like a miniature of the entrance hall of Arinmede! However did they make the stained glass so tiny? Isn't it marvelous? The sun sets off all the colors just as it does at the manor. I've never seen anything so exquisite."

Reginald stopped stiffly in front of the window to allow her to admire the artisan's handiwork. "Your cousin has talented hands. It's about time he applied them to something useful," he said gruffly, not daring to touch her.

But he didn't refuse her hand when she slid it into his palm, Marian felt his fingers tighten around hers, and she dared turn him an expectant look. Jessica would have been terrified by his stern demeanor, but she knew Reginald had a habit of hiding himself behind that expression and his cynical attitude. And she loved the man he tried to hide. She smiled and watched his gaze grow wary.

"Surely you don't mean the marquess? Gavin might set a regiment of soldiers in line with a single word, but he could never make anything so exquisite as this. And if it is Michael's doing, how do you know it? I think it would be easier to catch a leprechaun than to catch Michael."

"He fancies himself Irish," Reginald hedged, not yet certain how to breach his news. "That's why he calls himself O'Toole instead of Lawrence."

Marian made a moue of distaste. "You need not be polite with me, you know, Reginald. It's not as if I haven't questioned Gavin thoroughly on the subject. He is as evasive as you, but it does not take a great mind to see that Michael doesn't believe he shares the same father as Gavin. I shall ferret out the entire story sometime, but it is of little account. Their mother was married to my great-uncle or whatever when Michael was born, so his name is Lawrence no matter what he believes."

Reginald almost managed a smile, but his eyes were still wary as he watched her. "His birth does not matter to you? You would claim a thief and a street magician for family even if he may not be related?"

Marian shrugged and turned back to the fascinating display in the window. "I understand they led hard lives after their parents died. I don't think Michael is really bad, he just has a different set of values than we do. And if Gavin claims him as brother, that is enough for me. I've never had the privilege of cousins before. I'm rather enjoying the sensation. They are my protection against your avalanche of relations."

"I trust no one in my family has been hurtful to you?" Reginald's thumb moved back and forth across her wrist as he continued to hold her hand.

"No, they have been lovely. Your sister-in-law is a delight, and I am dying to meet your nephew, and all the others have been more than proper. I do adore your brother. I wish I had been there when you returned home after the duke's ball. The way Lord Witham tells the story raises terrible images. I cannot believe Michael could have created such chaos so quickly. Were some of the ladies really undressed? Your brother does not say so, but there is this gleam in his eye . . . "

Reginald finally grinned and squeezed her fingers. "I shall never tell, and you are above all naughty to ask. Suffice it to say that Michael will be paying for that episode for a long time to come." The grin slipped away. "That is not why I brought you here today."

Marian turned her gaze up to him. "I've been waiting for you to tell me. Am I supposed to beguile you out of whatever it is that is bothering you?"

He winced. "No, witch, I would rather not be twisted between your manipulative little hands. I'll take your honesty any day. I only wish I'd had the courage to give you the same from the start. Now we are so thoroughly embroiled I see little way out, and I fear you will despise me for the rest of our days."

Startled, Marian removed her hand from his, only to place it on his arm instead. "Are you feeling quite well? I thought we had come to some understanding over these last weeks. I like you too well to ever despise you. Surely you know that." She paled a little and removed her hand. "Unless you have found someone else, someone you can truly love. Is that why you wish out?"

With a muttered curse, Reginald grabbed her waist and hauled her toward the door. "That might be easier for all concerned, but no. It is not I who wishes out of this arrangement. You are the one who will be sorry. I have debated every possible way of not telling you, hoping you will never know, hoping if nothing else I can make you so enamored of me that you will not care, but I cannot do that to you. I've come to love you too damned much to deceive you like that. You will have to know the truth before it is too late for you to cry off."

Head spinning with the impossibility of that one little phrase, Marian ignored all the surrounding words and allowed herself to be shoved through the door of the emporium. The boy behind the counter looked up from waiting on a customer to give them a respectful nod of greeting. Jacobs came hurrying out at the sound of the door, then shrugged and returned to the back at the sight of them. Marian thought it rather odd that he did not wait on them, but she was too confused by Reginald and his behavior to question anyone else's.

Holding her waist tightly in his arm, he steered her toward the back of the store. Marian began to resist. "Where are we going?" she whispered. "We can't go back there."

"We can do anything we like in here." Reginald grabbed up a crystal paperweight and lobbed it at a marble statue. His throw nicked the crystal, sending it bouncing against the Turkish carpet, while nearly toppling the statue. Marian held her breath, waiting for it to fall, waiting for someone to come out screaming at this desecration. The boy raised

an inquiring eyebrow, his customer slinked out the door
and away from the madman, but no one protested Reginald's reckless destruction.

"Reginald, what are you doing?" Aghast, Marian
watched as her betrothed helped himself to a selection of
leather bound books from behind the counter. She clasped
them to her when he dumped them in her arms, fearful he
would throw them like the paperweight if she gave them
back.

Once her hands were otherwise occupied, he set himself
to decorating her with every exquisite jewel his eye caught
on in the display case. He placed a glittering tiara on her
hair, adorned her ears with diamond bobs, wrapped golden
necklaces around her throat, and clasped a jeweled band
around her wrist. Marian struggled desperately with the precious volumes in her hands, returning them to the shelves
before he made her into a walking display of valuables.

"Reginald, stop this at once!" she commanded with a
hiss when he enveloped her in a cloth of gold cloak that
looked vaguely familiar.

"Why should I?" he asked disinterestedly. "They belong
to me." He adjusted the cloak. "Or your cousin, in the case of
this item. He has generously allowed me to sell his posses-
sions on consignment, so I needn't come up with the cash to
buy them all. My commission will keep us very comfortably
for many years if I am successful in selling them."

It was the way he said it more than his words that made
Marian stop and listen to what he was really trying to say.
She fingered the costly bracelet on her wrist and looked
with interest at the fascinating variety of titles on the shelf
in front of her. Her gaze drifted back to the miniature in the
window, and with a swirl of her golden cloak, she stalked
behind the counter and through the doorway she had
thought only for the shopkeeper.

The room beyond was a fascinating assortment of books
and maps and antiquities too delicate to be left unattended
in the main display area. An open staircase led to another
story, and glancing over her shoulder at Reginald's blank
expression, she daringly started up it as if she owned the
place. He made no objection.

The cloak swirled around her as she ascended the stairs and entered what was evidently a large work space. Old wood covered this floor rather than valuable carpet. Shelving littered with odd bits of hardware and tools, legs off old tables and chairs, heads of crumbling statues, and any number of oddities collecting dust filled the walls. Beneath a gabled window on one end of the room sat a table cluttered with myriad bits and pieces of metal and fabric and glass—and her cousin Michael.

He glanced up, startled, at her entrance. He seemed to be working on a replica of the exterior of Arinmede Manor, but Marian gave him little notice. She stalked to the far end of the work area where she had spied a door with a glass transom. Michael watched without expression as Reginald raced up the stairs after his cousin, following her with a dangerous look in his eyes as he crossed the room. Only after they disappeared into the far room and slammed the door did he grin and return to his work.

Marian swung around, swirling her cloak with a dramatic ripple as Reginald followed her into his office. With a theatrical gesture, she unfastened the cloak and let it fall to the floor. She stepped over it, dropping a bracelet on its gleaming folds. Unfastening necklaces and earbobs and bracelets and letting them fall as they would, she approached her betrothed.

Gold and jewels littered the path she made toward him. Reginald remained frozen where he was, unheeding of the fortune in valuables scattering across the floor, his gaze focused entirely on the woman in the center of these treasures. His eyes narrowed dangerously as Marian reached him and placed both hands on his chest.

"Are you going to make love to me now?" she whispered huskily.

His body responded as she meant it to, but Reginald was made of sterner stuff. He held himself stiff and unresponsive, not touching her. "You don't understand yet, do you?" He swung his arm. "This is my office. This is my shop. I own this place. This is how I earn my living. I, my dear, am a shopkeeper."

"And I, my bumble-headed ninnyhammer, will be a shopkeeper's wife." Marian slid her hands over his shirt, beneath his habitually unfastened waistcoat. She really was quite fascinated with the feel of him beneath the fine cloth, and the scent of him. Reginald had a fascinating scent of male flesh and a lime fragrance and occasionally the musty odor of old books. She could recognize him in the dark just from his scent, she was certain.

His hands slid reluctantly to her waist, attempting to hold her away. "Is a bumble-headed ninnyhammer better than a braying jackass?" he asked inquisitively, just for the record.

"Not better, just more endearing."

She leaned into him, and Reginald didn't stop her. She felt good cuddled against his chest, her head tucked under his chin. He warmed his arms by wrapping them around her back. "You aren't paying attention, my love," he reminded her. "If society finds out what I do, we will be ruined. We will be scorned by family and friends, cut from all entertainments, mocked by all around us. This is what I would bring you to if we married. I'm not a wealthy man, Marian. You must consider what you are doing before you make that fatal step. You are the daughter of a marquess. You can do much better than me."

She sighed and played with a button on his shirt. "You buy and sell books and things?" She felt him nod. "I buy and sell books and things, too. So does Gavin. I much rather buy than sell, but one has to live. I don't see any difference."

His hands stroked her back. "You and Gavin sell the occasional oddity when you need funds. You don't make a habit of acquiring things to sell for profit. There is a distinct difference, my dear."

"I could make a habit of it," she said thoughtfully. "It could be very challenging. Just the other day I heard Lady Agatha wish for an old lorgnette she once owned. I saw one that would be just perfect for her in a Covent Garden stall. I could buy it from that vendor and sell it to Lady Agatha for easily twice as much as I bought it. I think it would be rather amusing."

Reginald ran his hand into her hair and dug his fingers deeply into her thick coiffure. He tilted her head back until she met his eyes. "I love you even if you are insane. You will not go down to Covent Garden to buy Lady Agatha a lorgnette. Is that clearly understood?"

"Even if I do love you enough to be classified insane, I will not let you bully me, Mr. Montague. If I wish to sell Lady Agatha a lorgnette, I shall. And no amount of kissing will make me change my mind."

"No amount?" His eyes gleamed as he studied her.

"No amount," she answered firmly.

He lowered his head and found her deliciously full lips. "If I kiss you enough, will you love me more?" he murmured against them.

"Insanely," she agreed as his mouth closed over hers.

In the work area beyond, Michael whistled a happy tune and polished a piece of glass for a tiny mullioned window. He lifted an eyebrow at the sound of a piece of furniture in the office bumping against a wall.

The old sofa in there was none too comfortable. He'd give them another window or two before intruding. After all, he had no desire to end up back on the streets again. These London streets were damned damp even at the best of times.

And illusion held little comfort when compared to the genuine emotion he saw between those two lovers. He rather imagined his little cousin was a true original, one who didn't mind being a shopkeeper's wife. He wouldn't mind finding a woman like that for himself one day, a real woman, not an illusion.

But in the meantime, he found it extremely amusing to sit back and watch this pairing of the noble marquess's daughter with a man who made his own living. He rather liked to think that he was partially responsible for the sounds of love emanating from that room right now—he and the ruby necklace, anyway.

Whistling, he snapped his fingers and produced a tiny gem to install in the miniature desk drawer waiting for its place in the manor. Ruby red sparkled in the sunlight from the window, and the magician grinned.

Now that Montague possessed the genuine article, he wouldn't miss this piece of glass.